Protecting Her Heart

Other Proper Romances
by Nancy Campbell Allen

My Fair Gentleman
The Secret of the India Orchid

Steampunk Series

Beauty and the Clockwork Beast
Kiss of the Spindle
The Lady in the Coppergate Tower
Brass Carriages and Glass Hearts

Hampton House

The Matchmaker's Lonely Heart
To Capture His Heart

PROPER ROMANCE

Protecting Her Heart

NANCY CAMPBELL ALLEN

For my angels:
Kari, Solveig, Julie, Ragnhild,
Ragna Amanda, and Maude

Visit us at shadowmountain.com

Library of Congress Cataloging-in-Publication Data

Names: Allen, Nancy Campbell, 1969– author.
Title: Protecting her heart / Nancy Campbell Allen.
Other titles: Proper romance.
Description: Salt Lake City: Shadow Mountain, [2023] | Series: Proper romance | Summary: "Longtime friends Dr. Charlotte Duvall and Director John Ellis work together to solve the mystery of Charlotte's mother's death while also navigating their developing romantic relationship." —Provided by publisher.
Identifiers: LCCN 2023022990 | ISBN 9781639931699 (trade paperback)
Subjects: LCSH: Women physicians—Fiction. | Police—Fiction. | Nineteenth century, setting. | London (England), setting. | BISAC: FICTION / Romance / Historical / Victorian | FICTION / Romance / Clean & Wholesome | LCGFT: Historical fiction. | Romance fiction. | Detective and mystery fiction.
Classification: LCC PS3551. L39644 P76 2023 | DDC 813/.54—dc23/eng/20230601
LC record available at https://lccn.loc.gov/2023022990

Printed in the United States of America
Publishers Printing

10 9 8 7 6 5 4 3 2 1

Prologue

My dearest Charlotte,

I am not well—my heart is failing, but it is time you knew the truth. I have kept secrets from you. Perhaps I am nothing more than an old fool, but my days are numbered, and they are filled with the ghost of your mother. She haunts me, you see, because circumstances of her death are not as I have maintained these long years.

I dare not commit details in this letter; I must see you in person. I would give anything to embrace you once more, to see Katherine in your face, to explain why I have kept these secrets.

I dare not confide in your brothers. They believe my mind is confused, and perhaps it is, but regarding your mother, I am clear as a bell. I have a packet of information stashed away safely—proof of my claims.

There is danger, you see, in raising the specter of her death at this time. I have kicked a hornet's nest, turning over stones and sending messages that could prove problematic for some who have a very long way to fall. However, I cannot leave this earthly realm without making a clean breast of it—without bringing the guilty to justice. Yet I am a coward in that I have waited until now when I am nearing my end and expecting you to finish this task if I cannot. I realize asking you to come home is no small thing. If it were not so urgent, I would not ask it.

Your mother's life was so different from mine—her friends were important people destined for greatness, and she was the glittering jewel at the center of every gathering, while I was happiest sitting in the library with you, reading our fairy tales. That she ever fell in love with me, a humble man with five sons, still awes me.

Near her end, however, I believe Katherine was tiring of her social whirl. Her friends were not always friendly. The poison of jealousy sometimes kills immediately and sometimes is administered slowly over time. The end result, though, is always the same.

Come home and I will explain. We will seek justice together. You were robbed of a mother and I of my dearest love. The time has come to make it right.

Ever and always,
Papa

Chapter 1

Charlotte Elizabeth Duvall stood at the steamship railing, looking at the vast ocean beyond. The water was dark gray, as was the sky, and before long, the two would blend on the horizon. The wind had picked up and made a mess of her hat, and then her hair. The long, auburn tendrils blew back from her face, and she knew she must look like a red medusa from behind.

In one hand, she held her hat, which she absently registered as having been important to her when she purchased it six months earlier upon graduation from medical school in Pennsylvania. She'd been so happy that day; the only sad spot was that her family had been unable to attend the commencement celebrations. In her other hand was the telegram the ship's purser had handed her an hour ago. Her father was dead.

The last letter she'd received from her father had unsettled her enough to take an extended leave of absence from her new job in a New York women and children's clinic and book passage on the next available steamer.

But she was too late.

She clutched the telegram in tight fingers, her wrist braced against the railing. Two weeks earlier, she'd been in her New York City flat, debating whether she ought to make her new residence there a permanent thing. Aunt Sally wanted her to return home to England, as did her cousins, her father, and her friends. But she'd spent four hard years attending one of the most rigorous medical schools in the world—one established by women who insisted a medical education ought to consist of more than the few months of training required for a simple medical certificate. Charlotte's professional colleagues and contacts were in America, as were her prospects for a promising career.

Then she'd received word from her eldest brother, Thomas, that their father was ill, that he'd suffered a heart issue—angina pectoris—and the prognosis was not promising. If she wanted to see him alive, she must return home immediately. Not two days later, the strange letter from her father arrived, and her thoughts began spinning in confusion and concern. She'd quickly settled her affairs, made arrangements at St. Anne's clinic, pre-paid a few months on her apartment lease, and contacted her friends and acquaintances to alert them of her changing circumstances.

It had all taken time. Too much time. And now he was gone.

The tears in her eyes were a combination of grief and the result of wind that whipped and swirled around her in biting gusts. Rain began to fall, cold and sharp. She couldn't catch her breath, couldn't see through blurred vision that obscured the definition of the waves. The ship dipped, and she fought for her balance, grabbing the railing and losing her hat in the process. She looked behind her as it flew across the deck and disappeared over the other side.

"Miss!" a purser shouted at her, waving to catch her attention. "You'll be wanting to get below deck! The storm promises to be a bad one!"

She nodded, brushing her flying curls away from her forehead and around her neck. "Of course." She didn't move, though. She couldn't think of where to go, of how to get there.

Charlotte was never at a loss for something to say or a plan to put into action. Death was permanent—she'd seen that firsthand. She'd spent four long years learning to combat it. She couldn't fix her father.

There was nothing to be done. He'd sent that cryptic letter warning of danger and secrets, and now he was gone. She wondered—if she threw her arms wide, would the wind carry her away like the hat?

The purser gestured. "Come, I'll escort you."

She took his arm, noting the absence of any other living soul on deck. How long had she been standing there? How long would she have remained there? She attempted to gather her hair in her free hand as they turned toward the stairs. Her fingers, threaded through the man's arm, still clutched the telegram that by now she'd crushed into a ball.

They reached the stairs, and she paused. The purser frowned at her as she pulled her hand free, turning with the wind. She opened her hand, and the telegram shot from it, hitting the far railing before disappearing into the dark water below. Fighting for breath, she reached again for the man's arm and descended.

CHAPTER 2

London, 1889

Johnathan Albert Ellis, second son of the Earl of Ashby, and director of the Metropolitan Police's Criminal Investigation Department, took in the gathered mourners at Mr. David Duvall's funeral. His regrettably late arrival placed him at the rear of the old chapel, which gave him an unobstructed view of several political dignitaries of note—people he'd not been aware were acquainted with the Duvall family.

He'd not noticed them straightaway, however; his eyes had immediately gone to the family gathered in the front two pews, and to one person in particular whose thick, braided twists and curls were dark red in the chapel's dim light, but which he knew would shine like a deep red wine shot through with gold in sunlight.

Charlotte had returned.

Charlotte Duvall, niece of Sally Hampton (of the Notorious Branch of the Hampton family), and cousin to the wives of two of the CID's best detectives. Amelie, Eva, and Charlotte—the Hampton trio had been missing its third piece in recent years, and John, to his surprise, had noted her absence keenly.

Charlotte was a force of nature once her mind was set on

a task. To her benefit, and those around her, her judgment was usually sound. That which she couldn't understand or master, she pursued until she could. Her move to America was proof. She'd felt the better education, especially for a woman, lay across the Atlantic, and after a year of training in London, she'd gone after it.

She turned her head, revealing her profile. Her black hat, rather than giving her a morose appearance, merely accentuated her red curls. The hem of the attached mesh veil hung just below her eyes, obstructing their intense emerald green. What a shame it would be if the world were denied a glimpse of that color. Knowing Charlotte as well as he did, he knew she'd not tolerate the veil for long.

He noted the subtle strain on her face as she leaned closer to Sally Hampton, listening to something her aunt whispered. John didn't know how close Charlotte had been to her late father, but he didn't imagine it was a joy to return home for a funeral rather than a reunion.

Five years earlier, Detective Michael Baker had met the Hampton House cousins, who became embroiled in an investigation, resulting in a near death and then a marriage for Amelie Hampton and the detective. The following summer, Detective Nathan Winston had entertained Eva Caldwell at a seaside holiday where she'd nearly died. They'd married that December.

The detectives and the cousins had made a comfortable social set of six, with John and Charlotte as the only unmarried pair. Platonic, the two of them? Absolutely. They'd not nearly died or fallen in love. Fond of one another? He comfortably assumed he could speak for himself and Charlotte if he also answered "absolutely" to that question. They'd become friends, and he cherished their friendship. A regular exchange of letters during the last four years had only solidified the friendship. She was straightforward, honest, and, beneath a fairly blunt exterior, was unfailingly kind at her core. She was fiercely protective of family and friends, and he would unhesitatingly call upon her in an emergency.

Then Charlotte had gone away for school, building a new life far away, and he didn't know if she'd be returning to it. It wouldn't signify to him, not really, if she left again. The Bakers now had two young children, and the Winstons had one toddler in addition to an adopted fourteen-year-old son, Sammy; the days of attending the theater and enjoying dinners into the late evening hours were a thing of the past. Their social lives had shifted, and it was not as though John ever felt like a fifth wheel to his friends. He didn't need Charlotte to stay behind to again round out the group; besides, his career didn't allow for much socializing. Seeing her again now, however, sent a pang through his heart as he realized how much he'd noted—and tried to ignore—her absence.

Charlotte turned her face forward, head bowed, and John willed the vicar to bring the service to an end. Mr. Duvall's body would be interred in the small cemetery outside, and close guests would retire to the family home for condolences and food. While he couldn't deny the prospect of good food was a motivator for his impatience, he also didn't want Charlotte to be sad for a moment longer than necessary. She was vibrance; she was life. She was not one for wallowing in despair, and as her friend, he hoped she would soon find solace in work or other pursuits. It was always better to look forward than back.

The organ struck a chord, and with a quiet sigh of relief, John stood with the congregation. He fumbled through a hymnal to find the closing song, mumbled through the words, and finally gave it up for lost and closed his mouth. He was at the back of the chapel—nobody would notice the breech of propriety. He saw so much death in the course of his career that he had little love for funerals. The hymns always seemed like cold comfort, the words hollow. Sentiments like "eternal rest in the arms of the Divine" did not fill the gaping hole left behind when someone died. Perhaps the only consolation here was that Mr. Duvall had lived a full life, a father to six sons and a daughter. At least he'd not been cut down in his prime.

The song drew to a close, and guests remained standing as the casket was carried down the aisle. The family walked slowly behind, a long slew of Charlotte's brothers and their wives, followed by Sally, who threaded her arm through Charlotte's. Their faces were solemn, and John noted the quiet breath Charlotte blew from between pursed lips.

He willed her to look up as they neared, and miraculously, she did. His late arrival had meant he'd not had an opportunity to speak with her, and he wanted her to know that he cared enough to be there. He saw the moment when she recognized him. She lifted the veil with black gloved fingers, and her eyes brightened. He swallowed. She was leaner and carried more of an air of maturity than when he'd last seen her. The stress around her eyes and mouth were obvious, but even still, the corner of her lips turned up as her gaze locked on his, and she put her hand to her chest as if to say, "Thank you."

He tipped his head to her and offered a small smile as she passed. His eyes followed her as she exited the building, and he absently registered Amelie and Eva walking behind her. It had been some time since the six friends had been together; his own schedule was tight, as were Michael's and Nathan's, but perhaps they might find an evening to reconnect.

During the internment, Michael found his two friends—technically his subordinates at the CID but friends nonetheless—who stood some distance back as the family gathered close to the grave. He quietly joined them, and they moved apart to accommodate him.

"Good of you to join us," Michael Baker whispered out of the side of his mouth, which tilted in a partial smile.

John considered offering the man a rude gesture but refrained. They stood on sacred church grounds, after all. "Where are your hellions?" he whispered instead.

"With Winston's sisters at the country house."

Nathan Winston nodded. "They've given us carte blanche to enjoy the evening all to ourselves."

"What will you do?" John asked.

"A lot of nothing, hopefully." Nathan rotated his head and massaged the back of his neck. "Except supper somewhere quiet."

John's lips twitched. Fatherhood had settled well on his friends, and he had to admit, the children were quite adorable, but the *noise.*

Mercy, the noise.

It wasn't as though he didn't imagine himself married someday, but it remained theoretical, a far-off notion. He simply hadn't the time. His profession ate up most of his waking hours, and sometimes his sleeping hours as well, and what little socializing he did was either as part of his work duties or at the behest of his mother, who was disappointed with his decision to pursue law enforcement rather than a military commission, as all good second sons were expected to do. He was required, regrettably, to natter at all political and social levels, and more often than not, found the process tedious. That his mother frequently found ways to introduce him to eligible ladies on the marriage hunt only made him dread the events even more.

At least Winston's mother had given Nathan fair warning of her intentions to move the matrimonial train along, and while

Mrs. Winston may not have introduced him to Eva, her machinations proved a success.

The crowd shifted, and John caught a glimpse of the three cousins, their backs to him, standing together by the grave. He was happy for his friends, and their wives were amazing women he was glad to call friends. He relied heavily on Amelie to keep his office and schedule organized; her weekly visits saved his sanity, and she was worth every penny of her salary. His gaze rested on Charlotte, who stood between Eva and Amelie. She leaned forward and tossed a clump of earth onto the casket as the vicar droned on, and then straightened, rotating her head on her shoulders. John smiled. It was her telltale sign of impatience. Amelie put an arm around Charlotte's shoulders and gave a squeeze.

Finally, the service was complete, and the crowd began dispersing. Amelie and Eva wove through the guests with relative ease, while Charlotte was caught multiple times by well-wishers. The five friends waited for her to eventually find a clear path to them, and as she neared, John noted her fatigue.

She extended her hands to him. "Hello, John," she said, her polite smile softening as it reached her eyes.

"Hello, friend." He took her hands and kissed her cheek. "Condolences that you must arrive home to a sad occasion."

She straightened and squeezed his fingers. Her eyes grew bright through tears he'd rarely seen her shed. "I've missed you all so much. Come to the house, won't you?"

"Of course," John said, pleased when she threaded her hand through his arm as they began to walk to the carriages.

"Your letters these last years have been a boon," she said, looking up at him. "Something from at least one of you five seemed to arrive on days when I needed it most."

"Grueling?" John put his free hand on hers where it rested against his arm.

"Extremely." She nodded. "But I did it."

"Absolutely, you did it," Michael said. "Never doubted you for a minute."

As they neared the carriages, a light rain began falling. They all quickened their steps. She would probably ride with family back to the house, and John realized it might be some time before they would be able to fully converse. There were many things he wanted to ask about her experiences, but the most important question of all hovered on his tongue and he couldn't hold it back.

"Are you staying here?" he asked. "Permanently, I mean? Or will you be returning to New York?"

The others paused, and he wondered if they'd all been thinking the same thing.

She frowned. "I initially thought to return straightaway, but there are"—she paused, brow wrinkling—"issues to settle here. Additionally, I'm uncertain whether the clinic will be able to hold my position for me." She offered a wan smile. "Competition is fierce."

"We are all well-connected," Winston said to her. "We shall see your career flourish here if you wish it."

She nodded but didn't confirm an intention to stay in England. Now that she was here, John realized he didn't like the idea of her leaving again. Her face at Nathan's suggestion, however, shifted to an expression John recognized. It was a light in her eyes, the notion that there was a plan of action in place she could follow.

"Thank you, Nathan. Very much. Will you all ride with me? Let's find a larger carriage."

They walked through the guests until they found a conveyance that would accommodate them all comfortably. The couples took opposite sides, with John and Charlotte sitting across from each other. As he settled in, John observed her. Something was bothering her. She had just lost her father, and her career in a new land across the ocean was now in question. And yet, he sensed it was something else. Something he couldn't quite put his finger on.

He narrowed his eyes as the carriage rocked into motion, and Charlotte rested her head against Eva's shoulder. She exhaled quietly and rubbed a furrow between her eyebrows. She caught John studying her, and she sat up straight with a tired smile.

"What is it?" she asked.

"That is what *I* am wondering." He lifted a brow.

"My mind is full of many, many things."

"Understandably."

"So much has happened in the span of a few days."

"Of course."

She chuckled. "You are interrogating me, Director Ellis."

He smiled. "I most certainly am not."

"You are asking questions using minimal phrasing and then waiting for the subject to fill the silence."

John stretched his leg across the carriage, resting his foot beside hers. If they hadn't been friends, the familiarity might have been unseemly, but there was something on her mind, and he was frustrated at his lack of ability to simply take her hand and lead her off somewhere to talk about it. Encourage her blunt honesty.

He nudged her foot gently. "What is it?"

She sighed through her nose. "I received a letter from my father that prompted my return. I was already on my way home when Thomas sent word of his death." She paused, and the silence lengthened. "My father said something about my mother's death, implied that it was not as it seemed. Said he had compiled a 'packet of evidence,' but I have no idea where it is or what it contains. However, Robert said my father had been going through old papers and journals, moving things from the attic to his bedroom."

Eva looked at her, frowning in question. "What sort of things?"

Charlotte returned her gaze. "My mother's things." She paused and looked again at John. "I fear much of my life has been a lie."

CHAPTER 3

Charlotte smiled at the gentleman who handed her a drink of punch, wishing she could escape the funeral visitors and close herself in a room with only her friends. She was exhausted and yet strung tighter than a bow.

"I apologize, your name, again?" she asked the man.

"James Carter," he said. "I was a friend of your parents."

Charlotte was jostled from behind, and Mr. Carter took her elbow, moving out of the way with her. "Goodness," she said, wiping spilled punch from her hand. "If only the weather would cooperate, we might spread out to the garden. We're awfully pressed for space."

"Shame this isn't a regular social event, no? It's quite the crush—a grand feather in the cap of any good hostess." Mr. Carter chuckled at his own wit.

Charlotte managed a wan smile, and Mr. Carter looked over his shoulder at a woman who was clearly nudging his arm. He cleared his throat and nodded at Charlotte.

"At any rate, Miss Duvall, I offer my condolences on behalf of myself and my wife." He gestured to the woman, who looked strangely nervous. She smiled, but it faltered as her gaze snagged on someone behind Charlotte. Mr. Carter had paused, perhaps waiting for his wife's response, but then said, "This is Phillipa. As I said, we were friends with your mother and father."

Charlotte's ears perked up, even as she looked over her shoulder at a crowd of strangers, wondering who had caught Phillipa Carter's attention. The woman had gone quite pale. "You knew my mother?"

"I should say so." Mr. Carter smiled broadly with a nod. "Quite the group, we all were. Would you not say so, dear?"

Phillipa nodded, but she looked so uncomfortable Charlotte couldn't help but pity her. "Do you spend time in Town?" she asked the couple. "Perhaps we might have tea sometime, and you may share your memories with me?"

"Splendid," Mr. Carter beamed. "We are always in Town for the Season and often between. Carter Textiles is headquartered there, of course, and I am never far from the office."

Charlotte realized why the name had sounded familiar. Carter Textiles was a successful enterprise, second only perhaps to Winston Textiles, owned by Eva's husband's family.

"I look forward to an invitation," Charlotte said to Mrs. Carter, as though the idea had originated with the other woman. "Tea would be delightful."

Charlotte's intention was not to put Mrs. Carter in an uncomfortable position, but her head was beginning to throb. Someone else bumped up against her, mumbling an apology, and she worked to keep a scowl from her face.

She looked across the parlor at her brothers, most of whom were duly visiting as they'd all agreed as siblings they would do—share the burden, feed the guests, clear them out. Thomas looked particularly pained as a gentleman Charlotte didn't know guffawed and elbowed him in the ribs, laughing about the women who had visited their father in recent months.

"Ever a gentleman for the ladies was our David," the man said.

Charlotte raised a dubious brow. She'd not known her father to be one to hold court with the ladies; he'd always been rather withdrawn. Though Charlotte would have been happy had he remarried. Perhaps it would have chased away some of the shadows that had lingered in his eyes for as long as Charlotte could remember.

Charlotte narrowed her gaze on the gentleman with Thomas—was he a member of Parliament? She recognized him, but surely her father had not counted such high-profile men amongst his friends. And yet here were the Carters, quite esteemed and socially connected. She'd not been home for years, though, so perhaps her father had changed his social habits.

She frowned as Thomas's wife, Joan, swooped in and ushered the MP away with a plate of pastries. The entire event felt surreal as the chatter continued. Faces belonging to people she'd never met entered and exited as though on stage, blurring from one to the next until Charlotte wondered if she'd taken a tumble down the rabbit hole. The home was familiar, everything about it was the same as when she'd left, but her father was gone and in his place were strangers who uttered platitudes or claimed relationships of which she'd never been aware.

She realized, belatedly, that she'd gotten distracted and not said an official farewell to the Carters, who had disappeared. She hoped they did not think her incredibly rude. On the other hand, she mused, perhaps she'd done Mrs. Carter a favor by allowing them to slip away. The woman clearly had been uncomfortable.

She spied her aunt, Sally Hampton, and Eva's mother, Esther Caldwell, chatting with a group of well-dressed and clearly wealthy women. The look of them standing together like a flock of fine birds set Charlotte's back up. She wasn't one to judge unfairly—at least she made a conscious effort not to do so—but the expressions on most of the women's faces varied from boredom to mild distaste as their gazes scanned the parlor and its décor. They did not seem to be the sort of people who would have spent time with her father, but perhaps they were merely the wives who were obliged to accompany their husbands as they paid their respects.

Charlotte frowned into her glass of punch. Most of it had spilled on her hand and, regrettably, down the front of her long skirt. At least the fabric was black. It should clean up easily enough. From the corner of her eye, she spied Amelie, who peeked at her through the almost-closed French doors leading into the smaller study off the parlor. She motioned to Charlotte, who set down her cup on a sideboard and made a beeline for the study. She would apologize to her brothers later for shirking hostess responsibilities; besides Joan had things well enough in hand. This dereliction of duties wouldn't drop Charlotte in her sister-in-law's estimation—Joan rarely had anything good to say about anything Charlotte did.

She put her head down and made her way across the room, hoping she wouldn't be intercepted. As she passed the throng surrounding her aunts, she heard a muted gasp but didn't slow her progress. Probably one of the esteemed ladies had noted décor that was hopelessly out of fashion. *Quelle horreur!*

Charlotte slipped between the glass doors, which were covered by a heavy lace curtain, obscuring the view between the rooms. She was relieved to see both of her cousins, their husbands, and John Ellis in the study. She quietly clicked the doors closed and then smiled her thanks at Eva, who handed her a fresh cup of tea.

She'd not had a moment to relax in the four days since

returning to England. She'd missed her cousins and their husbands desperately, and John Ellis, who was handsomer than ever. She'd have not imagined four short years could give someone an increased air of command, but somehow it had with John. If she hadn't known him personally, she'd have been intimidated, and she was not easily intimidated. His career was not an easy one, though, and she sensed, rather than saw, an additional thread of stress in his demeanor.

With the noise from the parlor dampened, Charlotte breathed a sigh of relief and sat back in her chair.

"How fares the mingling?" Amelie asked.

"People mean well," Charlotte muttered, then sipped her tea as the others settled around her.

Amelie chuckled. "However?"

Charlotte shook her head. "More often than not, the commiseration lends itself to the sentiment that I must feel awful at having put my education above my father's health. From the women, of course, which is doubly galling. Oddly enough, the gentlemen don't breathe a word of it."

John, seated on an ottoman next to her chair, chuckled. "Likely because they were unaware you were gone, or why." He winked at her. "The older set, at least."

"Fair amount of the younger set, too," Eva remarked drily. "The faces of new constables when I appear at crime scenes with my photography equipment—quite priceless."

Charlotte smiled. "I imagine that part of the business has slowed since your cherub arrived, no?"

Eva tipped her head and looked at her husband, a smile on her lips. "Slowed, yes, but there are times I simply must get some fresh air."

Nathan smirked and put his arm around Eva, rubbing her neck. "Gruesome crime scenes amount to 'fresh air' now."

They all laughed, but Charlotte understood her cousin completely. A woman did not cease having other interests in life by giving birth; the notion was embraced by suffragettes and bluestockings, but still rubbed up against tradition held by many.

"You can take pictures and still be an exceptional figure of motherhood," Charlotte told her with a smile.

Michael and Amelie had settled next to each other on a small divan, and Amelie leaned against her husband's arm with a yawn. Two children kept her busy all day, although her cousin still maintained the spark Charlotte had always adored in her.

"Amelie, where do you find your fresh air these days?" Charlotte asked, taking another appreciative sip of the tea. She still felt the chill from the cemetery despite the warmth of the fire in the hearth.

Amelie pointed at John. "With that one."

Everyone laughed as Michael shook his head, bemused.

John shrugged. "I make no apologies. She's still by far the best assistant I've ever had. I'm willing to take whatever I can from her." He winked at Amelie, and Charlotte laughed again. How she'd missed them all!

Charlotte looked at the other two couples, seated close to each other, and nudged John gently with her knee. "Seems as though we're still the bachelor and spinster of the group. We must be too set in our ways by now for matrimonial bliss."

He looked at her with a half smile. "No hope for us, I fear."

He really was too handsome for words. Dark hair, hazel eyes, broad through the shoulders, tall. How he'd not yet been ensnared—whether due to family pressures or his own efforts—was a mystery to her. She didn't much like the thought of him sitting here with a wife, though; she supposed her affection for him was making her proprietary.

"Can you get away for supper at the café later?" Amelie asked Charlotte. "We're staying with the Winstons and Eva's mother, and they're shepherding all the children for the evening."

Charlotte nodded. "The only person who might have issue with me going anywhere is Joan, and that's because she is a crone." The others laughed, and Charlotte rolled her eyes. "She was among the first to express her dismay that I'd put my interests above family duty, and she hopes desperately I'll forgive myself someday."

Charlotte's brothers—six of them in all—had been the bane of her existence for as long as she could remember. Now that she was an adult, twenty-six years of age, for heaven's sake, they ought to have accorded her at least a modicum of respect. She would always be the youngest, and a girl, and her father was no longer here to shush them when they teased.

A wave of sorrow washed over her, and she closed her eyes. When she'd left for school, her father had embraced her tightly and whispered in her ear how proud he was to be her father and that her mother was surely looking on from heaven with equal love and pride. He had written to her regularly in the beginning, but his letters had grown less frequent and more disjointed.

She had yet to speak with any of her brothers about his last letter, in part because her father had not confided in them himself and also because she didn't know which of the lot would be the most helpful. They were busy with their own lives, and she wasn't certain how closely any of them other than Thomas had been with her father in his final months.

Her friends watched her expectantly, and she knew she owed them an explanation for her declaration in the carriage.

She sighed and set her tea on the table, looking at her cousins. "Speaking of my family . . . I don't know that I've ever explained to the gentlemen the circumstances surrounding my mother's death." She rose and went to the mantel, glancing at the closed French doors before retrieving her reticule she'd placed there after the funeral.

She returned to her seat, admitting, "*Nobody* seems to know exactly what circumstances surrounded my mother's death." She took a deep breath. "My mother was not my father's first wife; my five older brothers were the first wife's sons. After she died of a prolonged illness, my father married my mother, who was substantially younger than he was, and she bore him my brother, Robert, and then me. I was four years old when she died. I have only vague memories, a daguerreotype, and a small painting my father had commissioned of her."

She frowned, looking at the reticule in her lap. "I don't know about the dynamics between my parents—I was much too young to understand—but I know from the little bits Aunt Sally has told me through the years that my father changed when my mother died. He drew in upon himself. He became a different person."

She looked up with a small smile. "It makes sense, of course. We change when we lose a loved one. But Sally has implied that the change was . . . severe. Stark."

The room was still except for the crackle of the fire.

"My parents were in Town for a friend's celebration. They had brought Robert and me with them. We were in the nursery the morning after she died, when my father joined us there. I remember being surprised—he never so much as darkened the door of the nursery—and then he said Mama had gone to heaven, and we would never see her again. When I grew a little older, he told me my mother's death was an accident, that she drowned in the Thames."

"She drowned?" John asked quietly. "Was that the official cause of death?"

"As I understand it." Charlotte frowned. "There are so many things I wish I would have asked him, and now it's too late." She paused, forehead creasing as she examined the paper in her hand. "I share this with all of you in the hopes that you can help me make sense of it." She swallowed and withdrew her father's last letter from the reticule. She read it aloud; the silence in the room was punctuated only by the occasional crackle from the fire.

When she finished, she looked at John. "What on earth am I to do with this information? Do you believe—as my brothers do—that he might have been suffering from senility?"

John frowned. "I did not know your father well, but the letter sounds coherent, if a bit veiled."

"I hoped to do a deep search in his library for this 'packet of information' he has stashed away somewhere, but I haven't had time alone." She folded the letter into a small square. "Thomas and Joan are moving into the home soon, as my father left it to them, and Joan has already staked her claim over much of everything in it." She shook her head. "I do not want her meddling in this."

She looked at her cousins, who watched her with sympathetic eyes. "I have questions for Sally too, but she must return to Town tonight. Eva, has your mother ever mentioned anything suspicious about my mother's death?"

Eva frowned and shook her head. "Only that she drowned, and that always surprised her because Aunt Katherine was an exceptional swimmer."

John straightened, regarding her carefully. "Charlotte." He

paused. "Your father's letter seems to be implying . . . murder." He pointed to the paper she still held. "Did he ever mention your mother having enemies?"

She shook her head. "Nothing. I wish he would have written the truth. All I have are suspicions and vague hints." She bit her lip, lowering her voice. "Perhaps he *was* suffering from senility." The thought of her father's bright mind having deteriorated made her feel ill.

She looked at John. "Perhaps this is nothing. But perhaps . . . perhaps I've learned nothing but lies about my mother's death."

John, Michael, and Nathan exchanged glances. She'd seen that look on each of their faces when working on various cases. Their investigative instincts were never far from the surface, and now that the word "murder" had entered the conversation, the energy in the room felt different.

John reached for her hand and clasped it. "Perhaps do some digging for this packet of proof your father claims to have compiled." He turned to Amelie and added, "I'll leave a signed request for you to access the archives next week when you come to the office. Can't hurt to look for information." He squeezed Charlotte's hand and gave her a little nod. "We'll get to the root of it."

Now that Pandora's box had been opened, Charlotte wasn't certain she wanted to look inside.

CHAPTER 4

Charlotte changed into her dressing gown later that evening and sat at the vanity in her childhood bedroom. She let her hair down from its pins and twists with a sigh and massaged her scalp with a wince. Her hair was thick and heavy, and while vanity permitted her to enjoy it, the relief at dismantling the elegant configurations that formal events required was immense.

She viewed her reflection—so different from the last time she'd sat in that very place and thought with optimism and hope about her future. In truth, reality had surprised and surpassed what she thought she might do with her life, and she was embarking on a career full of challenges she'd never have dreamed of. She was pleased and proud, and she was glad her father had lived long enough to receive word of her college graduation.

She'd expected to feel sadness upon arriving home for the funeral, but the element of unease was worse. She brushed out her hair, looking at the room's reflection in the mirror. It was reversed—each item properly in place, but then again, not. Everything was backward, flipped, and was a perfect analogy for the state of her reality.

Everything felt off.

She had always believed her mother had died in an accident,

had fallen overboard while on a ferry ride down the Thames and drowned.

Now, Charlotte's father had written to her of secrets, and she had questions. Who could have wanted to hurt her mother? And for what reason? Had it been storming that day on the Thames? Who had been with her mother at the time? Had her father witnessed the "accident"? John had said the letter implied murder, which was a difficult concept to consider.

She remembered prying for details in her childish innocence in the months following the death, but her father had cried, and so she'd learned to avoid the subject. She couldn't bear to see him upset. It had become a habit, then. She did not ask about her mother's death, did not even ask Aunt Sally about it. Sally shared details about her sister's life when Charlotte asked, but they did not discuss the ending of it. Sally had been the youngest of the Hampton children and had adored Katherine. Would Charlotte soon find herself tasked with informing Sally that her sister had secrets—even enemies—that resulted in her death? Her heart clenched.

A quiet knock on the door pulled her from her thoughts, and she answered it to see Thomas standing there.

"Are you well?" he asked.

She blinked. "Am I . . ." Thomas had never asked about her welfare before.

He shifted his stance. "Joan mentioned seeing you leave the gathering before the guests had left. She was wondering if you were ill."

"Ah." Charlotte smiled. "Please convey my thanks to Joan. I was suffering from an aching head, but I feel much better now. I convalesced for a time with Amelie and Eva."

His lips pinched. "I see."

"I was still entertaining guests. They are family, after all, who came to pay respects."

"Your family."

Charlotte blinked again. "My . . . ?"

"They are *your* cousins. Your mother's nieces."

She was stunned into silence. When she finally found her voice, it was flat. "I was unaware you considered Katherine Duvall anything but a mother. My memories are scant, but I was under the impression that we all referred to her as 'Mother.'"

He flushed. "It was complicated, Charlotte, and I was much older than the rest of you."

The silence between them stretched. She didn't want to ask for his insight, but the sense of urgency her father had created left her pride little choice. "What sort of things occupied Father's time in the months before he died?"

Now Thomas blinked in surprise. "Things? His customary pursuits, I suppose. Bird-watching, word puzzles. He spent time sitting out at the pond, feeding the ducks." He frowned. "He was at the pond when his heart failed. He'd fallen in."

Charlotte's mouth dropped open. "He fell in the pond?" Her thoughts raced. "What were the autopsy results?"

"Autopsy results?" Thomas scoffed. "There was no cause for autopsy. His doctor had visited only days before and told me Father's days were numbered. He finally suffered an angina pectoris and died. Honestly, Charlotte, all of that studying has made you rather gauche."

"I am a doctor, Thomas." She kept her voice even. "I did more than just 'study.' I am also David Duvall's daughter, and I have a right to know the exact cause of his death."

Thomas shrugged, spreading his hands. "What difference does it make? He was dying, Charlotte! If you'd bothered to come home, you'd have realized it. Joan was the one who cared for him those final weeks, though it ought to have been his own daughter."

Charlotte felt emotion rising and tried to swallow it back. Her anger was spurred by guilt, by her belief that he was right. She rubbed a hand across her forehead and chose her words carefully. "I received an odd letter from him just before I returned. He spoke of conspiracies and danger. Something about my mother's death."

Thomas frowned, and the bafflement on his face told her he knew as little as she. He finally sighed. "His mind was fading. He wasn't himself. He thought Joan was a scullery maid and I was a footman. I wouldn't put much stock in what he may have said to you before he died."

Charlotte nodded. "Very well." The words of the letter swam in her head, and she wondered again if they were the product of a man who'd lost his concept of reality.

Silence stretched as they both gathered their thoughts. She imagined herself and Thomas each taking a deep breath and a mental step back. As she shifted her weight to bid him good night, she remembered another thing she'd wanted to ask. "I met some people of consequence today following the services. I wasn't aware Father kept such august company."

Thomas lifted a shoulder. "I was surprised, myself. They were mostly your mother's associates, apparently. MP Worthingstone mentioned spending many social functions with them in the early years. Said it was only right to pay their respects to the husband of a lifelong friend."

There was an edge to his voice, an unuttered implication that Katherine had been Charlotte's mother, not his.

She nodded. "Good night, Thomas. I'll be in Town for the near future but shall return soon to pack my belongings. Please tell Joan I appreciate her patience with the delay."

Thomas nodded stiffly. "Good night."

She closed the door with a soft click and returned to the vanity, sinking slowly onto the padded stool. She would have to decide soon which path she wanted to pursue. She couldn't expect her employers in America to hold her job indefinitely, but she couldn't leave England without knowing for certain what her father had meant in his final letter.

The first year of her studies in London had included volunteer work at Delaney Hospital, which treated London's poorest populations. She'd developed a warm relationship with both the matron and the hospital president and had maintained the connection during her years away. On impulse, she pulled a piece of paper from her stationery set and addressed a short letter to them both, asking if she might call on them soon. Though she didn't know where it would lead, the simple fact that she was taking action, that life wasn't just happening to her, calmed her nerves.

When she finally turned down the lights and climbed into bed, sleep remained elusive, tired though she was. Her father had left her with questions that might never be answered.

CHAPTER 5

Charlotte was increasingly in John's thoughts the next several days. Perhaps she was tired from four years of rigorous schooling and living far away from home, or that her return brought with it a flood of unexpected questions. In his mind, however, her father's letter left little room for doubt about what David Duvall believed had happened to his young wife. He didn't know if Charlotte was prepared to accept it, though. Perhaps when John had a moment to review the police file, he would have answers for her.

Charlotte Duvall was the most levelheaded woman John had ever known. His first interactions with her, when Amelie had found herself the target of a madman, had impressed him to no end. She was practical, direct, and what he would describe as "tough," despite being a woman of gentle rearing.

He thought about her as he tied his cravat in his dressing room. He occupied the townhome he'd inherited from his mother's side. His elder brother, Edgar, was their father's heir and lived with his family near their parents. John had never coveted his brother's position, and in fact, much preferred his own. That he'd chosen a career in law enforcement over the military was a sticking point with his parents, but his strong will had always matched theirs, so that was that. It didn't stop them from insisting he make a suitable social match, however, and they'd had more conversations about the matter than he could count.

Tonight, he was obliged to attend a political gathering disguised as a ball and anticipating it had caused a headache to form behind his eyes that was spreading up into his forehead. He'd known when becoming the CID director that a certain amount of political pandering was part of the job. As much as it irritated him, he often found it useful; though, if given the choice, he preferred direct conversation in a club or office. Combining work with social settings where his mother would manipulate him into dancing with women he'd already met—and who agreed with him that their match was unsuitable—was tiresome.

Sally Hampton might be in attendance, as she frequently was, and he found her conversation refreshing. Perhaps because she reminded him of Charlotte. His mother had little good to say about "*those* Hamptons," but he was usually able to ignore her criticisms. His head was hurting tonight, however, and if he didn't soon swallow a pot of black tea, he feared the pain would bloom into something incapacitating. Then his hopes for keeping his mother's snide comments from bothering him would be put to the test, and he feared he'd lose.

He straightened his neckwear, satisfied with his appearance. His valet appeared at his side with a cup of the requested tea, and John took it with a nod. Piping hot, no sugar, barely a splash of milk. Casting up an unuttered prayer of hope it would do the trick, he drank it quickly before heading down the stairs, his valet at his heels.

"Mason, I shouldn't be much past one o'clock," he said as Mason helped him into his overcoat and brushed off his shoulders. "Even so, do not wait up. I can manage."

"You're certain, sir?" Mason had been with John for a decade, so he knew him well. He would see the strain around his eyes and the headache settling there. "I shall leave laudanum at your night table."

"Yes, thank you." He hoped he wouldn't need the medicine—it made him tired, and he had work piled high on his desk for the morning. As he stepped out into the crisp autumn evening and waited for his carriage to be brought around, he smelled the city air and wished to be back in the country.

His carriage stopped in front of him, and John gave the driver the address before climbing in. It was another difference from life in the country; there, he'd have ridden his horse to a social gathering, enjoying the freedom of his own control. The carriage lamp burned low, and he turned it up slightly despite the pain in his head, then reached for one of the evening edition newspapers that lay crisply folded for him on the seat.

Sensationalism, much of it, but he made a point of glancing over as many publications as he could throughout the course of a day. Knowledge was power, and knowledge of London and its denizens was crucial to his success. At the bottom of the stack lay *The Marriage Gazette.* He smiled. Sally Hampton had purchased the failing publication a few years earlier and employed her three nieces there. She also provided them room and board at the cozy, respectable Hampton House in Bloomsbury. It had been her desire to see the young women begin their adult lives as Women of Independent Means, as Amelie liked to say, and Sally's successes in that endeavor were impressive.

Amelie was the best assistant John had ever had, and he used her organizational skills as often as he could secure her time. Eva had built a reputation as an excellent photographer whose skills were in high demand despite the advent of personal cameras that had begun to circulate from New York. And Charlotte . . . John smiled. A doctor. She'd done it, though he'd never doubted she would.

He set the papers aside and turned down the light. Leaning back against the comfortable seat, he closed his eyes. He hoped Sally would be in attendance tonight. He wanted an update on Charlotte's plans.

The carriage came to an abrupt stop, and John winced at the sudden lurch. He looked out the window to see a large crowd entering the Fulbright home. Carriages lined the street, and John sighed as he exited his, telling the driver he'd walk the rest of the way. He put on his hat, wishing for a moment he could keep it on as the tension of the brim eased some of the pain.

He smoothed his features as he reached the front doors, nodding at people he knew and managing a smile as he tipped his hat to the Misses Van Horne, octogenarian twin sisters who were sought-after party attendees following the murder that had occurred in their home nearly five years back. Every hostess in London hoped that their eccentric appearance might spark *something* memorable that would make the gathering the talk of the town.

"Handsome as ever," Margaret said to Ethel, elbowing her as she looked John up and down. "Age sits well on you, Director."

"As it does with you, Miss Van Horne." He took her elbow as they stepped inside the brightly lit foyer of the enormous home. "I do hope both of you will allow me to ply you with refreshments later this evening."

Ethel muttered something to her sister that John couldn't discern but was certain was a bit ribald. His lips tightened as he fought a smile, wishing the ladies were decades younger and yet somehow relieved they weren't.

"I bid you a momentary farewell," he told them as he handed

his hat and coat to an attendant, "and pray you'll save me a dance." The ladies never danced, and he knew it. He also knew that *they* knew he knew it. It was an amusing game they played at each event, which delighted them to no end.

"Of course, we shall," Ethel answered, adjusting the grip on her cane. "Pray you do not take too long in searching us out. We shall likely be near the refreshments table, or perhaps with Lady Swinton. She usually faints during the second hour, you see, and we make wagers."

His mouth twitched, and he gave them a small bow.

"Too much more of that and you'll cause a scandal," a voice said at his elbow.

He turned to see Charlotte, and his heart tripped in surprise. "You're in Town?" He stated the obvious as he took her hands and kissed one.

"I am, indeed. Moving back into Hampton House while I contemplate my career." She rolled her eyes and lowered her voice. "If I'm able to create one at all. Mr. Auburn of the Medical Society has already given me the cut direct, and we've not even made it into the ballroom."

Satisfaction rose as he considered the implications. "You're staying in London?"

She nodded. "At least until I unravel this business about my parents. I do not know how long it will take, and if I am not working, I'll go mad. I've written to Matron Halcomb at Delaney Hospital and arranged an interview."

John put his hand on her back and led her toward the wide-open doors of the ballroom where music played, a cacophony of voices sounded, and the gasoliers shone brighter than the sun. He winced at the noise. "You'll find yourself employed in no time—with Dr. Auburn's approval or without it."

She looked up at him and paused, long enough that he looked down at her in question.

"You have a headache," she said.

He nodded, but even that hurt.

"John," she murmured. "You should be at home."

"I must speak with a certain member of Parliament. Quincy's proposal for restructuring the police fund has the potential to impact my department severely."

"Surely you can schedule an appointment with him later."

They were bumped from behind, and he guided her farther into the room. "Charlotte, you know as well as I do that it's much better to raise such a matter initially in a neutral setting, preferably one where he is either already into his cups, losing badly at cards, or desperate enough to escape his wife that he welcomes the distraction."

"That is true, but I don't imagine the impression you'll leave if you vomit on his shoes will be favorable."

"Perhaps not, but as you've said, it will be memorable." He smiled at her quiet chuckle.

"Do you see him here?"

John was tall and had a good view through the crowd despite a profusion of feathers and ribbons adorning a multitude of feminine hats. "Not yet, but we've only just arrived."

"Suppose we circle around to the balcony? We can avoid the worst of the din, and the cooler air will do you good."

"Is that your order as a physician?" He smiled at her, but to his consternation, silver flashes appeared in his vision and partially obscured her face. She must have seen it in his expression; she'd been present once before at the onset of a megrim.

She paused, stood on her toes to see through the crowded

room, and with a huff of frustration, took his arm firmly. "Come with me."

Nausea was settling in, and he followed her willingly as she carefully guided him back through the doors and down a hallway to the left. They walked for some time before she tried a door that opened into a cooler room. A library, with a few lamps burning low in the far corners.

"Cause a scandal for certain," he murmured as she guided him to a deep leather sofa.

"Haven't you heard? I am a Notorious Hampton; people expect nothing less." Her voice was soft, and he heard her stripping off her gloves. "Lean back," she said, placing cool fingertips against his forehead and exerting light pressure.

He did as she ordered, closing his eyes in relief at the coolness of the room. He heard her cross the floor, followed by a collection of sounds: water poured from a pitcher, a rustle of fabric, the sound of water droplets hitting a tray. She returned to his side and sat gingerly next to him.

"I'm going to place a cool cloth on your forehead," she said, her voice low, soothing.

"You're very good at this," he said, wondering if his words were making sense. The pain was excruciating.

"I ought to be." She placed a cool stretch of fabric on his forehead, and he nearly groaned in relief. "I'm going to mix a powder for you to drink. It doesn't have the heavy effects of laudanum and won't completely cure the pain, but it should remove some of the edge."

"You travel with an apothecary?"

"I have suffered more headaches than I imagined possible over the last four years. I never go anywhere without it." Her voice was wry, and he heard the sounds of fabric whispering, paper crinkling, and a spoon clinking efficiently in a glass. "Here, drink it."

"Yes, ma'am." The thought of refusing her never crossed his mind. "Is it true that in the United States, the term 'doctor' applies to both physicians and surgeons?"

"That is true."

"So, the title is considered one of distinction, regardless of specialty."

"Correct."

"Here, a surgeon worth his salt would never be addressed as anything but 'Mr.'"

"That is also correct." He heard the smile in her voice.

"Which do you prefer, then? You've trained as a surgeon."

"Hmm." She paused. "I worked quite strenuously for the distinction of 'doctor.' No matter the difference in status here, hearing that honorific does make me smile."

"Then, Dr. Duvall, I must confess something."

"Yes?" He heard the smile in her voice again.

"I've missed you dreadfully, friend."

CHAPTER 6

Charlotte refreshed the cold napkin she'd placed on John's forehead and smiled at his sigh of relief. It was the third such sound he'd made since arriving in the quiet library, and as one who'd suffered plenty of head strain, she could relate.

"How long do you suppose we can hide in here before our absence is noted?" She sat next to him on the leather sofa, one elbow resting on the back of it, facing him.

"Hmm. Considering the attentiveness of not only our esteemed hostess but also my mother, I'd guess we have another twenty minutes before tongues begin wagging."

She laughed quietly. "Perhaps nobody saw us enter the home at all."

"Wishful thinking, my dear."

"It wouldn't be seemly for the director of the Criminal Investigation Department to be sullied by his association with the scandalous lady doctor who spent four years in America doing who knows what."

He lifted the side of his makeshift bandage and tilted his head, cracking open one eye. "My reputation can only be enhanced by keeping company with the smartest, most stunningly beautiful woman in London."

To her surprise, she felt sheepish at his compliment and her cheeks warmed. To hide it, she wrinkled her nose at him. "I don't remember you as one who plied women with false flattery, John Ellis."

"False?" He snorted and repositioned the cloth over his eyes. "I don't remember you being one who lacks self-awareness, Dr. Duvall."

"Smartest?" She laughed softly. "Perhaps I'll own that one."

"The other is equally true, and I would have you know that, as well." He reached over and found her fingers, giving them a squeeze. "The world is not kind, but sometimes we are cruelest to ourselves." He rested his hand on her leg.

She smiled and lowered her head on her arm, which was still crooked on the back of the sofa. "I am sorry for anyone who cannot boast of an acquaintance with you, Director."

He chuckled. "Ah, words that can be spoken only by one who is fond of another. Plenty of people wish they could *not* boast of an acquaintance with me."

"How are you feeling?" She was close to him and, despite the low light in the room, had a clear view of his profile.

Handsome as sin, this one.

She wondered if she should tell him that. He'd paid her a very nice compliment after all, even if it was, as he'd said of her, "words spoken by one who is fond of another."

"I'm feeling fractionally better," he murmured. He removed the cloth and turned to look at her, still resting their clasped hands against her leg. "Your apothecary-in-a-reticule has come to my rescue. The pain is lessening enough that I should be able to stand in the ballroom without embarrassing myself."

"Good. We should return, then."

"We should." He smiled, and she had the absurd thought that he was close enough to lean in for a kiss.

"Scandal," she murmured, her lips curving upward.

"Indeed." He paused. "You and I are so very similar, Charlotte," he whispered. "I suppose that accounts for our friendship."

"Similar, how?"

"We are driven, obsessively so, to succeed. We've taken obscure paths despite the good opinions of those around us." He drew his brows lightly together, his eyes tired but clear. "We've little time for the customary pursuits that polite society requires."

"You speak of marriage and family, of course." Charlotte thought of her cousins and their children and smiled, surprised to feel a little wistful.

"Some things come at a cost."

"Yes." She was growing increasingly aware of the warmth of his body, his arm, his hand on her leg. Her chest slowly rose and fell, and she was loath to move away. "I will cherish my role as the 'favored aunt,' then. Nurses are required to remain single to keep their employment, and until convention changes, the same holds for women doctors." She sighed. "Besides, I'm quite on the shelf, you know."

He laughed through his nose. "Absurd. You are more alluring than any young girl just out of the schoolroom."

Her eyes locked on his, and she felt herself sinking into their hazel depths. Her heart thumped in response to his compliment. Rather than indulge it, however, she whispered, "Your personality would crush a girl just out of the schoolroom."

"Who would I not crush?" His expression was serious but unguarded. Gone was the consummate professional, the man who commanded a room and everything in it with his presence alone.

"Someone equally fierce."

"Where would I find such a person, I wonder?" He lifted their joined hands and placed his lips on her fingers.

Mercy.

She ought to have guessed he would be potent in his close regard of a woman given his notice of detail, his scrutiny of the individual. When he did settle, the future Mrs. Ellis would be the luckiest woman alive. To have his undivided attention, his unfettered affection—it was certainly more than she could ever expect to find. He was one of few men who didn't view her as a threat, who didn't believe her education had made her less feminine.

A voice sounded in the hall, faint, but enough of an interruption that she sat up. He released her hand. She smiled, searching for equilibrium. "I'm sure you'll find your perfect match."

He straightened, folding the damp cloth, and arched a brow at her. There it was. His mask was back in place. The vulnerability was gone.

"I don't suppose you'll help me find her? You did work at *The Marriage Gazette*, after all."

"I did not realize you were looking." Once again, as she'd noted after the funeral, the thought of him with a wife did not sit well with her.

"Neither did I."

She tilted her head. "I am confused."

He gave her a half smile. "As am I. I am not looking."

"Nor I." She didn't know why she felt the need to tell him.

"Good."

"Good! How could I remain employed after all my hard work if I ruined it with marriage?"

"Indeed." He nodded seriously.

"Besides, we've already established that I'm too busy and much too unconventional to please an average man." She was talking in circles.

He winked at her. "He'd best be above average, then."

"Perhaps I ought to make use of *The Marriage Gazette* for myself," she muttered.

"I did not think you were looking."

"I'm not!"

He smiled broadly, and she laughed. Good. They were back on familiar footing. She didn't know what kind of bewitched web had wound itself around them in the library, but she would be well advised to avoid such close communion in the future. It wouldn't do at all to develop feelings deeper than friendship for John Ellis.

She rose, and he followed her from the room, offering his arm when they reached the hallway.

"You are feeling better?" she asked.

"Much. This was just what I needed."

CHAPTER 7

John and Charlotte parted when they reached the ballroom, both nodding politely at each other. He wasn't certain what had happened during the thirty minutes they had been in the library, but he didn't think he was the same man who'd entered.

He'd wanted to kiss her. His friend. Of course she was beautiful, and of course any man would want to kiss her, but their relationship had always been different. They'd regarded each other largely with suspicion when they'd first met, but they had both softened, becoming friendlier over time. Humor infused their friendship, and they enjoyed common reflections on life, believed the same things were important. He couldn't count the times while she had been away that he saw or heard something he knew she'd appreciate, making sure to include a note about it in a letter to her.

His was a deep regard for a cherished friend, not something frivolous. Kiss her? Kiss his friend? The notion was absurd. The headache must have muddled his thinking.

They had been sitting so close—they'd never sat so close to each other—in a darkened room, speaking softly, becoming reacquainted and falling back into the same comfortable pattern they'd always enjoyed.

They'd danced in the past, and he'd offered his arm when the six friends went to the theater or dinner. He pulled out her chair, helped her with her overcoat. She'd often held his gloves while he situated his hat. But those were things friends did. They were not like Nathan and Eva, who had been so obviously enamored of each other before they realized it themselves. Charlotte was not like Amelie, who had been starry-eyed and full of the conviction that romantic love was a fundamental human right.

John and Charlotte were *friends*. That was all.

He'd forgotten for a while that their association did not include that invisible pull, the yearning, the quickened breath. He could certainly be forgiven for that momentary lapse, because he was a man in his prime, and she was . . . exquisite.

Strains of a waltz sounded from the musicians on the far end of the room, and as he looked around for Mr. Quincy, a member of Parliament and the reason for his attendance at the ball in the first place, he saw a flash of Charlotte's deep auburn hair. She was dancing with a gentleman he knew, Franklin Frampton, who was a perfectly affable fellow. Frampton smiled and said something Charlotte must have found amusing, because she laughed, genuine delight showing in her deep green eyes.

John's head began to ache again, and he realized he was clenching his jaw. And his fists. He shoved his hands into his pockets and maneuvered through the crowd to an empty spot on the wall which he claimed for himself. Regrettably, he still had a clear view of the dancing couples, and no sooner was Charlotte out of sight as Franklin spun her around than she reappeared. Still smiling, occasionally laughing, perpetually lovely.

John exhaled quietly and pinched the bridge of his nose. He should have insisted he wasn't well enough to leave the library. Then he wouldn't be forced to watch Frampton being friendly with *his* friend.

A woman appeared at his side, and he turned to see Sally Hampton, dressed in the latest designs and looking at him beneath her fashionably cut dark fringe. She was a pretty woman in her forties and always at the forefront of society's trends. She'd turned down at least two proposals that he knew of, both from men of means and reputation. Sally had her own money, though, and her own reputation. She need not acquire them from external sources.

"Director," she said to him with a smile. "Lovely to see you out and about at one of society's finest events. Glad your work pursuits do not consume every moment of your life. It can be so tedious, I find. Wouldn't you agree?"

"I would agree, Miss Hampton. As a fellow member of the working class, I know I have a kindred spirit in you."

She laughed lightly. "And as a fellow member of high society families, I know we share a kindred love-hate relationship with these kinds of events."

"I do wish I could claim to be here this evening strictly to observe social pleasantries," he admitted. "I am here to solicit good will."

"Ah. I suspect you're here to chat with our esteemed Mr. Quincy?"

John smiled ruefully. "You are correct, of course. Have you seen him this evening?"

She shook her head. "Regretfully, no. I hear he suffers from a touch of rheumatism, and the cold air has kept him home."

"I've heard of his rheumatism complaints, and I don't mind telling you that the good MP seems stricken with its complications rather conveniently during events his wife favors."

Sally's lips twitched. "I suppose you'll be obliged to seek him out at his offices during daytime hours."

John sighed. "I was hoping to kill two proverbial birds with one stone this evening."

"MP Quincy being the first bird?"

He nodded, and at Sally's raised brow, answered, "The second is a show of good faith to my parents."

"Of course. Proof of due diligence in keeping up the social obligations."

"Exactly." He watched Charlotte finish her dance with Frampton, and the pressure around his chest eased. He didn't know why. She was hardly a wallflower, which meant he would be forced to watch her take to the floor many more times before the night was through. Perhaps he might slip out unnoticed by his mother.

"And then there is that one." Sally had tracked his gaze to Charlotte, who was searching for someone now that the dance had concluded.

John frowned, concerned. "How so?"

"She is preoccupied with something, and I've yet to drag it from her." Sally's brow knit as she observed her niece.

John knew Charlotte had planned to speak to Sally about the allegations in Charlotte's father's letter, but clearly she hadn't yet. It wasn't his place to mention it, so he remained silent. He watched Charlotte, wondering who she was hoping to find in the crowded ballroom.

He felt Sally's attention return to his face, and he looked at her. She was studying him rather as a scientist might examine a specimen under glass.

"Yes?"

"She confides in you and in her cousins."

"I suppose," he said carefully.

"Her cousins are not here."

"That is true."

"That leaves me with you." She narrowed her eyes. "Tell me what you know."

John couldn't help but laugh. "Miss Hampton, surely there's no secret your niece would share with me that she'd not also entrust to you."

"That's hardly an answer, Director Ellis, and I'll thank you not to use your evasive detective maneuvering on me."

He held up a hand in surrender. "I would never dream of it." A smile lingered on his lips. What was it about the company of the Hampton women that lifted his spirits despite his head pain?

He hesitated to reply, wanting to choose his words carefully. He did not wish to breach Charlotte's confidence in him. "Following the funeral, Charlotte mentioned a desire to speak with you about your late sister."

Sally glanced at the crowd, then back to John. She looked puzzled. "Perhaps with her father's death, Kat has been on Charlotte's mind. She's only been in Town for a day, and much of that was spent moving back into Hampton House. She's not had time to seek me out."

"Her father wrote to her just before he passed. He had some interesting things to say—not all of which were entirely clear." He didn't add that the most interesting tidbit about Mrs. Duvall's death had piqued his own concern; instead, he addressed a minor issue the group had discussed. "I believe Charlotte is concerned about her mother's ability to swim, given that she had been told her mother had drowned."

It was indelicate to speak to a woman about the tragic death of a family member while standing in a glittering ballroom, he was sure of that. He was fortunate his own mother was nowhere to be found. Her disgust in him would have known no bounds.

Sally looked at him in open surprise. "Kat was an exceptional swimmer. She was conscientious about her health. She liked being active, and she never drank; it made her ill." She offered a small shrug. "It was the head wound that accounted for her drowning."

As clearly as if someone had struck a match at the end of a dark tunnel, John's intuition, already on alert, leapt fully to life. "Head wound?"

Sally nodded. "Witnesses said she slipped on the deck of the ship and hit her head before falling into the water. It was dark, and from what I understand, crowded and confusing on the boat. A few people jumped in after her, but it was too late."

"Was Mr. Duvall witness to the whole of it?"

She shook her head. "He'd been in the ferryboat's salon, if memory serves. He went up on the deck after hearing the commotion."

Silence hung between them as John imagined the scene. "I'm sorry for your loss, Miss Hampton."

Sally lifted a shoulder, but a frown creased her brow. "I was home packing my trunks to leave the next morning." She paused. "Kat and I had been arguing during those final days, and I'd decided to call on her to apologize before leaving Town. When I learned of the accident—" She shook her head. "My grief and anger both were overwhelming."

He wanted to pursue the matter further, but Charlotte appeared, subtly shoving her way between two large matrons who were waving fans as though they stood in the Sahara.

Sally missed only a beat before fixing a smile to her face. "There she is!" She grasped Charlotte's hands and kissed her cheeks. "I do hope you plan to visit me tomorrow at the *Gazette*. I'll book the tearoom down the street for luncheon."

Charlotte nodded. "I've a meeting with Matron Halcomb and

Mr. Corbin tomorrow morning, and then I'll come straight to you. We've much to catch up on." She smiled, but it was strained.

John wondered if she was already dreading the conversation about her mother.

"Director, I believe I see your mother headed this way. Perhaps you'll hit one of those birds you were aiming for." Sally tilted her head toward John's left.

John's head throbbed at the thought, but rather than be conspicuously rude to his mother, he didn't look in her direction. Instead, he took Charlotte's elbow. "A dance, Dr. Duvall? You would be doing me a great service."

Charlotte gave him a half smile and raised a brow. "Will your headache support so much movement?"

"We'll turn in slow circles." He nodded to Sally and made his way with Charlotte around the chattering masses to the edge of the dancers.

"What's all this about aiming at birds?" Charlotte asked as she settled into his arms. They began very gentle movements of the waltz.

"I need to show my mother I'm out socializing."

She chuckled. "Dancing with me is hardly going to satisfy her demands; in fact, these efforts may do more harm than good."

"Nonsense." She was right, of course, but he didn't care about his mother's opinion of him. However, Lady Ashby could make things uncomfortable for Charlotte, and that did cause him concern.

"Very well," Charlotte said. "You ought to find a suitable debutante to dance the next set, however, to neutralize the effects of this one." She gently adjusted the sweep of his turns and tightened the area they covered on the floor. She sought to minimize the spinning in his head, which he appreciated.

He looked down at her, taking in the green of her eyes, the hint of a smile on her upturned face. She was close enough to kiss, and he was again surprised at the impulse. He found himself pulled back into the closeness he'd felt with her in the library. "I thought we'd already decided I am unsuitable to court a debutante."

"Their loss, of course."

As they turned, she looked up at him through lowered lashes, her head tilted just slightly enough to be considered flirtatious. She'd looked at him that way before, but only in jests designed to produce laughter. Now her eyes hinted at maturity, a nuanced *something* that seemed to be shifting. The ballroom lights glinted across her hair, reflecting a sheen of golds, reds, and a deep auburn that was nearly purple in the shadows.

The music slowed and came to a gradual stop. She dropped into a curtsey, and his breath caught in his throat. "Charlotte," he murmured. He wanted to take her away from the crowd, be somewhere with her alone. "I—"

"You see, she is here!" Franklin Frampton appeared, dragging two young women with him. He was smiling broadly, and the women squealed in delight, one of them clasping Charlotte in a quick embrace.

Charlotte overcame her surprise well enough, even as her eyes widened at the exuberant greeting. "Inez Shelton?" She looked at the woman, and her smile became genuine. "And Louisa Wilhite! I've not seen you since the Winston seaside holiday!" She turned to John and pulled him closer to her side, adding, "Director Ellis, have you met my friends?"

The women nodded as John said, "We met at the same house party. I believe I've seen you both in passing since—I hope you're well."

Both women nodded, all smiles, and Louisa held out her hand for Charlotte's inspection. "It is Anderson now, not Wilhite; I was married last year! My husband is on the Continent . . ."

John quietly said his goodbyes and made his escape. He walked the long way around the room to the exit and out into the foyer where the cool air from the front entrance greeted him like a welcomed guest. He really ought to have made time for his mother, but he'd visit her later in the week. As it was, his head was muddled with thoughts of auburn hair, dimly lit libraries, and his strange feelings. He needed a quick bath, a warm cup of tea, and then sleep. He'd reason through everything in the morning when he would be back to regular mental footing concerning his friendship with Charlotte.

Yes—by morning, things would be back to normal.

CHAPTER 8

Charlotte entered Delaney Hospital's receiving room and a sense of nostalgia washed over her. The last time she'd been there she'd been a new medical student, full of hopes and apprehension for her future. She was glad now that she'd been unaware how challenging the path would be. She smiled, imagining the ghost of her younger self walking wide-eyed through the halls.

Nurses wore dark dresses with crisp, white aprons and white caps. Their movements were brisk and efficient, as well trained as a military unit. The receiving room contained several rows of benches and a tall desk to one side where a doctor consulted with the matron, who made notes in a ledger. The benches were full of people waiting to be seen—mothers with feverish, listless children and coughing adults of all ages. Down the hallway to her right, she noted three men who seemed to have been in an accident being wheeled away to surgery.

The building was an older structure that had formerly served as a veteran's hospital after the Crimean War. Florence Nightingale's revolutionary ideas about basic cleanliness and sanitation had changed hospital procedure decades earlier, and the medical field was now well-versed in the sciences of germs and bacteria as causes of illness as opposed to miasma, or bad air.

Delaney wasn't much different from the hospital where she'd

trained in Philadelphia. It had served the same population for years and was funded by philanthropists who put their millions to good use. Even if their outward claims of compassion and care for the poor and widowed was sometimes nothing more than a pretty façade, their money was very real, and it kept the hospital running. Such financing was crucial to the survival of the institution, and yearly fund drives, much like those conducted at Delaney, were grueling but necessary.

Charlotte noted Matron Halcomb's expression tensing as the doctor spoke to her; she bore the expression of one who must acquiesce but did not want to. Charlotte made her way across the room, wondering who would have the temerity to question the matron's good sense or opinion.

The surgeon was new—at least he'd not been at the hospital four years earlier. He looked up in impatience at Charlotte when she reached them, and he then looked at the matron in surprise when she let out an exclamation of delight and moved from behind the desk to clasp Charlotte in a tight embrace.

"My dear girl! You've grown up!" Matron Halcomb's face beamed as though she were Charlotte's mother. The woman was middle-aged, had never married, but had dedicated her life to the nursing profession. She had dark chestnut hair beneath a small lace headpiece, and her black dress, with its high collar and long sleeves, was impeccably pressed.

She brooked no nonsense and ran as tight a ship as any captain, and her hospital wards were tidy and sterile. She inspected each morning with a white glove, looking under beds and behind curtains.

"I should say, 'Dr. Duvall,' though," the matron continued, placing her hands on Charlotte's shoulders. "You're no longer the same young girl I knew."

"I've not changed much." Charlotte smiled. "I've no doubt you could still put me soundly in my place."

Matron chuckled, but then paused. "But no, you've also trained as a surgeon! So, you're actually 'Miss Duvall.'"

Charlotte tipped her head. "I only hope for employment in either capacity."

"Is this our candidate?" the man standing behind the desk asked.

Matron inhaled but barely missed a beat as she looked at him and forced a tight smile. "Miss Duvall, allow me to introduce Mr. Stanley. He has been with Delaney for a year and became head surgeon after Mr. Call retired."

Mr. Stanley gave Charlotte a curt nod. He was trim in stature, and handsome enough. Something about his eyes, however, suggested he might be the sort of person who bullied his way through life believing his appearance and wit would always carry the day. She would wager her pending inheritance on the fact that he would bristle if referred to as a mere doctor.

Charlotte smiled and extended her hand. "A pleasure to make your acquaintance, Mr. Stanley."

He took her hand after a pause that was just long enough to imply insult and gripped it a touch too hard to be considered polite, and her eyes narrowed through her smile. Matching his clasp, she gave a good squeeze before dropping her hand. A muscle moved in his jaw, and she knew she'd just made herself a nemesis.

"We ought to make our way upstairs," Matron Halcomb interjected. "Mr. Stanley will sit in with Mr. Corbin and me for the interview."

"Delightful," Charlotte said with a tight smile and a sinking heart.

"I shall be along momentarily," Mr. Stanley said.

Charlotte fell into step with the matron as they climbed the stairs up two flights.

"Odious as the day is long," the older woman told Charlotte as they neared the top. "That man is condescending to my nursing staff and has run two doctors right out the front door in the year since his arrival."

"He must be a good surgeon to justify his employment here," Charlotte said.

"He is mediocre, at best," Matron Halcomb scoffed, lowering her voice as they passed a few staff members in the hallway. "Two other surgeons on staff are obliged to pick up anything he drops."

"Then why—"

"He is the personal physician to the wife of the hospital's most influential benefactor."

"Ah."

"Yes." Matron Halcomb knocked on the door to Mr. Corbin's office. "And so, we exercise patience and diplomacy."

The door opened to reveal a man in his late fifties, with hair a bit grayer than the last time Charlotte had seen him but his broad smile was exactly the same. "Miss Duvall!" He clasped her hand with both of his and led her into the office.

"Mr. Corbin," Charlotte said, surprised when her eyes suddenly stung with happy tears. "I am so glad to see you again. Your letters during my time away were a welcome boon to my spirits."

Mr. Corbin had five daughters, each accomplished and headstrong, and his acceptance of Charlotte's plans as a new medical student had been surprising and more than welcome. She had come up against person after person who'd attempted to dissuade and discourage her efforts that first year in school before leaving for America, so much that she'd nearly decided to quit. Mr. Corbin had encouraged her, and, because he held a position at one of London's largest hospitals and was a good man of influence and compassion whose opinion she valued, she began to hope her dreams might come to fruition.

"I am glad to hear it," Mr. Corbin said and led her to a chair opposite his desk. He patted her hand again, shaking his head. "I can hardly believe the time has passed. Look at you! Miss Duvall, you've matured and learned much; I can see it in your face. Tell me about your experiences."

Matron Halcomb took a seat next to Charlotte, and Mr. Corbin poured a cup of tea for each of them before settling into his chair. Charlotte handed him her packet of references, school marks, and relevant experience. She told him about her classwork and practical studies in the hospital and clinics in Pennsylvania, and about her employment at St. Anne's clinic in New York just before her return home. He listened, meeting her eyes, asking questions, and taking a few quick notes as he flipped through her portfolio.

They were interrupted by a quick knock at the door, and Mr. Stanley let himself in without bothering to wait for admittance.

"Mr. Stanley, do come in," Mr. Corbin said needlessly. "I've begun Miss Duvall's interview. Your appearance is well-timed."

"You did not wait for me to arrive," Mr. Stanley commented and pulled a chair over to the group.

Mr. Corbin checked his timepiece. "We began at the prearranged time, but I do understand that you may have been delayed. Please, do not feel badly for arriving late."

Charlotte bit the inside of her cheek.

"We've covered Miss Duvall's formal education, which was quite extensive—her diploma required more rigorous study than some of our own doctors—and her practical experience, which is also very impressive. We were about to discuss her surgical experience."

"I hardly think that is necessary," Mr. Stanley said. "We have two surgeons already in addition to my services. Mr. Call, though retired, is also available for emergencies. We are short two doctors, however. If we are to continue down this road—and I've already expressed to you my reservations—we hardly need assume Dr. Duvall would be involved in the surgical theater in any capacity."

Charlotte raised one brow but kept her mouth closed. Maintaining a bland expression was a skill she'd perfected over the last five years. If Matron Halcomb was correct, the reason the hospital was "down two doctors" lay with the good Mr. Stanley himself. She kept her hands folded in her lap—unclenched—and looked at Mr. Corbin.

Mr. Corbin lowered his voice. "You are aware that your inclusion in this interview is a courtesy I am extending at your insistence, Mr. Stanley." He gestured to Charlotte. "Continue, Miss Duvall. I'd asked about your surgical experience in emergency settings, and you indicated you have worked alongside experienced surgeons performing amputations, childbirth emergencies, and some internal abdominal work treating both knife and gunshot wounds." He turned over a few sheets of paper and glanced over her recommendations from attending physicians in Philadelphia.

Mr. Stanley extended a hand for the stack of papers. "May I?"

Mr. Corbin glanced at the man in clear irritation but scooped the papers together and handed them over. "Miss Duvall, why is it you seek employment at Delaney, specifically? There are dozens of hospitals and medical clinics in London." He folded his hands together on his desk and smiled at Charlotte.

"Delaney appeals to me because of the population it serves," Charlotte said. "I have been blessed with a life of privilege and comfort, and the more experience I gain, the more I recognize the chasm between myself and others. I appreciate the effort Delaney makes to bridge that chasm." Charlotte swallowed past a lump in her throat.

Mr. Stanley tossed her file back onto the desk and folded his arms. His smile was little more than a smirk. "Impressively altruistic, doctor. Would that all of the medical community cared so for the poor and destitute."

"Clearly you must, Mr. Stanley, because you work here among the least of the least. I find it admirable." She smiled. "Perhaps we are like-minded, despite minor differences."

His gaze dropped from Charlotte's face and traveled the length of her body before returning to her eyes. She steeled herself to keep from reacting to the insult. He would only use it against her.

"I would not describe our differences as minor, dear lady. It must be clear to each of us in this room where I stand on the matter. I make no secret of my disapproval of women playing at doctor duties, let alone surgical. I need not confer with you in private, Mr. Corbin, and am informing you directly before this candidate that I cast my vote against hiring her."

Mr. Corbin assessed his head surgeon with raised eyebrows before stating, "I appreciate your vote, Mr. Stanley, but it was never yours to cast. The hiring of doctors and surgeons falls under my purview, and I accept feedback from Matron Halcomb alone. As a favor to you, I will take your opinion under advisement, but as there are nearly one hundred women doctors practicing medicine in this country—a number that will only increase—you might consider revising your view."

Charlotte did not look at Mr. Stanley in triumph but kept her attention trained on Mr. Corbin. He turned to her and said, "Miss Duvall, we are desperately short-staffed, and your qualifications are stellar. Matron Halcomb"—he nodded to the woman sitting next to Charlotte—"has given me her opinion already. As the lead administrator of Delaney Hospital, I hereby extend to you an offer of employment as a doctor and substitute surgeon."

Charlotte released a slow breath of relief, even though she'd suspected the interview would go in her favor. She rose with Mr. Corbin and shook his hand with a smile. "I accept, sir, and will do my best to be an asset to this institution."

Mr. Stanley stood, then turned on his heel and left the office without saying a word.

"Don't mind him," Mr. Corbin said in an undertone. "He'll come 'round. You do your job well, and he'll have nothing further to say."

Charlotte had known men like Mr. Stanley, and their bark was almost always worse than their bite. The only problem with this particular man, though, was his tie to a hospital benefactor. She resolved to treat his ego with care to avoid upsetting the financial boat. Money always dictated the course of things.

Matron Halcomb took Charlotte to the different wards, introducing her to the nurses. Nearly all of them were new to Charlotte, but they welcomed her warmly. Their friendliness went a long way toward making up for Mr. Stanley's rudeness, and as Charlotte continued her tour with the matron, she was walking on clouds.

She met three other doctors, all of whom were busy with patients but who greeted her professionally enough that she was hopeful for a good working relationship.

Matron Halcomb led Charlotte to her office, which was just beyond the receiving room. She'd just handed Charlotte a satchel of papers and a few supplies one of the other physicians had left behind, when a courier approached with a sealed message.

He gave it to Matron Halcomb and asked, "Do you know who this is?"

The Matron examined it in surprise and then gave it to Charlotte, whose name was scrawled on the front in an unfamiliar hand. Only family and her friends knew she would be at the hospital for her interview—she figured the message must be from one of them.

"Thank you," she said to the boy, handing him a coin from her reticule.

He tipped his hat with a grin and darted away.

Charlotte gave Matron Halcomb a final hug, then placed her portfolio of papers in her new satchel and left the hospital. She stepped out into the brisk air, feeling satisfaction at having a good plan in place. She would work at the hospital, continue her career, decipher the truth of her father's veiled secrets, and decide whether she would remain in England or go back to the United States. She had plenty of time.

She looked down at the message in her hand and walked down the street away from the congested hospital receiving doors. She didn't want to set her satchel down in the muddy street, so she balanced the letter against her leg and fiddled one-handed with the seal. Finally opening it, she squinted at the few words scrawled in a cramped handwriting.

Your father was a madman. Leave well enough alone.

Her heart pounded, and she looked around, suddenly feeling as though she was being watched. She hoped to see the boy who had delivered the message, but he was nowhere in sight. As she scanned the crowded streets, everyone who made eye contact with her was suddenly suspect. One woman finally nudged past her, muttering, "What're ye lookin' at, missy?"

Charlotte swallowed and folded the message in half, tucking it into her satchel. She made her way to the train that would take her to Bloomsbury and the stop near Hampton House. As her heartbeat returned to normal, she realized that if someone was concerned enough about the "hornet's nest" her father said he'd been kicking before he died, then warning her away from it only gave it validity.

But it raised another concerning question: since the note had not come from her family, who else had known she would be at the hospital?

CHAPTER 9

Charlotte took the cup of tea from Hampton House's gruff housekeeper, Mrs. Burnette, with a smile of thanks. "The chamomile will put me right to sleep," she said to the older woman, who nodded briskly.

"You cannot be staying up all night when you're on the train early for your new job." Her tone was stern, but Charlotte saw the pride in the woman's expression—pride she would undoubtedly deny if pressed to acknowledge. Mrs. Burnette had always seemed to feel it was her job to keep the Hampton House tenants humble; she had made an impressive career of it.

"I'll be right as rain in the morning."

"Shall I awaken you with a knock?"

Charlotte headed for the stairs, carefully carrying her tea while also lifting the skirts of her housecoat and nightdress. "I do appreciate the offer, but it is unnecessary."

"Very well." Mrs. Burnette sniffed. "I'll be awake just the same if you need me."

They said their good nights, and Charlotte climbed the stairs to the first floor where there was a large sitting area in the center with windows that overlooked the front garden and street below. Doors flanked the sitting area, two on each side, leading to four bedchambers, three of which once had been occupied by

Charlotte, Eva, and Amelie, while they had been working at *The Marriage Gazette* with Sally in their early London days together. The time had been magical, though Charlotte wasn't sure she'd realized it then. They'd been in such a hurry to move into adulthood, to become Women of Independent Means, but as she reflected on it, she remembered the fun they'd had, evenings out or staying home, sitting on each other's beds and laughing late into the night.

The floor was currently unoccupied, which had worked well for Charlotte, who simply moved back into her old room. She was warm with nostalgia, if not a little lonely for company. She entered her room and set the teacup on a small table near the hearth. She'd put away most of her belongings, but a few items were still strewn over the open armoire drawer and lower shelves. The lights were low enough for relaxation but still bright enough to read by, and she went to the vanity for a novel she'd placed there.

She thought to read, but after picking up the book, she put it back down and sat at the vanity instead. She brushed through her hair, looking into the mirror and seeing the room in reverse. She was restless, feeling unsettled about the note she'd received.

Your father was a madman . . .

Charlotte had brought a few items with her from the country house, one of which was her mother's trunk that her father had retrieved from the attic. Her eye landed on the reflection of the cedar-lined chest seated on the floor at the foot of her bed. The name of the company, Kiel, was backward to her view in the mirror, the letters slanting the wrong way, the broken lock lifting from the wooden surface on the right side instead of the left.

She put her brush down and turned, viewing the large box

as it truly was. The broken lock had given her pause. Her father must have misplaced the key after having stored the trunk for more than two decades. She imagined him trying to open it without causing damage to the trunk itself. He'd always been so careful that way.

She moved to sit next to the trunk, tracing her finger along the nameplate. She'd seen the chest in the attic as a child when playing games with her friends. It had always been locked, and she'd never had a peek inside. Now knowing that it was a treasure trove of her mother's things, things she could have enjoyed through the years growing up without her, she couldn't help the sense of betrayal she felt. Had the loss of Katherine Hampton Duvall been so tragic for her father that he'd been unable to bear more than the portrait of her that hung downstairs in the parlor? She suspected now that he'd allowed that only as a nod to decorum.

She lifted the lid, closing her eyes as the combined scent of cedar, old paper, and a light perfume she barely remembered from childhood wafted up. This had been her mother's hope chest, full of items she'd have embroidered and collected in her younger years and put away for safekeeping upon her marriage. Charlotte had a similar chest, but it had been neglected over the years. Her governesses had tried, bless them, but growing up in a household of brothers had not been conducive to adequate hope-chest-filling.

Charlotte traced her finger along the smooth cedar planks. Copies of what she assumed were her mother's favorite books—*Persuasion* and two books of poetry by Byron—sat next to a multitude of letters tied in separate stacks with fine pink ribbons. There was a scrapbook filled with playbills, calling cards, purchase receipts for custom hats, and notes from friends and admirers. Sets of finely embroidered linen napkins, pillowcases, and table runners filled one corner. Small bundles of fine lace that must have cost a fortune were wrapped in tissue paper that crinkled quietly when Charlotte touched it.

Remnants of an entire life contained in a solitary box. Charlotte felt a stab of sorrow so complete that her eyes burned, quiet tears spilling over her cheeks and dripping onto her hand. There was no noise in the room save the quiet ticking of the ormolu clock on the mantel. Ticking away the seconds of her life. Would this be all Charlotte left behind, as well? Would she leave behind loved ones too bereaved at her passing to ever speak of her again? Would she even *be* missed? Would she leave anything of substance behind, anything that would prove she had been in the world and left it better than she'd found it?

She blew out quietly through pursed lips and sniffled, wondering absently if there was a handkerchief in the box she could use. "A jest, Mama," she whispered. "I'll not sully your precious work." And it was precious—the small, neat stitches and beautiful patterns were perfection, and a far cry from anything Charlotte had ever been able to produce. "Except for in surgery," she said aloud. "My surgical stitches are second to none." She smiled, wondering what her mother would think of her now.

Proud . . . so proud . . .

Her father's parting words to her when she'd left for America echoed quietly in her head, and she hoped, so *desperately* hoped, that they were true. She missed him so much it was like a physical ache in her chest, and the hole inside her that once held her mother's memory felt ragged and raw.

A tiny music box in the corner of the chest tickled a memory, and she tipped open the lid with one finger. Strains of a song she'd not heard for years filled the room, and she heard the words in her head, a nighttime song Katherine had sung to her in the nursery.

Under the starlight and far from the sea,
My darling sweetheart waits gently for me;
Under the pine boughs and flowers so free,
My heart's secret treasure lies waiting for me.

She carefully closed the lid, and the fading notes lingered in the air. She picked up the music box, thinking to place it on her nightstand, but one small leg was caught on something. She moved closer, using both hands to untangle it from a pale green ribbon that was stuck in the corner between the bottom panel and the side.

Frowning, she set aside the music box, then clamped the end of the ribbon firmly between forefinger and thumb. She tugged, but it held fast. She sat back, perplexed, and looked at the corner of the chest from the outside. It sat flush on the floor, with no feet to elevate it, but the bottom of the box was two inches higher on the inside.

She tried again to free the wedged ribbon, then quickly removed the items from the chest, stacking them high on the floor. Before long, she was surrounded by fabric and paper, books and boxes. Now that the box was empty, she could see light scrapes against the sides in large arcs, as if something had been continually lifted and then replaced. She traced her finger along the seam where the bottom of the chest met the sides. There were no ridges or indentations showing where it might lift up, and further efforts with the ribbon proved fruitless. Maybe it wasn't meant to lift.

Under the starlight and far from the sea . . .
Under . . . Under . . .

Her frown deepening, she rose and retrieved her scuffed, worn medical bag, settling it next to her on the floor. She withdrew a clamp and placed it at the bottommost part of the ribbon where it was lodged. She worked gently and slowly to avoid tearing the ribbon, angling the clamp by the smallest of degrees until a telltale creak of wood suggested movement.

She continued, patient despite growing anticipation, until the bottom of the trunk slowly inched its way upward. The ribbon tore slightly, and Charlotte winced, reaching into her bag for small scissors to use as a lever. The thick sheet of wood from the foundation of the chest creaked and groaned as it scraped against the side, but it finally shifted to a point where Charlotte was able to grasp it with her fingertips and walk it upward a little at a time.

The ribbon slipped free, and Charlotte could see where it had been attached to the bottom of the board at the center of it. A simple but clever mechanism designed to make the task easier. The tip of the fabric had gotten lodged in the corner as though someone had hastily closed the false bottom without ensuring the ribbon could be easily accessed again.

She lifted the false bottom completely out of the trunk and set it aside. Her heart pounded as she looked at dozens of letters that had been hidden from view. They had not been carefully tied or organized as those in the main body of the trunk had. Reaching into the hidden compartment with fingers that shook, she brushed the letters together, revealing a journal and several loose postcards.

Charlotte looked at the door to her bedroom as though she was about to be caught doing something wrong. Acting on instinct but feeling foolish, she rose and turned the key in her bedroom door, locking it.

She knelt by the chest, heart beating quickly, and picked up the thick journal. These things were probably nothing more than additional treasures from Katherine's childhood—silly letters from prospective beaux or missives from school friends. Charlotte understood the yearning for privacy and had a few treasures of her own that she'd prefer nobody ever saw.

When she opened the journal and looked at the date atop the first entry, her suppositions about Katherine's childhood treasures was quickly proven false. The entry had been written just before Charlotte was born. She flipped through the pages to the last entry, dated just before Katherine's death. Charlotte caught her breath at the remaining hauntingly blank pages.

> *I am taking Charlotte and Robert with me to London, and David and three of the boys will join us in two days. We've been invited to a reunion of sorts—the Paddletons, Fineboughs, and Worthingstones are in Town for the Season, and we will celebrate the Carters' engagement.*
>
> *Sometimes I wonder why I torture myself by attending events where I know J will be present. There are times when I look up to see him staring at me, the longing in his eyes palpable. Still, I dance and sing and smile, determined to be happy. Perhaps placing permanent distance between us would be the best for all concerned, especially for my own well-being. David knows—he has always known—but where before he was patient, now his jealousy flares. He is such a kind, good man, but sometimes I worry he will reach the end of his rope. How long will a man watch in the shadows while another man covets his wife?*

Charlotte's heart pounded painfully, and she slipped from her knees to sit hard on the floor, staring at the page. The words, while veiled, were heavy in their implications. She swallowed and drew in a shuddering breath.

Oh, Mama. What happened to you?

CHAPTER 10

Charlotte's first day at work was exactly what she thought it would be: exhausting, endless activities, complaining, sometimes hostile patients, and very little time to stop or eat or sit for any length of time.

She loved it.

It was everything she'd hoped for, and it had the added benefit of keeping her from thinking about the discoveries she'd made the night before in her mother's trunk. Between her mother's journal and her father's letter, which she'd now read so many times she knew it by heart, it was too much to sort through while busy, and she was glad for the distraction.

Her colleagues, Doctors Stevenson, Leatham, and Tribe, were every bit as professional as she had hoped they might be. They seemed to have decided to reserve judgment until seeing her at work, and once she began to prove her skills, they were satisfied.

One of the nurses she had known before, Maggie Petersen, made a point to bring Charlotte a cup of tea and a biscuit, which was generous given that the nurse was busy enough for three people.

To her delight, she did not see much of Mr. Stanley. If they could keep some distance between them, perhaps their mutual annoyance wouldn't continue to fester. She caught enough veiled comments and eye-rolling from other colleagues throughout the day to confirm that she was not the only person to be frustrated with the opinionated surgeon.

She was walking through the receiving room at the end of her shift when she caught sight of the boy who had delivered the note to her the day before. Quickly, she dashed over to him and grabbed his shoulder, spinning him around and guiding him into a corner of the room.

"Who gave you the message you brought here yesterday?" she asked him, breathless.

His eyes were large, and he shrugged away from her grasp. "I don' remember!"

"It is very important that I find out," she insisted. She reached into her pocket and produced two large coins. "Can you at least tell me where you met with him?"

The boy eyed the coins and finally nodded. "Tallulah's." He gave her the address to the pub, which was in easy walking distance.

"Do you know his name?"

He shook his head.

She frowned in frustration. "Can you find out for me? What did he look like?"

"I don' ask too many questions," the boy mumbled, still looking at the coins.

"I'll pay you double this if you can learn his name, or anything about him." She placed the coins in his hand and wrapped her fingers around his. "Anything at all. You know where to find me—I'm here nearly every day." She paused. "What is your name?"

"Donovan."

"And where do you live?"

He lifted a shoulder. "'Round." He was thin and slightly shorter than she was.

"How old are you?"

He straightened. "Fifteen."

She nodded. So thirteen, at most. "Thank you for your help. And if you ever need anything in return, come here and ask for Dr. Duvall."

He nodded and headed toward an older woman in the receiving room. Perhaps she was a relative? Charlotte climbed the stairs to the first floor and turned a corner to the tiny room that served as her office. To have personal space at all was a boon. The doctors' offices were scattered throughout the hospital wherever there might be an empty room. Mr. Stanley was the only staff member with an office that rivaled the size of Mr. Corbin's or Matron Halcomb's.

She changed her clothes and freshened up, noting on the clock that she had enough time to walk by the pub Donovan mentioned, having changed her plans to meet Sally for supper across town.

The days were growing shorter; it was already deep twilight. The air outside was colder than it had been that morning. Fall was deepening in earnest. She turned up her collar against a brisk breeze and made her way down the street, checking addresses and hoping she knew where she was going. After passing it and then doubling back, she finally found Tallulah's, which smelled of an odd combination of fish and chips and Greek food.

She debated entering, not knowing who she was looking for, but figured she wouldn't learn anything hovering at the door. She made her way inside, allowing her eyes to grow accustomed to the dim light and smoke-filled interior.

She spied a woman directing two sullen-looking servers who

resembled her enough that they must be daughters. The proprietress? Charlotte hesitated. One might assume that approaching women for information would be a safe option, but one might be mistaken. Charlotte had learned that lesson more than once in New York.

A man stood behind the scratched and dented wooden bar, and he finally motioned to her. She stepped forward, deciding a direct approach would be best. She leaned close to him, shouting to be heard over the din. "I'm looking for someone."

"'S an awful vague description, miss."

Charlotte nodded. "Someone hired a boy named Donovan to deliver a note to me. My name is Charlotte Duvall."

He eyed her for a moment before shaking his head. "'Aven't a clue."

She nodded again, resigned. It had been a very long shot. "Thank you." She stepped away from the bar when the man called out to her and beckoned her back with his head.

"Folk sometime meet in the alleyway." He jerked his thumb over his shoulder.

"Thank you very much." She smiled and left the cost of a pint on the bar before making her way back outside. Nothing in blue hades would entice her to enter an alleyway where mysterious people needing secret messages delivered met with errand boys. She wasn't stupid—she would return to the pub later with John perhaps. No, not John. Every inch of him screamed "detective."

She frowned, stepping away from the pub, checking her timepiece.

"Duvall." The voice was almost a whisper, but it was close enough that she heard it.

She jerked her head up. It hadn't been more than a murmur, but blast it all, it seemed to have come from behind the pub.

In the alleyway.

She pursed her lips. As she slowly approached the rear of the building, she withdrew a thin scalpel from its pocket inside her medical bag. She held it carefully in her right hand, hidden behind the folds of her skirt.

Daylight was gone, and lights in nearby buildings flickered to life but did little to illuminate the darkened alley. She knew she couldn't take down a seasoned criminal bent on murder and mayhem, but perhaps with a sharp instrument in her hand—and knowledge of where to effectively wield it—she might survive long enough to find out who sent the message, and why.

She hesitated in the shadows, drawing a shuddering breath, and strained to see if anyone stood behind the pub. The back door opened with a bang, and she jumped. Light spilled onto the muddy ground, and the bartender dropped a crate of empty glass bottles near the door before pulling the door shut, again throwing the alley into darkness.

Charlotte sighed in relief. In that brief instant of illumination, she'd not seen anyone else lurking there.

As she turned around, someone grabbed her from behind, strong fingers encircling her right wrist and squeezing painfully. Her scalpel dropped from suddenly numb fingers. His other hand gripped the back of her neck. He rushed her against a stone wall on the alley's far side, and her head smacked so hard that stars clouded her vision.

She cried out in pain and dropped her medical bag, trying to fight free with her left hand. He pressed her harder into the wall until she thought her spine would crack. She flailed, trying to stomp on the assailant's instep—anything to loosen his grasp—but he held firm and kept his foot just out of her reach.

"What do you want?" she managed. "Who are you? Who sent

you?" She thrust her left elbow back, hoping to catch his ribs, but he quickly moved so her arm smashed awkwardly against her chest. She kicked backward, trying to hit his groin or his legs, but she was quickly entangled in her own skirts.

"You do not follow instructions well," the man said quietly in her ear. He sounded American. "You were told to leave well enough alone." The grip on the back of her neck tightened until she gasped in pain.

"Who—" she gritted through the pain, fearing he would crush her temple against the stone. "*Who sent you*?"

"You have family, Dr. Duvall. I've seen them. Sure would be a shame if they came to harm."

Fear sliced through her at his words, followed quickly with fury. "Leave my family alone!"

"That depends on you."

"Have you been following me from *America*?"

"Sent you a letter to stay put, but you'd already gone. There's nothing for you here," he continued in his low voice, as calm as if they were taking a stroll in the park. "Your father was old, but he stirred up a heap of mess before dying. Go back to New York, to your little apartment and your work at St. Anne's clinic. Nobody else has to get hurt."

He paused but didn't release her.

Her breath came in pained, stunted gasps, and her head hurt beyond description.

"Do you understand?"

She managed a strangled, "Yes." If he didn't stop squeezing, he would break her wrist. She knew how many bones her wrist contained, and exactly which ones were suffering the most under his assault. Bones, tendons, muscles—she would be bruised and painfully swollen.

"No more questions."

"F—fine."

"I'm going to lean down, and you're going to lean down with me. I'm going to pick up your fancy doctor knife. If you make any sudden moves, I will gut you with it. Do you understand?"

"Yes." The tears that formed were a result of anger as much as pain. She slowly bent down with him, her head scraping against the wall as he allowed her very little movement. He picked up the scalpel, holding the edge to her neck as they both stood back up. She closed her eyes, angry that her assailant had the satisfaction of seeing her cry.

"I'm going to leave, and you're going to stay right here against the wall and count to fifty. Then, you can go home to Bloomsbury and make arrangements to return to New York."

She clenched her teeth together hard to keep from screaming at him. She wanted to whirl around and demand he tell her who had hired him to stop whatever it was her father had begun. If he thought she was going to trot back obediently to New York he didn't know her at all. She longed to tell him so, but the press of the scalpel against her neck kept her quiet.

"Understand?" he snapped.

She gave a slight nod.

"There's a good girl."

Her nostrils flared, and she closed her eyes to keep from rolling them. True, she was terrified, but his condescension was more offensive than his threats.

He released her neck and backed away.

She forced herself to be still, placing her left hand on the wall and gripping the stone to anchor herself against spinning around to catch a glimpse of his face. She wouldn't be able to unravel her father's final message if the assailant killed her now. She didn't doubt he would do it—he'd been eerily calm, as if he couldn't have cared less if she lived or died.

She shook her right hand, wincing at the pain, and then cradled it against her chest. With her other hand, she felt the side of her face where blood trickled in a steady stream. She was dizzy and disoriented, and she felt a lump forming on her temple. She retrieved a handkerchief from her pocket with shaking fingers and held it to her head.

She counted to fifty as she'd been ordered to, then picked up her bag and slowly turned, half expecting to see a madman with a scalpel in the shadows.

Nobody was there. Voices still carried around the corner from the activity in the pub and beyond. No one had witnessed the attack, or if they had, they'd turned and headed the other direction. She sniffled and wiped her nose and eyes, and then walked slowly from the alley. She forced herself to hold her head up—she'd no doubt he was watching. He'd been watching before. He'd observed her closely enough when she approached the alley to know she'd placed the scalpel in her right hand.

Doing her best to ignore the pain in her wrist, in her neck, and in her head, she walked in as straight of a line as she could manage, wobbling and stumbling only a bit. A passerby laughed and told her it was early in the evening to be so far in her cups. She licked her dry lips and pressed toward the street where she saw two cabs, one of which was empty and starting to pull away.

"Wait!" she called, and the sound rang like an explosion in her head. Mercifully, the driver stopped and waited until she climbed in.

"Where to?" he asked and clucked to his horse.

"The Yard." She sat back against the cold seat and closed her eyes.

CHAPTER 11

Night had fallen, and John was jotting down a few notes for the following morning when he heard one of his sergeants call out in concern. He frowned and looked out his office window to see the officer approaching a woman who held a blood-soaked cloth to her head. Her red hair gave him pause, and his heart thumped. Surely not . . .

She exchanged a few words with the sergeant when he reached her side, and he looked toward John's office and nodded.

The woman continued across the room, and with sickening clarity, John realized it was Charlotte. Her hair was mussed, long auburn curls hanging free of their usual tidy coiffure, and bright spots of red dotted her shoulder and the bodice of her jacket.

His heart pounded in alarm as he made his way to the door and yanked it open. "Charlotte!" As he approached her, he told the sergeant, "Bring a pitcher of water and the medical chest from the locker room."

The sergeant nodded, wide-eyed, and hurried away. Voices sounded in the stairwell signaling the arrival of officers and staff working the night shift. John wrapped an arm around Charlotte and urged her into his office. He pulled out a chair, and as she sank into it, he closed the blinds to preserve her privacy.

"What happened? Do you need a doctor?" he asked, pulling

another chair close and gently cradling the side of her head. "Was it an accident? Were you run down in the street?"

She made eye contact with him, and the size of her pupils gave him pause. Wincing, she removed her handkerchief from the wound, exposing a number of cuts and scratches from temple to chin. A large bruise had formed on her temple and was spreading to her forehead, and blood seeped from a deep abrasion.

John swallowed and withdrew a clean handkerchief from his pocket, gently touching it to the oozing wound. "What happened?" he whispered.

Tears slid down Charlotte's face. Her cheek was swelling, and he imagined her entire head must hurt like the dickens.

She sniffed and placed her hand atop his, and he moved to let her hold the cloth. She winced again, and he noted the state of her hand, which was as bruised and swollen as her face. He placed his fingertip at the cuff of her jacket sleeve and pulled it back to reveal discoloration extending down her arm.

"I was attacked," she finally said, then cleared her throat. "I am very angry."

"Who did this?" He felt his temperature rise with a surge of anger. "A patient?"

"No." She began shaking her head but clearly thought better of it with a wince and a quiet exhalation between pursed lips.

A knock sounded at the door, and John retrieved the medical kit and water from the sergeant. "Stay close, if you please," he told the young man, who nodded. He quietly closed the door and set the medical box on the table near Charlotte's elbow. Retrieving a clean cloth, he dipped it in water and wrung it out, forcing himself to keep from peppering her with questions.

After a few moments, she finally began speaking, explaining everything that she could remember about the last hour.

He cleaned the wound as she spoke through tears, which seemed to be more a source of frustration than the attack itself.

"Charlotte, it is not a weakness to cry, you know." He met her eyes, worried to see them glaze over as though her vision was fuzzy. "I believe you should see a doctor," he told her, holding a fresh, damp cloth against her head.

"He will tell me I have a head injury," she mumbled. "Which I already know. I knew it as it was happening. He will also tell me to drink plenty of tea and get plenty of rest."

"You may require stitching."

She focused on him with some effort. "I'd hazard a guess that it's an open abrasion, so there really isn't much to stitch." She sighed quietly. "The bleeding will slow—let me see the cloth."

He moved it away from her head, and she studied it.

"It's already slowed." She smiled weakly. "Your treatment is as good as anything I'd offer my patients. Have you any clean, dry bandages?"

He retrieved a long, white strip of cloth from the medical kit and folded it on itself, then placed it over the worst of the wound that still seeped blood.

"Just tie it around my head, for now," she said, motioning a circle with her left hand.

He followed her instructions and then leaned forward, carefully holding her hands. "Tell me everything you remember about the attacker."

"He was taller than I am, by several inches, I would guess." She closed her eyes.

"Did you see anything—clothing, gloves?"

"I saw his hand on my wrist as he held it against the wall." She swallowed. "He was wearing gloves."

"Did you smell anything?"

"Musty, as though his coat had been in storage somewhere damp." She blinked, meeting John's eyes. "His voice was low, but he sounded like an American southerner. A slight accent to his words."

"Did he admit to being an American?"

She frowned. "Implied more than admitted."

He rose and retrieved a paper and pen from his desk. Sitting down with her again, he recorded her recollections. A picture formed in his head, but it lacked too many pieces to be complete. He suspected it all hinged on her father.

"Did anyone else know about the things your father said in his letter to you?"

"I don't think so, but he admitted he might have put me in danger. Whomever he'd been pestering for 'justice' for my mother must assume I am here to pick up the cause." She paused. "That is what I find confusing. I've not spoken of it to anyone except to you, my cousins, and Michael and Nathan at the funeral. I've barely even broached the subject of my mother's death with Aunt Sally."

He frowned. "I suppose someone may have overheard the conversation we had after the funeral. It isn't as though the French doors separating the parlor from the study provided a proper sound barrier." John made a note to question Charlotte's brothers about the identities of the guests at the funeral. "I've been thinking I could make time to revisit her last days here in Town. That might provide a clue as to whose cage your father was rattling these recent months. I do wish we knew with whom your parents socialized."

Charlotte's half smile seemed sad. "I believe I have an idea of who that might have been. I found some things in my mother's trunk that she'd been keeping secret. A journal and some letters."

She bit her lip. "I do not want you to think ill of her—indeed, *I* do not know what to make of it. I cannot bear the thought of her reputation being tarnished." She lifted her chin.

He cradled her uninjured cheek. "I would never think ill of the woman who gave birth to you." The sight of her, battered and bruised, twisted something in his heart. Underlying the tumble of emotions, cold anger had taken root. "I am going to find the man who did this to you, and if I am feeling generous, I'll allow him to live to see his day before a judge."

She smiled, and he saw a shade of her regular self. "You are not judge, jury, and executioner, Director Ellis."

"Oh, I do not speak of myself as an officer of the law when I say I am going to find the man." He smiled at her and placed a soft kiss on her forehead.

"Perhaps you should allow someone else to investigate."

"Now where would be the satisfaction in that? Come. Let us get you home."

"I can manage," she said, waving a hand in his direction and then wincing, holding her injured wrist with her other hand.

He shot a look at her that he usually reserved for his subordinates. "You are not going anywhere alone until this matter is settled. Is there a room available at Hampton House?"

She wrinkled her brow. "Yes, but who do you suggest should move in?"

"Me."

CHAPTER 12

John tied his cravat clumsily the next morning using a mirror that stood in Eva Caldwell's former dressing chamber at Hampton House. Upon arriving the night before, he'd informed Mrs. Burnette that he would be renting Eva's old room for the foreseeable future, and one look at Charlotte's face cancelled any protests the housekeeper might have voiced.

He gathered his greatcoat and the leather case he used to carry files to and from his office. He paused outside Charlotte's room, but he couldn't hear her moving around. He thought of knocking but decided to let her sleep. It had been late before Mrs. Burnette had been able to clean her up and put her to bed.

He made his way downstairs to the dining room where Hampton House's other residents—two elderly men named Mr. Roy and Mr. Croft—dined in companionable silence. One of the maids, Sarah, noted John's presence and gestured to the sideboard where breakfast was laid out.

"I'll eat in a moment, thank you. Is Mrs. Burnette available?" he asked.

Sarah retreated to the kitchen, and when Mrs. Burnette appeared, he took her by the elbow and led her to the parlor.

"Is Miss Duvall not doing well?" the woman asked him with clear concern.

"She is fine for the moment. I have sent word to Matron Halcomb at Delaney Hospital that she requires a day of recuperation at home following an accident."

Mrs. Burnette frowned. "She'll not be happy about that."

"Which is precisely why I obtained Miss Duvall's permission first." She'd been too tired to make much of an argument, that was true, but John had gotten enough of an agreement from Charlotte to cover himself for future defense. "I understand you've been advertising the three vacant rooms on the first floor, but I'd ask that you pull the advertisement for a time. I've hired a man to accompany Charlotte when I cannot be with her, and he will require use of one of the rooms across the common area."

Mrs. Burnette blinked. "You're suggesting I allow two unmarried men and one unmarried woman to cohabitate on the same floor of this exceptionally respectable boardinghouse?"

"Bear in mind you'll be well compensated in rents."

"I do not care a fig for the rents!" The woman lowered her voice but punctuated each word as though shouting. "I'll not have Hampton House gain a reputation as a house of . . . of . . . ill repute!" She blushed on the last phrase, and he wondered if she'd ever uttered it before.

"Do you remember Miss Duvall's condition when I brought her home last night? Would you like to go upstairs with me now and take another look at her face?" He'd also lowered his voice but felt his irritation rise. "You have my word that the *temporary* living situation on the first floor of this hallowed house is not to perpetuate nefarious activity but to keep Miss Duvall from being killed."

Mrs. Burnette pressed her lips together, and although she may not have approved, she also did not argue further. "Very well," she sniffed. "I shall inform Miss Sally Hampton of the *temporary* arrangements."

"Much appreciated, Mrs. Burnette. If I might be so bold—had I not devised this solution, I believe Miss Hampton would have suggested one similar. I suspect she will wholeheartedly approve."

She nodded, frowning.

"The gentleman occupying Miss Amelie's former room goes by the name of Dirk. He is set to arrive within the hour, and I will orient him to the house and his duties."

"*Dirk?*"

"Yes. Dirk."

She narrowed her eyes. "A man who provides personal security is conveniently named 'Dirk'?"

"I do not question the name he may or may not have been born under. He is exceptional at his profession, and I trust him with my life." A knock sounded at the door, and John smiled. "I suspect that is the man himself."

Mrs. Burnette left the parlor to answer the door, and John knew his supposition was correct when he saw the woman's head tip back to take in the visitor's tall stature. Before long, she ushered the man into the parlor, where John greeted him with a warm handshake.

Dirk was a former police officer, Scottish, who had formed an independent security service. What had begun as a one-man operation had bloomed into a team of seven with Dirk at the helm. Their work was discreet and professional and had grown to the point where Dirk had the luxury of being selective in his company's clientele. John had worked by the man's side on multiple occasions and had him to thank for saving his life.

"Follow me, if you will," John said, and the large, muscled, blond man nodded as he took in the surroundings with his sharp blue eyes. He'd yet to utter a word, and John knew that would remain the case until absolutely necessary. As they made their way up the stairs, John explained the layout of the first floor. They sat in two comfortable chairs in the common area, and he gave Dirk details of what he knew so far about Charlotte's situation, the letter from her father, and the attack the night before.

"Her routine mostly includes travel between here and Delaney Hospital?" Dirk asked in his distinctive Scottish burr.

"Yes." John frowned. "I know she is intent on learning who was behind the attack, but I do not know what that will mean for her movements outside work and home. Her schedule has, in the past, included social events—dinners, balls, musicales, soirees. Nothing you haven't handled before."

Dirk nodded. He had an uncanny ability to make himself invisible unless he wanted to be seen. He'd mastered the art of blending in as a domestic servant to an impressive degree.

"Either of these two rooms is available to you," John said, gesturing. "I'll coordinate my schedule with yours so we're not overlapping. Leave any invoices or expenses with me, and I'll see to them immediately."

"Not with Miss Duvall?"

"No. I'm handling the costs."

Dirk nodded but kept any opinions to himself. "Very well. Is Miss Duvall aware of my assignment?"

John opened his mouth just as Charlotte's door opened. "She is about to be," he said with a wry smile.

Charlotte emerged from her room wearing a simple day dress and pale blue housecoat. She'd fashioned a makeshift cold bandage the night before by lining her reticule with baking parchment and a block of ice chipped from the cold cellar. It seemed to have helped with the swelling, but bruises and cuts still adorned half of her face. She'd affixed a smaller bandage to the deepest of the cuts and, to John's relief, no blood had seeped through.

"Hello," she said as both men rose. She looked at Dirk, eyes curious, and automatically offered her wounded right hand, which was now splinted. "Oh," she said, pulling it back. "Apologies. I am Charlotte Duvall—and I seem to have intruded on a tea party."

Dirk tipped his head and offered her his left hand, which she took with a broadening smile. "Dirk," he said. "I believe Ellis was just going to explain the reason for my visit."

"A Scotsman," she said, waving them both back to their seats as she took the settee adjacent theirs. "Welcome to Hampton House."

"Dirk is going to be your shadow for a time, Charlotte, when I am unable to be with you." John tensed, awaiting her response.

"I see," she said slowly. She lowered the ice packet and rested it on her wrist in her lap.

The sight of her battered face solidified John's determination to solve the matter at hand, and quickly. "He'll take Amelie's old bedroom and keep an eye on things while we investigate. That way you can continue to go about your life without fear of another attack."

The silence stretched, and suddenly the ticking of the clock on the wall sounded loud.

"I certainly appreciate the idea," Charlotte finally said, "but that seems an awful amount of fuss. I've committed to keep away from alleys and strange pubs. As long as I do not *overtly* pursue the identity of my attacker, I should be fine."

"Which indicates you plan to *discreetly* pursue the identity of your attacker." A muscle worked in John's jaw.

Charlotte sighed. "I sincerely doubt I shall have much time to do anything but work. I'll leave the detective work to you." She turned to Dirk. "I apologize if Mr. Ellis has brought you here unnecessarily and wasted your time."

Dirk studied her for a moment and then lifted a finger, indicating her face. "This happened to you last night within twenty minutes of leaving the hospital? Because you asked one person about the identity of a message sender?"

She pursed her lips and nodded once.

"Pressure on your father's enemies will only increase as Ellis investigates a twenty-year-old murder. This will get worse."

Her lips were still pursed, but she remained quiet.

"I am here as a favor to Ellis. I've never known him to be overly cautious. If he feels there is a justified reason for security, only a fool would dismiss it."

She bit the inside of her cheek and finally the corner of her mouth lifted. "You knew just the right words to use, Mr. Dirk. Very well, John, as I am no fool, I graciously and gratefully accept your efforts to keep me safe."

Whether or not sarcasm laced her words, he wasn't sure, but John was impressed with Dirk. His blunt approach had accomplished more than an hour's worth of cajoling on John's part would have.

"I'll keep you both apprised of anything new I learn," John said. "I have unavoidable meetings today and an obligatory supper with my parents, but I've asked Amelie to dig into the archives for any files on your mother's death."

Charlotte nodded. "Thank you." She took a deep breath. "I am restless already; perhaps I'll go into work for a few hours."

"Allow yourself one day to rest, Charlotte," John said,

exasperated. "One day." He moved to the settee beside her and looked at her eyes. "I'm no doctor, but you still seem a bit cloudy."

"My pupils are much smaller this morning," she muttered with a scowl.

"Much, but not normal." He took her left hand. "One day. All right?"

"Very well." She looked at Dirk. "I'm afraid you're in for a boring time, Mr. Dirk."

"It's just 'Dirk.' And I've plenty to keep me occupied. Please don't think you need to entertain me."

"That really is a lovely accent," Charlotte said, smiling at him.

John suppressed a groan. He'd been witness to more than one woman becoming dazzled by the handsome, rugged Scotsman. He had nobody but himself to blame if he lost his best friend to the man.

She *was* his best friend, he realized as he stood and made his goodbyes. He didn't think he would ever recover from the shock of seeing her last night after the attack. He would move heaven and earth to keep her from ever being hurt again, and as he heard Dirk's low voice say something, followed by her soft laughter, he hardened his resolve.

Thoughts of Charlotte dominated John's mind throughout the day, distracting him from his meetings. Eventually, the day wound down to suppertime, and as much as he wanted to return to Hampton House for a quiet meal in the cozy dining room, he instead made his way to his parents' large town house.

He reminded himself that it was important to maintain familial ties as they joined around the table for supper. His father's contacts in Parliament were also important to success in his own career, much to his regret.

His elder brother, Edgar Ellis II, and sister-in-law, Hortense, were in attendance that evening, which only strained matters further.

"Delightful to see the Hampton woman returned to Town," Hortense said with a glance in John's direction. "There was a time when they and your detective friends formed your only social circle."

"Darling," Edgar interjected, "those 'detective friends' are John's subordinates. We mustn't forget he is the director of the CID."

It was a predictable pattern of attack. Hortense's salvos usually contained thinly veiled criticisms of his social choices, and Edgar's invariably contained a cut at John's profession. It was tiresome, and the thought of that exact scene replaying itself decades into the future was enough to turn his stomach.

"Oh, John, surely you're not going about again with those people," his mother, Adele, said. "I saw you dancing with the girl at the Fulbrights' ball, which was to be expected as it was her first appearance since returning to Town. But to have it continue, just as before?"

"Those people, my 'subordinates,' as you call them, Edgar, are exceptionally well socially connected. The women are Hamptons, and Detective Winston has enough money to make even the queen blush. I should think that alone, while crass, would be enough to put your mind at ease about the company I keep." He speared a piece of lamb and chewed it thoughtfully.

Hortense opened her mouth, but he lifted his fork and added, "I seem to recall even you, dear sister, have sought an invitation to Mrs. Winston's seaside holiday charity the last three years running. As I am on favorable terms with Mrs. Winston, I shall put in a good word for you next year. Perhaps your hopes will be realized."

Hortense closed her mouth, and two spots of color appeared high on her cheeks. John wished he could find it within himself to regret embarrassing his brother's wife, but he was tired, Charlotte was on his mind, and he was not in the mood to hear her disparaged.

"While I never venture to assume the meaning behind any woman's thoughts," John's father, Edgar Ellis, Earl of Ashby, said, "I presume Hortense disapproves of your friend's choice of hobbies."

John continued eating but spared his father a flat look. "By 'hobbies,' do you reference the fact that Miss Duvall is a medical doctor?"

"Hardly suitable for a woman, John," Adele interrupted, "and you well know it. You pretend ignorance to our disapproval, as if you can't imagine why we should feel such a thing, and it is tiresome." She scowled at him before resuming her meal. "I would dearly love for this family to enjoy a meal together just once that does not involve bickering. You've again dragged us into disagreement, John."

"Now, Mother," Edgar said, a smile on his face as he winked at John, "we mustn't blame all our ills at John's feet."

"Thank you, Edgar," John said, waiting for the insult that was sure to follow.

"Of course, brother. You spend your time with criminals and common folk; 'tis no wonder you find yourself surly at the end of the day."

"There it is," John said, lifting his glass to Edgar in salute. "Masterfully done."

Edgar arched a brow at John as he put a forkful of food into his mouth and slowly chewed. There was no love lost between the brothers. Edgar was the elder by nine years, so by the time John had arrived, Edgar was already being groomed to inherit their father's title one day. John was never sure if his brother's resentment was genuine disgust at John's career choice or envy that he'd been free to choose his own path.

After a few minutes of silence punctuated only by the scraping of silverware, Ashby asked, "Is she looking to obtain work at a hospital in Town?"

"Do you mean Miss Duvall?"

Ashby's nostrils flared slightly, and John had to admire his father's successful effort to not roll his eyes in irritation. "Yes."

"I believe she is."

"Which hospital?"

"I've not the slightest idea." The lie fell smoothly from his lips. He wanted to keep a fair distance between Charlotte and any meddling his family might concoct. He couldn't imagine his father cared one way or the other who John's associates were as long as they didn't sully the family name or interfere with Ashby's status in Parliament. The influence Ashby wielded was extensive, however, and John didn't want Charlotte's career sabotaged in any way.

The meal continued in merciful, albeit awkward, silence. Adele and Hortense eventually left the dining room so the gentlemen could enjoy a glass of port, and John counted the minutes until he could make an acceptable exit. But it seemed his father was not quite finished with the subject of Charlotte and her profession.

"I'm happy to provide a character reference for your Hampton friend if you wish it. I know the board members of several hospitals and clinics in Town."

"Thank you, sir, but I admit confusion about the sudden interest in Miss Duvall's career."

"You're so suspicious, John," Edgar interjected, lazily swirling his port between two fingers. "Can we not simply offer support for someone whose company you seem to enjoy?"

John imagined the satisfaction he'd feel in knocking loose Edgar's drink by lobbing the gravy boat at it. He almost smiled at the thought. "I am suspicious of ulterior motives. As you said, I work with criminals on the daily; you'll forgive me for assuming the worst."

Ashby remained quiet, and John regarded his father while taking a sip of his drink. His father collected information—bits and pieces on everyone and everything that crossed his path—and used it to his advantage. John suspected that trait, which had passed to him, was one that so often led John to success in his work. It was also the reason why he couldn't assume his father was taking an interest in Charlotte out of the random goodness of his heart. Nothing with Ashby was ever simple.

"Frankly, John," his father finally said, "I couldn't care less with whom you choose to socialize privately. It would benefit appearances, however, if you would begin to pay attention to suitable women of matrimonial material. You're into your thirties; you've had time to enjoy bachelorhood."

"I shouldn't think my marital status would be of import to anyone—Edgar is your heir, and he has two sons. Even were I to remain single for decades, it should be no cause for concern."

"My patience with your glib attitude will stretch only so far." Ashby's tone was quiet but sharp. "We've a family name to protect, and I'll not have my progeny sully it. We marry suitable women and maintain a respectable reputation." He paused, and at John's silence, added, "I am well aware you make liberal use of the family name and connections to me in furtherance of your investigations. I've never taken issue with it because it is not something you've abused. Think about what I've said, however; I should hate to be forced to tell my colleagues that additional funding for the police would be a wasteful use of Her Majesty's coffers. Or that cooperating with any future investigations would be ill-advised because my misguided son has leanings that would prove harmful to the party."

John carefully set his glass on the table, studying the pattern on the tablecloth beneath it, gathering his thoughts. He cast aside a dozen retorts that sat ready on his tongue, and in the end, smiled.

"Well? Have you nothing to say?"

"The one thing you need never concern yourself with, sir, is the prospect of my causing a public scandal. I think if nothing else; you should know that about me."

Edgar sat forward in his chair. "Continued fraternization with a . . . a woman doctor—let alone one who studied in America—is hardly conventional. You know the kind of surgeries women doctors perform!"

"An unflattering lie, propagated decades ago by cheap, ignorant literature."

Edgar's face reddened with frustration. "Come now, John, it was one thing when she was younger and you were sowing your oats, as it were. Now, however—"

Reaching the end of the proverbial rope, John straightened in his chair. "I don't care for your tone or your insinuation, Edgar. Charlotte Duvall's reputation was, and still is, impeccable." He felt his temper surging and decided the time had come to make his farewells. "If you'll excuse me, Father, I'm afraid I have work that requires my attention."

John found his mother in her parlor and kissed her cheek, as was expected. She was still irked with him, as evidenced by the tight smile she gave him, but she did say, "I hope you'll attend the Davises' soiree next week. Lady Compton has twin daughters who are enjoying their first Season, and I'm certain they would enjoy a gentleman's polite conversation."

He grimaced a smile and glanced at Hortense, who barely looked up from her needlework. As he left the parlor and made his way across the spacious foyer to the front door, he couldn't help but compare the tomb-like quiet of the large house with the noise and joy he always found in his friends' homes. Even the children playing underfoot was preferable to the farce of a family gathering he'd just endured.

He accepted help from the butler, Jones, as he shrugged into his coat. Nodding his thanks to the aging man, he put his hat on and stepped out into the cold. This house had been his primary residence except when he had been away at school, and while familiar, he never felt the pang of homecoming so many poets wrote about. In fact, he mused as he climbed into his carriage, he could pinpoint the time when his life had begun to change, when he'd learned the joy that could be found when relaxing with genuine friends. It was when Michael Baker had met the Hampton cousins and pulled John and Nathan along with him into their world.

He leaned back and closed his eyes as the carriage bumped along through the streets to Bloomsbury. Although the reason for his temporary residence at Hampton House was unfortunate, he couldn't help the sense of rightness he felt at going home at the end of the day to wherever Charlotte Duvall was. His heart thrummed in anticipation of seeing her, glad she'd acquiesced and allowed Dirk to help keep her safe.

As the carriage arrived at Hampton House, he gathered the documents and files Amelie had pulled from the archives. He was hopeful he'd find something useful for Charlotte regarding her mother's death, but he also knew he may have to disappoint her. As that was the last thing he ever wanted to do, he resolved to not leave even a stone unturned. She was the only person he could think of whose trials would keep him up late willingly. It was just as well, he mused wryly as he exited the carriage. He'd thought of little else since her return.

CHAPTER 13

Charlotte was resting when John arrived home, and rather than disturb her, he changed his clothes and settled in the first-floor common area with the files Amelie had found. Dirk joined him, and between the two of them, a harrowing picture began to emerge. After an hour, John sat back and pinched the bridge of his nose.

"This will get ugly," Dirk said. "Now that we know the players involved, it's a miracle she even made it across the Atlantic."

John nodded. "It also explains why her attacker was an American. He was likely hired by one of these families to prevent her from returning home."

He shook his head. What had her father been thinking? He'd told Charlotte he might have put her in danger, but if he'd mentioned to his enemies that she was returning to England to help him then he'd effectively painted a target on her chest.

"When she left the United States so quickly, the assailant had no choice but to follow. Finish the job."

"What, exactly, was the job?" Dirk asked. "Intimidate?"

John nodded slowly. "I think so. Perhaps at first to keep her from returning to England, but now that she's here, scare her into returning to New York so she doesn't ask any more questions about her mother's death." He frowned. "Her father supposedly collected information, but it's not turned up."

"That would be useful." Dirk yawned and rubbed his eyes.

"Thank you for your help," John told him. "Why don't we turn in for the night."

Dirk was to his door when Charlotte's opened, and she squinted at the light. Dirk looked at John in question, and John waved him on. He patted the sofa next to him, and Charlotte joined him, carefully rubbing her tired eyes.

"What's all this?" she asked.

He sighed. "Pieces of the puzzle. Are you too tired? I can wait until tomorrow to show you what I've found."

"Now, if you please." She nodded and leaned toward him, holding her sore wrist to her chest.

"This is the initial accident report. Amelie found it in the Thames Division archives. Interestingly, the clerk she spoke to commented that she was the second person this year to request the old file."

"Who else asked for it?"

He lifted his shoulder. "The clerk didn't make note of it, but it was a man. He was allowed to peruse the contents but not remove the file from the building."

He handed her the initial incident report and watched her eyes fly along the lines written there. The facts were simple: Authorities responded at 10:30 p.m. to activity near the Waterloo Bridge where they found Katherine Hampton Duvall had been pulled from the water after falling overboard from a chartered river ferry. One person whom the officer didn't name claimed to have heard a splash. Everyone else present was in the salon, unaware the victim had been alone on the upper balcony deck. The report also listed the names of everyone at the scene.

Charlotte tapped her fingertip to the top four names. "James Paddleton, MP. James Worthingstone, MP. James Finebough, MP. James Carter." She bit her lip. "I spoke with Mr. Carter and his wife after the funeral. She was as nervous as a cat in a room full of rocking chairs—an American patient told me that one." She smiled faintly.

"Worthingstone and Finebough were in attendance at both the funeral and the gathering afterward," John said. "I believe I saw Paddleton only at the funeral." He studied Charlotte's face. "You seem unsurprised to see these names. If you were unaware of your parents' social circle, may I ask how you know these men?"

"My mother wrote in her journal that all of them would be together for the Carters' engagement party. It was her last entry." She shook her head ruefully and gave a dry laugh. "And all them are named 'James.' That doesn't help much."

"What do you mean?"

She licked her lips and stared down at the papers in her hand. "My mother wrote in her journal that 'J' would be there, and I got the feeling that she was afraid something might happen."

"And you think the J stands for James," he said.

Charlotte nodded absently, chewing again on her lip. She pointed to another line in the report. "This mentions a head wound—a lump on the back of the decedent's head that caused blood to seep through the shroud the coroner's office had placed her in. This Sergeant Dane makes a note that it will likely come up in the coroner's report."

"I saw that too." John shook his head. "The sergeant isn't wrong—I'm certain the coroner would have seen the wound, but I am surprised there wasn't more vigorous follow-through in questioning the witnesses about it on-site."

"Do you have the witness reports?"

John nodded and flipped through the files. "There are statements from all four men, along with statements from each man's wife or fiancée, as well as the crew and captain. There were also two witnesses on the bridge who claimed to have seen everything—a Mr. Evans and a Mr. Sheen. Those aren't much help, though, as the constable says they were 'drunk and disorderly, and barely coherent in their speech.' Claimed they heard shouting and a scuffle, but then weren't sure if it had happened on a boat or on the street."

Charlotte read through them all, then hesitated. "And . . . my father? Was he . . ." She cleared her throat. "Did he give a statement?"

John wordlessly handed over another piece of paper.

According to the statement, David Duvall had been in the salon below the upper deck and had not witnessed his wife's fall. He was unsure how long she'd been in the water before the alarm sounded. He said resuscitation efforts had been attempted but failed. It matched what Sally had told John, and he shared the details of the conversation with her.

She absorbed the information, silent for a moment before returning to the issue of her father's presence. "He never said he *wasn't* there," Charlotte murmured, her brows pulled tightly together. "I suppose I always assumed he would have said if he had been—especially the one time I asked him about it."

John felt the urge to reach for her, offer her some comfort, but she was entirely focused on the reports in her hands.

"They're all so similar. Why was my mother the only person on the upper deck when everyone else was in the salon? Who noticed she was missing? Nobody seems to know. They found her and pulled her out of the water so quickly, but she was already gone." She paused, forehead wrinkling.

John loved watching how her mind worked. She had seized on the same details that had bothered him when he'd read the reports.

"Perhaps the similarities were because there was pressure to close the matter," he said. "Also consider, none of these men had yet risen to the positions they now hold."

"No, but they were from families of incredible influence. Families who would do anything to keep their names from any hint of scandal. Even proximity to an accident resulting in a young mother's death would carry notoriety with it." She scowled. "People would expect a Notorious Hampton to come to a notorious end." Charlotte sat back against the sofa and looked at him, lips pursed in thought. "I wonder how long they all stood together and talked before the authorities arrived."

"By that you mean how long did they have to concoct a consistent story?"

She nodded. "But would my father . . ." She swallowed. "Would my father have been party to some kind of hushed-up story?"

"Perhaps he was busy attending to your mother," John said, wanting to give her some peace. "There was likely a lot of confusion, a lot of noise. Crowds gather, conversation can be either lost or hidden. If there was a 'story' concocted, your father probably knew nothing of it."

She inhaled slowly and quietly exhaled. "But perhaps he did, and that is the reason he decided to bring it to light before he died." She closed her eyes. "Did I ever really know him?"

"Charlotte." John leaned close and put his hand on hers. "What reason would your father possibly have for colluding with these other men? Considering all the Jameses had been your mother's childhood friends, this entire social circle was largely hers." He paused, and when she didn't reply, added, "What does your intuition tell you about your father's nature?"

She thought for a moment. "He was quiet. Melancholy. Often lost in his own world. He left my brothers and me to our own devices, as though he'd given up on ever maintaining control of his household." Her expression was pained. "He was the sort to go unseen. He might have been with her on deck himself and nobody would have noticed."

John arched a brow. "You think your father would have watched her slip and fall and go overboard without attempting to rescue her?"

Charlotte stood and crossed the length of the room, still holding the papers and rubbing her forehead with one hand. "How did she 'slip and fall,' and *then* go overboard? Was there space enough to have slipped beneath a rail?" She was agitated, and with her agitation always came movement. John recognized the habit, had nearly forgotten it. Charlotte was unable to sit still if something was wrong.

"What if he pushed her?" She finally stopped and faced him squarely. "Suppose he grew tired of her love for this 'James,' and in a fit of rage, hit her and threw her into the water."

"How often did your father fly into fits of rage?"

She frowned and dropped the documents on the small coffee table in front of John. She rubbed her eyes with her fingertips and sighed. "Never. He never so much as raised his voice." She looked at him, troubled, but unflinching. "It happens though, does it not? You've seen all sorts in your work, John. You must agree that it could be a possibility. Placid people have been known to lose their wits when provoked to anger or jealousy."

He sat back, studying her and trying to buy himself some time. "It does happen," he finally admitted. "But you lived with your father for twenty years after your mother died. You knew his temperament. Do you honestly believe that is a viable scenario?"

She began pacing again. "I wouldn't have believed my mother had been in love with another man, but here we are."

"You didn't know your mother," he said gently. "You did know your father. Until we know exactly what happened that night, find comfort in the good memories of him."

She crossed the room to stand near him, eyebrows knit in thought. She was close enough to him that he smelled her light perfume and the laundered perfection of her night dress. Of course she was cleanliness personified—it was paramount to her job. It was also just *her*. Barely contained energy in a very neat shell.

If the notion took him, he could wrap his arm around her waist and pull her close.

He very deliberately set aside the notion.

He did see, however, the moment when she realized how closely she stood to him and observed with satisfaction her subtle inhalation. The corner of his mouth turned up by the slightest of degrees, but he kept it in check. The last thing he wanted to do was frighten her away like a timid forest creature creeping closer for inspection.

At that thought, he nearly laughed. Charlotte was as timid as a mother bear guarding her den.

He reached for her hand and pulled her knuckles to his lips. He placed the softest of kisses to her skin, lingering there for as long as he dared. He looked up at her, resting his chin on her hand. "We will find your answers."

"Suppose I do not like the answers?"

"You may not like them, but I don't imagine you shying away from them either." He inhaled deeply. "Are you prepared for a storm? If we start asking questions and the wrong people overhear, we could be looking at repercussions."

"Would the repercussions come down on you?"

"Possibly. But I can handle myself."

"I do know that," Charlotte murmured. "I'd hate to have you as an enemy."

"You, darling girl, could not be further from that." He smiled at her and placed another kiss on her hand, this one quicker and much more appropriate, before standing up. "As luck would have it, the coroner at the scene was someone we both know—Dr. Neville.

Her eyes lit up. "He was the one who sparked my interest in medicine! I watched him do that autopsy while Eva photographed, and I was absolutely hooked." She smiled in genuine delight.

"I suppose that would explain the odd friendship."

"What do you mean?" she asked as he gathered the papers and put them back into his satchel.

"My best women friends are taken in by autopsies and crime scenes. How could I not be intrigued?"

She laughed. "Will you schedule a visit with Dr. Neville, or shall I?"

"I will. I don't suppose I can convince you to take another day from work?"

"You suppose correctly. I nearly went mad today."

"Very well." He put his hands in his pockets to keep from reaching for her. His thoughts were venturing into dangerous territory. There was no future for them beyond friendship. She wouldn't be allowed to work as a married woman, and she thrived in the professional setting. He would rather die than destroy her career.

"Get some sleep," he told her. "Dirk will accompany you to work in the morning."

She smiled. "Funny man, that one."

He raised a brow. Funny? Not a word he would have used to describe Dirk. *Funny, in what way?* he wanted to ask. *Funny, charming? Funny, I wish he'd sweep me away to Scotland? Funny, I don't mind if he shadows me forever? That manner of funny?*

He rubbed his eyes. Ridiculous. He was being ridiculous. He waited beside his bedroom door for Charlotte to enter hers. She gave him a soft, "Good night," and clicked the door closed.

He rested his forehead against his door before finally turning the handle and going in. He'd best unravel the tangled web Mr. Duvall had left behind quickly lest he fall irretrievably in love with his best friend. That was not a road that ended well for either of them.

CHAPTER 14

Charlotte leaned against the comfortable sofa cushions in Eva's parlor and laughed at Amelie's retelling of her four-year-old daughter's latest antics. "By the time I reached them," she said, "Sophia had cut a lock of hair this long from Cassandra's head!"

Eva laughed. "I suppose we should consider the bright side—that Cassie didn't lose an eye to sharp shears."

A week had passed since Charlotte's attack, and she still felt off-kilter. She'd returned to work, but she could hardly keep the nature of her "accident" a secret; her bruised face was still a rainbow of garish colors. She'd given her colleagues the briefest of explanations for the reason she'd acquired a large Scottish shadow, but she told the entirety of the situation to the matron and Mr. Corbin. They supported the situation, but she detected uncertainty in their gazes as they passed in hallways.

True to his word, Dirk did not demand anything of her other than communication about her schedule and a promise to not "lose" him intentionally. She admitted to herself after the first day back at work that his presence was a relief, especially when she was anywhere outside.

Charlotte had yearned for an evening with her cousins since her return, and the thought of her father's enemies—*her* enemies—keeping her from it hadn't sat well. John had agreed to the "ladies' night," but only if he was allowed to attend. He promised to stay with Nathan and Michael in the billiard room, and Charlotte finally relented, even though Eva's and Nathan's home was fully staffed and buzzed with activity day and night.

John had also been true to his word; she'd not seen him since their arrival, although she occasionally heard creaking just outside the parlor door. If she could only have hidden her face, with its bruises and healing scratches, the evening of fun with her cousins might have been like any other they'd had through the years. She'd informed them and Sally shortly after the incident had happened, but she knew her face was a constant reminder of it, and she resented the assailant all the more for encroaching on her sacred space.

She was determined not to spare another thought for her attacker or the revelations she'd learned from John or about her mother's collection of Jameses. It was as though a storm hovered on the horizon—she knew it would eventually arrive. But not tonight.

She turned to Eva. "How is Sammy? Away at school?" Charlotte asked, referring to her cousin's adopted son, now a young teen.

Eva's smile faltered. "Yes, but we're bringing him home. His last few letters have hinted at what we assumed was teasing, but the headmaster contacted Nathan about the suspension of three older boys who have been harassing some of the younger ones." She winced. "The boy survives the first ten years of his life on the streets of London only to find himself preyed upon in a civilized setting."

"Hah," Charlotte said and rolled her eyes. "There is nothing civilized about a gathering of boys of just about any age, but especially the teenaged set. Will you hire a tutor for him?"

Eva nodded. "I had reservations about sending him away last

year, but he seemed to do well. This year means a different school with older boys, and I was doubly concerned."

"Sweet boy," she said with a concerned frown. It was Amelie who had first met Sammy and brought him into their fold. "I'd like to send some of the Yard's finest after the older bullies." She paused. "I do know a couple who would perform favors for a price."

Charlotte laughed, despite her anger on Sammy's behalf. "Imagine the headlines: Detective Inspector's Wife Charged with Assault-for-Hire."

Amelie scowled as Charlotte and Eva continued laughing. "I wouldn't be caught," she said. Her statement only increased the mirth in the room. "I know how to think like a criminal, now," she said, lifting her glass in salute. "You laugh, but won't you be surprised when Sammy is avenged and nobody is the wiser."

Charlotte nudged Amelie's foot. "Don't worry, dearest. Eva and I would never breathe a word of anything said in this room tonight."

Eva nodded. "It's true. The crown prosecutor could put me on the stand, and because I have such a demure, trustworthy face, they'd believe anything I say."

Charlotte laughed but had to acknowledge it was probably true. Eva was stunningly beautiful, and although she possessed a core of steel, her demeanor was a picture of polish and tranquility.

Eva cleared her throat. "And how are your housemates getting along?"

Charlotte felt herself flush and then was irritated because she had no reason for it. "They're fine, everyone's fine. Keeping me safe, protecting life and limb."

Eva nodded innocently. "I just wondered. Close proximity does breed such cozy familiarity. Just remember the three of us living there! We loved each other before but grew ever so much fonder after living together."

Charlotte scoffed. "Which one should I grow closer to? The big, silent Scot or my dear friend?"

"John Ellis needs a distraction," Amelie interrupted flatly, "or three. He works too hard, too much, and far too late into the night. He delegates, but not nearly enough. There are matters he could hand over to the newer detectives, but he mutters some nonsense about getting something done right by doing it oneself." She shook her head. "He may as well move into the office, considering how little time he spends at home. When he goes to social events, he ends up with a blinding headache for two days afterward. I feel like a pesky mother hen sometimes, but he doesn't take care of himself. If I didn't send Michael out the door with two lunches, I doubt John would take time to eat. Perhaps you can provide some balance, Charlotte, what with the new living situation."

"Temporary," Charlotte said absently and frowned, thinking of John working himself into an early grave.

"He needs a wife," Eva said. "A reason to go home at the end of the day."

"I suspect the sort of wife his family would choose for him might not be the kind to garner that result, which is why he's remained single." Amelie raised her hands as if to forestall any argument. "But that is only my opinion."

"You should fall in love with him, Charlotte," Eva said with a chuckle.

"What? Why?" Charlotte mentally kicked herself when she heard the defensiveness in her tone.

"I was only making a joke," Eva said. "We've teased the two of you often enough in the past, but perhaps it was unwelcome."

"No," Charlotte said, "I did not mean to snap, Eva. I . . ." She frowned. "My head is all a muddle since returning home. I feel as though the rug has been pulled from under me. Everything has gone sideways since I returned to London. Sitting close to John in the Fulbrights' library must have set the stage for mayhem."

The room grew instantly still. Amelie sat up straight, and Eva set her glass on the coffee table. "Sorry, what did you say?" Amelie asked.

Too late, Charlotte realized her blunder. "It was nothing—I was concerned for his health. We went into the library where it was dark and cool, and I gave him a headache powder."

"Sat close?" Eva echoed. "How close?"

Charlotte waved a hand and shook her head. "Not that close, and not for long. It was nothing, and as I said, my brain is all twisted in knots."

Her cousins looked at each other, and Charlotte wanted to slap her own forehead and drag her hand down her face. There was no reason at all for anyone to know she'd been feeling . . . things . . . for their friend, and she'd spoken without thinking.

"Of *course*!" Amelie said. "That's why he always watches until you're out of sight. He never does that with anyone else." She looked at Charlotte. "Oh, dear. This could either be very lovely or very catastrophic for our friendship circle."

"There is nothing to even think about," Charlotte said firmly. "He watches me until I'm 'out of sight' because he's taken my safety on as his responsibility. There is no reason to worry that our 'friendship circle' will change at all."

Silence.

"Of course he's watched me walk lately—I've been out of the country for four years, and we're very good friends! I watch *him* constantly!" She closed her mouth and wished for a very large hole to open up in the floor.

Eva looked at her in pity, and Charlotte wanted none of it. "Girls. I beg you, do not mention this further. I am trying to find my place here, to make it home again, and I do not need this sort of nonsense running amok in my head."

Both women nodded, and Eva belatedly said, "Absolutely. Not another word about it."

A toddler's cry could be heard descending the stairs, and Eva and Amelie looked at each other.

"Sounds like yours," Amelie said.

Eva nodded. "Little Henry has yet to sleep through the night in his new bed. I'd let Nathan handle it, but he'll fuss for me." She rose and her footsteps echoed out into the hall. "Young man," Eva said, her tone far from stern, "what are you doing away from your bed?" Her voice trailed off as she climbed the stairs.

Amelie gave Charlotte an arch look. "Good timing, there, Miss Charlotte. You must thank Henry in the morning."

"Ha. You're still here to torment me. Perfect timing would be if Sophia appeared in that doorway with a pair of shears."

Amelie grimaced, and then said, "Actually, I do believe I'll check on her. Can't trust that child for even a minute."

Charlotte breathed a sigh of relief once she was alone. Her only problem now was that she was imagining John, lingering at doorways, his eyes on her back as she left him. Heat rose in her cheeks that had nothing to do with her proximity to the fire. Unfortunately, it was a worthless endeavor to even imagine a future with him, with anyone. She'd chosen her path, and it was her career. She wasn't allowed to be married and work as a doctor or nurse.

Amelie was right. If she didn't keep her feelings in check, she could be headed for catastrophe.

CHAPTER 15

Charlotte's routine remained predictable for the next few days. Dirk guarded her during the day until John was able to join her in the evenings. She had not received any further messages or threats. She hadn't noticed if she was being followed by her American assailant, but her reliance on Dirk made her less observant. He'd not said anything, though, so her thoughts were free to wander.

Wander they did. Back and forth over the conversation with Amelie and Eva, wondering if she'd been foolish enough to begin developing feelings for her friend. John was on her mind constantly, and her heart beat faster each time she saw him.

She could feel it thumping as she sat with John in his carriage as they traveled to visit Dr. Neville at St. Vincent's morgue, where her mother had been taken after her death. The silence in the carriage was comfortable, if charged. Charlotte felt something in the air with him, something that seemed to have been building from the time in the Fulbrights' library.

She sat across from John—ever the gentleman, he'd taken the seat facing backward—but she wished they were side by side. She had only herself to blame for her speeding heart. He lived in the bedroom next to hers, now, so she saw him consistently, even if it was a mockery of an intimate relationship. They did not truly live together.

Still, she felt oddly vulnerable, like she was exposing a raw nerve. She'd seen that oftentimes patients fancied themselves in love with their doctors or nurses—perhaps that was the reason for her heightened awareness of him. He was the doctor to her dilemma, helping her find answers to questions. She'd do well to avoid casting him in the "rescuer" light; however, he was, literally, her rescuer.

But the night of the Fulbrights' ball . . . There was nothing to rescue then; in fact, he'd been the patient . . .

There was no hope for it, and no denying the expression in his eyes the night they'd discussed the police records in the first-floor common area. When he'd kissed her hand. Or rather, when he had caressed it with his lips. The warmth of his touch had shot straight to her core, and she'd been amazed to feel the quite clichéd weakness in the knees. She'd always thought such things were ridiculous, that she'd never "melt" or "swoon." Those words belonged in Amelie's vocabulary, not Charlotte's.

"What are you thinking, Miss Duvall?" John's face was in the shadows, but she saw his half smile.

"I am thinking I am fortunate to have such a well-connected friend." It was a partially honest admission. He *was* well connected, even if she'd only thought of it in that very moment.

"Your face suggests you seem rather perturbed."

"Does it? I suppose that must be my natural state."

He tipped his head back and laughed.

She smiled despite herself. "What on earth is so funny about that?"

"The absurdity of it. Your natural state as long as I've known you is curiosity. Excitement. You radiate energy. 'Perturbed' is not your regular state of mind. Of course, I may be misinterpreting you entirely."

"I've felt differing levels of perturbation since returning from the United States." She frowned. "My course was set during those years, with no question as to what would come tomorrow, or next week, or next month. I now have everything I've wanted for a long time, but my life is . . . unsettled."

"Understandable, given the questions you're trying to answer." He lifted the police file he'd brought along.

"Yes."

"Is there something else?"

Oh yes, you wretched man, there is definitely something else. "No, just adjusting to being home."

"Will you return to America?" His voice was carefully casual.

Would you mind? Would you miss me? "I was considering it. I had planned to remain at least six months at St. Anne's clinic in New York. It's similar to Delaney but focuses exclusively on women and children, which I enjoyed. I loved the challenge and loved working with my colleagues—all women. But then my father's letter arrived, and I came home and suddenly the notion of returning sounds . . . less appealing." She scowled. "Not to mention the fact that I'll not give my attacker the satisfaction of believing he drove me away. At least, if I'm ever unemployed here, I have family to rely on, much as I detest the thought of asking for help."

"Surely you had friends in America who would have helped."

She nodded. "I did, but would you wish to rely on friends for shelter and resources, all the while not knowing if another position would come along?"

"I would not." He paused. "I wouldn't want to rely on family either, but yours is much more gracious than mine."

"Psh," she said with a hand wave. "Not my brothers, certainly, but I could go to my cousins or Sally with less mortification. I'll soon be eligible for the trust that had been set up for me after my mother died, and my portion of my father's estate will also provide a nice cushion."

"Enough to return to the States if you choose." His tone was mild, and she couldn't read beyond it.

"Are you trying to convince me to leave, Director Ellis?"

"Far from it. I do not wish you to leave ever again. I would not be a good friend, however, if I didn't support your dreams."

She sighed. "I am living my dream. At least a variation of it, brutal assaults notwithstanding." She smiled. "Besides, a girl could do far worse than enjoy the company of a handsome gentleman." She tilted her head, adding, "Even if it means making a visit to a morgue."

"I can think of nobody with whom I would rather visit a morgue." His smile was subtle, just like everything else about him. He was understated, dry with his humor, and even now when he seemed to be intensifying their relationship, she was hard-pressed to put her finger exactly on what had changed. The way he looked at her, the affection in his tone—he seemed somehow different, but she struggled to explain to herself why she felt their friendship had shifted.

Charlotte didn't care for puzzles or riddles. She was impatient. Seeking to distract herself from the enigma seated across from her, she focused instead on her other problem. Regrettably, the other problem was more frustrating. With the former, if she truly wanted to know, she could ask John directly if his feelings for her extended beyond friendship. She could not, however, easily learn who had murdered her mother, or why.

She rubbed her temples and exhaled, suddenly feeling the strains of the day. Her muscles were tense, and though her bruises were fading, her wrist ached only occasionally. The cuts were nearly all healed, but she felt exhausted emotionally.

She looked out the carriage window at the steadily falling rain. The dark night hid layers of soot, mud, and dirt that covered the streets and pathways during daylight hours. If she were the pretending sort, she could imagine a world that was pristine and without blemish, simply sleeping in the cozy arms of darkness.

But pretending had never been Charlotte's strong suit. When her brothers had allowed her to play pirates with them, she'd been disappointed to realize they used wooden sticks instead of a sword and cutlass. Their responses had been little short of derision, which made no sense to her. "It's not as though I'll actually run you through," she'd said, at which point her brother Stephen had handed her a small, unimpressive tree branch and told her to keep her mouth shut if she wanted to play with them.

The carriage rolled to a stop in front of St. Vincent's, and John held her hand as she stepped from the carriage. He popped open an umbrella to shelter them, and they quickly made their way inside the old building of brick and arched stone.

"You did say he's available?" Charlotte said as John closed the umbrella, shaking the water droplets from it. "It is after working hours."

"I sent word earlier, and he answered that he'll be here late into the evening." He smiled. "The man is ancient as a fossil, but he'll probably die while conducting an autopsy, scalpel in hand."

"Convenient." Charlotte laughed. "They'll not have far to carry him." As they made their way to his office next to the morgue, she added, "Ancient as a fossil . . . I shall remember that one."

"First heard the phrase used by Winston," John said as they neared the office door. "In fact—"

"Who is this 'ancient as a fossil' fellow?" The grizzled voice came from within the office, and Dr. Neville appeared with his white hair and bushy eyebrows.

John chuckled. "Someone much, much older than you, good sir."

Dr. Neville looked Charlotte from head to toe, then smiled at her, holding out both hands. He didn't seem surprised by her bruises or scrapes, and she wondered if John had warned him earlier.

She clasped his hands and kissed his cheek, fighting a sting in her eyes. Meeting this man had sent her on a trajectory she'd never imagined possible.

"Officially a doctor, are you?" Neville asked, grasping his signature cane and making his way around his desk. He gestured for them to sit opposite, and they obeyed.

"Officially." Charlotte smiled.

The old man nodded once, briskly. "As I knew you would, even though you crossed the pond to do it." He gave her a flat look, and she stifled a laugh.

"I needed more schooling, if only to prove myself," she said. "You know what doctors are like."

"Psh. As I've always maintained, a village midwife has more practical medical information in her brain than I'll ever acquire." He opened a file on his desk and placed his spectacles on his nose. "You're here about your mother." He looked up at Charlotte, and she was alarmed to see sympathy in his eyes. She couldn't have that—it would be her undoing.

"Yes." She nodded and sat up straight, hoping to appear professional and unaffected. "I have some questions about the nature of her accident."

He nodded with a grunt, then looked at the file, lifting smaller papers she recognized as photographs.

She couldn't stop the gasp that escaped her lips, and she gripped the arm of her chair. "You have . . . It was so long ago . . ." She struggled to swallow with a dry mouth. "You have photographs?"

Neville tilted the papers toward his chest. "Dear girl, I am sorry. I ought to have thought." He shook his head. "You need some tea." He glanced to a sideboard where his assistants kept a pot perpetually warmed.

John got up and poured a cup for each of them as Neville explained the photos.

"We had only just considered the benefit of autopsy photos a few years before your mother's death. She was one of the first." He paused to sip his tea once John set it down before him. The poor doctor probably needed it more than she did.

She took a bracing drink from her own cup and managed a smile. "Please, forgive me. I was caught by surprise, that is all. I've only seen her likeness in a small daguerreotype and a portrait painted just after my parents' wedding. I never imagined there might be these . . ." She pointed at the photos that Neville had pressed against his jacket.

"I recognized you, you know," Neville said, his voice gravelly. "The first time I saw you. It was the hair, you see, but I couldn't recall until later, much later, and by then it hardly seemed appropriate to tell you . . . Well, you understand."

She swallowed past a lump in her throat. "I've seen your work, and the reverence with which you conduct it. I'm glad to know you were the last to see to her well-being." A tear formed and slipped free. *Drat everything under the sun.* "I was very young when she died, so my memories are few. I will not become a sobbing mess, I give you my word," she said as she quickly wiped away the tear.

In her periphery, she saw John extending a handkerchief, and she slapped his hand away. She thought he might have chuckled, but the offensive fabric disappeared.

"Why are you asking questions about this now?" Neville asked. He took another sip of tea, watching her expectantly.

"I've heard conflicting reports about her death." Charlotte shook her head. "I am simply looking for the truth."

"What do you hope will come of it? Justice, if warranted?"

She lifted a shoulder. "I must know. I'll cross further bridges when I reach them."

He nodded, seeming satisfied. "If your supposition is that her accident was no accident, then I say you would be correct."

Charlotte felt the breath leave her lungs, stunned to be receiving confirmation of what her father had suggested.

John leaned forward and tapped on the documents sitting in the open file. "We've read the police reports. They mentioned a head wound in addition to the drowning. What can you tell us about that?"

Neville finished the remainder of his tea. "According to the constable, Mrs. Duvall went into the water immediately, and there was, indeed, river water in her lungs. In my professional opinion, the head injury seemed the obvious cause of death, but authorities insisted on 'accidental drowning.'"

John frowned. "You said, authorities—plural. Were you visited by someone other than the constable?"

Neville nodded and thumbed through some papers in the file. "My personal notes, which I keep in addition to official records," he explained, selecting a sheet. He squinted at the document. "Apologies. My script has deteriorated with time, and I was never exceptional to begin with."

John took the paper and angled it so Charlotte could see.

"Visits from"—Charlotte read aloud—"Lord Worthingstone. Mr. Finebough." She blinked again, trying to decipher the hastily scrawled notes. "This here"—she pointed—"must be Mr. Paddleton."

John glanced at Charlotte, his face unreadable.

Neville handed over another paper. "Additional visits from the captain of the boat and two of her crew. And lastly, the Thames Division chief inspector. I know the captain was concerned about insurance matters and potential liability. Everyone else, if memory serves, came to see what I could tell them about Mrs. Duvall's cause of death."

"Why did they not just ask the authorities handling the case?" Charlotte mused.

"Exactly." Neville rapped his knuckles on the desk. "As she was a Hampton, I assumed she was a person of influence with many friends."

Charlotte took a deep breath and quietly exhaled. "May I ask about the head wound?" When he hesitated, she said, "I am a doctor, a professional."

Neville selected one of the pictures and gave it to her. The image showed the back of a woman's head with masses of curly hair pushed aside to reveal a deep gash surrounded by a darker shadow, undoubtedly blood.

Neville handed her a magnifying glass, and when she looked at him in question, he nodded toward the image. "Tell me what you see."

An odd sense of nostalgia washed over her. He had asked her that very question many times in the months during her initial year of medical school when she'd studied in London. He'd claimed she could learn much from a dead body as well as a living one, perhaps more.

Charlotte frowned and held the glass to the picture of the wound. "I see blunt impact, cracked skull, and . . ." She squinted and angled the picture toward the light. "And an extremely deep wound that penetrates the skull itself." She looked to Neville for confirmation.

He nodded. "As though someone had carved out a circular opening. Also notice the jagged breaks below the main wound, as though the object entered and then was forcibly removed. Additionally, consider this." He handed her another photograph.

This one showed several large bruises on her mother's back. "Whatever hit her head also caused these? They bring to mind a medieval torture device." She frowned. "It makes no sense."

"They look more like handprints to me." He pointed. "Do you see? I made note of it in my findings. I believe the bruising darkened after death, as though she received the impact just before she died. More than twelve hours had passed before she was brought here. This photo shows additional bruising on her thigh, possibly as a result of contact with the boat before entering the water."

Charlotte nodded. "Do you have any idea what would have caused this wound to the skull?"

"Something conical in shape. You can see how the wound narrows as it penetrates the skull. It is not entirely smooth, either. We would be looking for something oddly shaped but sharp enough to penetrate the skin and cut through nearly to the brain."

Silence settled over the room, and Charlotte's head swam with more questions.

Neville quietly cleared his throat and asked, "My dear, would you care to see the picture of your mother's face? There are no injuries on it."

She stared at him for a long moment. She'd not hesitated to

see the picture of the injury but looking at her mother's dead face was a different matter altogether. She finally nodded.

He handed her the picture, and she took it with a hand that shook, much to her disappointment. *Pull yourself together. It is only a photograph . . .*

When she finally looked at it, she saw a mirror image of herself. A flood of emotion rose up in her, and she was unable to stop the flow of tears that gathered and then fell down her face. She covered her mouth, but a quiet sound escaped anyway.

Neville extended his hand to take back the photograph, but she shook her head. "No," she whispered, "I am fine. I just . . ." She looked at the picture through blurry eyes. "My mother."

Sweet mercy, Mama, I miss you so. Why . . . why . . .

This time when John offered his handkerchief, Charlotte took it and wiped her eyes. She sniffed and tilted the photo to him and said, "This is my mother." Her tears kept flowing, blurring her vision.

He nodded, his face reflecting her emotion. "She was beautiful," he said, looking at the picture and placing a hand on her back.

She nearly laughed at the absurdity of it—oohing and aahing over an autopsy photo. Katherine Hampton Duvall had been beautiful, though, and Charlotte admitted it without hesitation.

"She loved me," she said unsteadily. "I remember that much."

"Of course she did," Neville said, clearing his throat and surreptitiously wiping an eye while mumbling something about a speck of dust. "She would never have left you, given the choice." He gathered the papers and stacked them together.

Charlotte traced her fingertip along her mother's collarbone, where the Y incision had been carefully stitched by the man who now sat with her, the man who had inspired her interest in medicine. It was an odd connection, but she liked it.

"Thank you," she said and handed the photograph back to him where he placed it atop the documents with the other one.

"I would never ask if we could remove official documents from the coroner's office, but . . ." John began.

"So don't ask." Neville pushed the file toward them and said, "I must ring for that night attendant. He's not been in here with a fresh pot of tea for over an hour."

John's lips twitched, and as Neville stepped into the hall, he deftly swept the file into his larger one containing information on her mother's case.

"Shouldn't those documents have already been included in the police report?" Charlotte asked.

"Not necessarily his private notes." John shot her a grin. "How odd that they got mixed into these other papers."

"Will you get into trouble?" Charlotte asked, surprising herself as soon as the question left her mouth.

John looked at her with one brow definitively raised and a half smile on his lips. "You? The filly who kicks against the paddock gate?"

She narrowed her eyes at him as they moved to leave the room. "Kick against *your* . . ." she muttered.

She heard him chuckle close behind, and he put a hand on her back as they bid farewell to Dr. Neville.

"You will keep me informed of any developments," the old man said, nodding at Charlotte.

"Of course. And thank you." She kissed his cheek.

"I am proud of you," he whispered gruffly, squeezing her hands. "You're a credit to us all."

"Oh no, you'll have me going again," Charlotte said, feeling tears in her eyes. She grasped him in a quick, tight embrace. "I shall visit soon."

John clasped Neville's hand. "Many thanks, sir."

Neville nodded. "Along with you both. I have work to do."

They made their way through the empty halls to the entrance, the sound of rain pattering on the roof louder here than it had been in Dr. Neville's office.

John retrieved the umbrella from the stand where he'd left it as Charlotte cracked open the door. A strong gust of wind pushed the door back, catching her off guard. She slipped back, but John was behind her, and his arms quickly encircled her.

She wondered if he could feel how fast her heart started beating at his touch.

He handed her the files, which she clutched to her chest, then pushed the door open, muttering, "Thanks be to Samuel Fox and his lightweight steel-ribbed frame," as he opened the umbrella against the storm.

Charlotte couldn't begrudge the rain as it forced John to wrap his arm tightly around her while they made their way to his waiting carriage. She lifted her skirts, trying and mostly failing to keep them from getting splashed in puddles that quickly filled the street.

"Where is the driver?" she asked as they neared the conveyance. The driver's seat was covered but still thoroughly wet.

"He usually finds a pub while I'm occupied, but I don't see one close by."

He opened the carriage door, and Charlotte saw the driver slip a flask into his jacket.

"Beggin' yer pardon," he said and scrambled for the door.

"Not to fret, Fitzhume," John said. "In fact, here—anchor it to the front if you can." He handed the young man the umbrella and ushered Charlotte inside.

John sat next to Charlotte and closed the door firmly. Putting his arm around her shoulders, he hugged her close. "Are you well?"

She wiped at a few raindrops that had fallen on her neck and shoulders. "I'll dry eventually, no harm done." He was warm and deliciously close, and she hoped very much he would stay where he was.

"I was not speaking of the weather."

"Ah." She did not want to discuss the fact that she'd cried in front of him, did not want to even think about it. She nodded and said, "I'm well enough. Thank you for arranging this meeting with Dr. Neville." She looked up at him, at his face which was quite close to hers, and wondered what he would think if she touched her lips to his.

Before she could give into the temptation, she turned her head and instead nestled comfortably against his side. He was merely acting as any supportive friend would. As a brother would. The thought nearly made her laugh when she thought of her own brothers and how different they were from solid, kind, and caring John.

Not a brother, then. But a very good friend. Until he said otherwise, expressed more of whatever he might be feeling, he would remain simply that, and she would behave accordingly. She wasn't about to ruin her friendship with John because she suddenly found him the most alluring man in the world.

Glad that the shadows in the carriage hid the heat she felt climbing into her cheeks, she turned toward the window as the carriage moved slowly through the streets. It had been a very long day, and she would need to be up with the sun for work. Allowing herself the luxury of relaxing against the solid, strong person at her side, she closed her eyes and sighed.

CHAPTER 16

John paced through his office feeling irrationally dissatisfied with his inability to travel back through time and interview the people who were present at Katherine Duvall's death. Of course, if he could travel back through time, he might as well go to the event itself and prevent it. At the very least, observe it.

He rubbed the back of his neck as he read over the witnesses' testimonies again. The sergeant who conducted the interviews had moved, but it would prove worthwhile to track him down and ask about his own memories of the event.

He heard laughing and good-natured bantering coming from the common area just outside his office, and then a knock sounded on the door. "Come," he called out.

Michael Baker and Nathan Winston entered, the former rolling his eyes as the latter chuckled. "It was a fair wager, Michael, and the lads clearly agree with me."

John frowned, pulling himself away from his papers and blinking.

"What's amiss?" Michael asked immediately.

"Something's amiss?" Nathan echoed and looked at John, his chuckle fading.

John shook his head, exasperated. "Why are you assuming something is amiss?"

Michael pointed a finger at John. "Your neck is stiff, and you've been pacing."

Nathan leaned against the round table, and Michael perched on the edge of John's desk. "More news of Charlotte's mother?"

John nodded and shared the facts he'd gathered, ending with the details Dr. Neville had shared.

Michael whistled low under his breath. "Someone did not want the details of this incident made public."

"Certainly looks that way," John agreed, tossing the papers on his desk and sinking into his chair with a sigh. "Three of the gentlemen present on the night of the death are current members of Parliament, and two of them are currently supporting additional funding for the Metropolitan Police. I do not imagine they would look kindly on a few pointed questions about whether one of them might have had been involved with an 'accidental drowning' that wasn't entirely an accident."

Michael gestured to the papers on the desk. "May I?"

"Of course."

He scanned the list of names and shuffled through the witness statements. He paused and glanced at Nathan. "You're acquainted with James Carter, are you not?"

Nathan nodded. "Carter Textiles. We were rivals for generations until both companies carved out their own places."

"What do you know of him?" John asked.

Nathan lifted a shoulder. "Decent fellow, seems straight with his business practices. Was rather hedonistic as a young man, if memory serves; made a bid for my mother once."

"Did she ever consider his suit?" Michael asked, amused.

Nathan snorted. "I should say not. She was already married to my father at the time. I remember my father speaking of the Carters with derision, but it wasn't until I got on in age and learning the mechanics of the family business that my mother shared the details."

"The fool is fortunate your father didn't thrash him," Michael remarked as he continued looking through the pages and then handed some to Nathan.

"He's fortunate my *mother* didn't thrash him. She has no time for nonsense."

Michael looked at John. "It says here that the boat was a small passenger ferry with a salon aft, atop which sat a deck with waist-high rail."

John nodded. "The captain was toward the center of the craft, but he had his back to Mrs. Duvall. The assertion is that she had apparently been drinking, then she slipped and fell, cracking her head on her way into the water. I've spoken with Sally Hampton, who asserts Katherine did not have a stomach for alcohol."

The men continued studying the file, each lost in thought. Nathan finally said, "I'll admit, I've hoped we would learn that Mr. Duvall was confused and that it was nothing more than an accident. But it seems clear that someone murdered Katherine Duvall and was never held responsible."

"Look at this list of attendees," Michael said. "It is full of money and influence. Three future MPs, whom we all know had parents that began their political ambitions for them in the cradle, the heir to a textile fortune, and their respective wives or fiancées, each of whom bears either titles or money."

John nodded. "Childhood friends of the Hampton family, each with ties to Katherine. James Carter was the only one of the four James's who hadn't known her for decades."

"What of David Duvall? How did he fit in with this group of socialites?" Nathan asked. "Charlotte said he was significantly older than Katherine. I would imagine his participation in these events was a means of placating his wife."

"Or keeping a watchful eye on her," John mused.

Michael raised an eyebrow. "Jealous older husband, beautiful young wife who had former romantic ties with a friend?"

"Or," Nathan added, "former romantic interest who couldn't stand to see her married to another."

"Perhaps a young wife who suspects a continuing assignation between her husband and a former lover." John stared into space, envisioning each scenario. It was when he imagined Katherine, looking exactly like Charlotte, that he winced.

On that thought, he asked both men, "As adults, have your wives or Charlotte crossed paths with any of these people?"

Michael lifted a shoulder and looked at Nathan, who pursed his lips in thought. "Eva has probably met at least one of them at events in the past few years. My mother is associated with the wives of several members of Parliament, many of whom often hail from backgrounds in trade, or their husbands do, so they do not have a harsh view of new money."

"Charlotte is the very image of her mother," Michael said, holding up the autopsy photograph of Katherine. "Are you wondering about their possible reactions to the sight of her doppelgänger?"

John nodded. "Charlotte is nearly as old as her mother was when she died. I'd love to see their reactions to her now. I didn't know to look during the funeral."

"What do you hope to accomplish?" Nathan asked.

John sighed and shrugged. "We do not have the resources to manage a full investigation of a crime that was committed more than twenty years ago, especially one that was successfully hushed at the time by people who have even more to lose now if the truth were known."

"There are implications for Charlotte, as well," Michael said. "If anything were to come to light that shines negatively on Katherine, Charlotte could suffer social consequences. She would say she doesn't care, but I daresay she would if it harmed her career."

Silence followed, and John felt a sense of futility, knowing full well that even if he were to uncover facts and evidence of the crime, he'd have a time of it convincing a crown prosecutor to pursue the case. Unbidden, he remembered Charlotte's face when she looked at her mother's autopsy photo, the unspoken anguish mixed with awe.

He shook his head, wondering how to handle a situation that was looking more impossible with every passing moment.

I must know.

That had been her answer to Dr. Neville when he'd asked exactly what Nathan had just asked John.

"I'll do what I can on my own," he finally told the two men, "regardless of outcome. Then Charlotte can at least rest easy knowing we tried." The statement rang false. Of course she wouldn't rest easy, and the look the other two exchanged suggested they knew it too. "Her safety is paramount. I hope to keep any responsible parties from thinking she is the person digging for old details. Perhaps then someone won't try to kill her."

Michael cleared his throat. "Amelie has suggested to me several times that I ought to ask if you've fallen in love with Charlotte."

"Of course, I have." John braced his elbows on his desk and rubbed the heels of his hands into his eyes. He heard what he'd said and slowly lifted his head. "That is, of course I love her, with the same affection I feel for all of you." Heat rose in his face. He couldn't remember the last time he'd blushed. What on *earth* had he just said?

Nathan stood and stretched, eyeing John dubiously. "If you start looking at Eva the way you look at Charlotte, we'll be having a talk."

"Don't be absurd."

Michael also straightened and dropped the papers back on John's desk. "It was obvious before she even went away to school, my friend." He gave John a half smile as Nathan opened the door. "Funny that I noted it before my romance-afflicted wife did."

"They don't always notice everything, you know," Nathan said as they exited the room. "Eva had no idea that my sister . . ." His voice faded as he closed the door.

John put his head in his hands and closed his eyes. He knew the two men weren't gossips, but their wives could pry information out of a rock. What would Charlotte think if his blurted non-confession made its way to her ears?

She would think what she'd always thought: that they were dear friends and that was that. She was practical. She'd never been giggly or insipid. She wouldn't corner him and say, "Michael said you're in love with me. Is that true?"

John wasn't stupid. He was well aware that he and Charlotte had been dancing dangerously close to crossing an invisible line. He'd nearly thought she might kiss him in the carriage after leaving Dr. Neville's office, and he'd desperately wanted her to. But she was vulnerable and had been crying, and he'd decided to be protective and brotherly. If *she* had kissed *him*, however, he'd not have objected.

He nearly laughed, and then groaned instead. Not have objected? He'd have been over the moon. Every moment spent with her and not touching her grew more difficult by the day. Michael said that John's growing affection for Charlotte had begun before she'd even left the country. Was that true?

Probably. He sighed, low and irritated. He'd missed her to the point of a physical ache in his chest. He'd forced himself to *not* write and beg her to come back home. And when she'd returned earlier than she'd planned because of her father's letter, he'd forced himself to *not* track her down before the funeral.

It was as if he'd known, beneath everything, how desperately he wanted her. Michael and John had teased Nathan years ago about his obvious love for Eva, but he'd insisted he wouldn't pursue it for fear of ruining the friendship. Something in that sentiment must have stuck in John's brain, because he'd done exactly the same thing with Charlotte.

He'd need to tread carefully from this point forward. He would follow her lead, because the last thing he wanted to do was sacrifice their friendship on the altar of his own desires. To not have her in his life at all would be worse than loving her from a safe distance. The biggest obstacle of all, however, was his personal devotion to her dreams. He would never ask her to give up her career for him.

He forced himself up, shoving on the desk for leverage, darkly amused at his state of affairs. He was in love with his best friend, whose mother had most likely been murdered by someone to whom John was beholden for political favors. His parents were rudely disdainful of her, she was embarking on a new career that left no options for marriage, and in the end, she had no idea he was enamored of her.

He hadn't known it himself before the last ten minutes.

He rotated his head on his neck, his muscles tight with stress. He donned his coat, checking his appearance in the glass.

He would be attending a ribbon-cutting ceremony for a Met-sponsored charity endeavor in the East End later. He gritted his teeth when his thoughts flew again to Charlotte, hoping he might catch a glimpse of her as he passed the hospital.

"As if she stands out front all day," he scolded his reflection. "You are ridiculous, man!" With that, he grabbed his hat and gloves, and left his office with a satisfying door slam.

Chapter 17

The week following her visit to Dr. Neville flew by in a blur that left Charlotte little time to think about her mother. She also saw less of John than she had in recent weeks. Some nights they chatted together in the sitting area following supper—sometimes with Dirk, sometimes alone—but they were usually both too exhausted to entertain long into the night.

After a particularly long day where Charlotte had argued twice with Mr. Stanley about his excessive use of anesthesia that nearly killed a small boy, she hurried home to change her clothes in preparation for Mrs. Winston's dinner party. With help from Sarah, one of Hampton House's maids, she donned an intricately beaded blue gown she'd not had occasion to enjoy more than once in New York. She piled her hair up with pins and allowed a few wispy curls to frame her face and rest on her shoulders.

Mrs. Winston's party was for an intimate group of seventy-five people, so Charlotte hoped she'd be able to sneak away without causing too much notice as soon as the meal was finished. The following day was her official "day off" of work, and she planned to sleep late into the morning.

She was looking forward to visiting with Nathan Winston's sisters again, and of course Eva and Amelie would attend, but she wasn't sure John would be there. He had been delayed by meetings more than one night that week. The disappointment she felt at thought of his absence caught her by surprise, and she shook her head as if to dispel the thought.

"I apologize profusely," she told Dirk, who had changed into tasteful dinner attire. "I cannot imagine you are looking forward to this."

He shook his head. "Part of the job." His mouth quirked, as it sometimes did, into an almost-smile, and she couldn't believe he'd never married.

She contemplated taking the carriage Sally made available to the Hampton House residents, but Dirk suggested they walk to the train station and ride back into Town. Luck was on their side as they found a cab just outside the train station, and in no time, she and her guardian stood at the Winston's large London home. Light spilled out onto the front garden, and strains of a string quartet were barely audible above the laughter and conversation.

Charlotte took a deep breath, hoping to harness the energy it would take to endure such a large event. She made her way up the steps and into the home, seeing Nathan's sisters mingling among the crowd, welcoming guests and directing traffic.

"Charlotte!" Alice Winston stood nearest the door and reached for Charlotte's hands with a wide smile.

Charlotte gave her a genuine smile as they kissed cheeks. She quietly introduced Dirk, and to her credit, Alice took the man's presence in stride. He followed as Alice swept Charlotte through the front hall.

"Alice, it's been an age! You look wonderful." By giving the compliment to Alice, she was essentially giving it to all of Nathan's sisters. The four were two sets of identical twins, and all four were nearly indistinguishable from each other. Olivia and

Delilah had brown eyes, while Alice and Grace had blue. That, plus personality differences, was the only way to tell them apart.

Alice was effusive and generous and had an energy for life unmatched by anyone Charlotte knew. It was infectious, and Charlotte immediately felt the joy.

"Now, you know many of the guests already, so I am taking you directly to the drawing room where several are already gathered, including Amelie and Eva. There are a few people still in the ballroom, and I believe I saw a large group of gentlemen making a beeline for the billiard room, but dinner will be served soon so I doubt they'll get much playing done."

"I don't know that they'd get much playing done anyway," Charlotte said drily as Alice handed off her outer coat to a footman. "They gather as though they are all experts, but really they just wish to talk."

"Exactly," Alice agreed. "And they say women are the chattering hens." She winked at Charlotte, showing a dimple, then linked arms with her. "Only a scant week ago, Nathan added four more couples to Mama's invitation list, and my supposition is that the only reason they were able to attend on such short notice is because the Van Horne sisters committed weeks ago."

Charlotte laughed. "Isn't it amazing how quickly schedules become uncomplicated when potential guests realize those ladies will be present?"

"Truly miraculous. Actually, it is rather miraculous these particular couples were able to clear their schedules. Three of them are members of Parliament and their wives, and the fourth, Mr. Carter, just returned from a trip abroad." She lowered her voice as though sharing a secret. "The Carters are in competition with our family business, of course, but we are cordial. Mama has known them for years, but to my knowledge she has never included them on any guest list." She shrugged. "Nathan must have his reasons."

Charlotte felt her heart skip a beat. Those were the four James's from her mother's life. John must have shared information with Nathan and Michael. She didn't mind, of course, but she would have liked a warning. Grateful that Alice had unwittingly warned Charlotte of a potentially awkward situation, she took a breath and quietly exhaled.

Alice escorted Charlotte into the drawing room, then bid her farewell with a quick kiss on the cheek and a promise to find her again to hear all about her adventures across the ocean.

Charlotte spied Eva and Amelie near the hearth, and as she maneuvered her way through the crowded room to her cousins, she heard a gasp and the tinkling sound of breaking glass. A ripple of surprise followed, and a footman hurried to the far side of the room. She heard nervous laughter, and then conversation resumed.

Amelie patted the spot next to her on a divan. "So happy you're here! We weren't certain you would have the wherewithal to attend after such a busy work week."

"Alice has infused me with enough energy to last for several hours, at least."

They laughed, and Eva nodded. "She does have that gift in abundance. She is the children's unapologetic favorite, and each of the aunties knows it." She glanced around. "Is your handsome Scot here tonight?"

Charlotte nodded toward the closest corner where Dirk was standing guard. "I feel horribly guilty that he must follow me everywhere. It's been an age since the attack. I should speak to John about releasing him from duty." The thought made her uncomfortable, but it no longer seemed necessary to keep the poor man on the hook. She changed the subject. "How are the children? Is Sammy home?"

Eva's lips tightened. "He is, and with a broken arm. It was treated and set at school, but they did not even bother to notify us. It happened the day the headmaster announced the older boys' suspensions, so there was not much delay, but I'd have ridden there myself to retrieve him that very night had I known."

Charlotte frowned. "Has he shared much of the incident with you or Nathan?"

Eva nodded. "He minimizes the effect it had on him, though. He tries so very hard to be manly." Her eyes were troubled. "Nathan is wonderfully patient with him, and I'm grateful Sammy trusts him. We're interviewing tutors next week." She paused. "Charlotte, would you be willing to stop by at your leisure to check the progress of his mending arm? Perhaps he might share with you if he has any other physical pains or problems."

"Of course, I would be happy to. Are you available tomorrow afternoon?"

Eva nodded. "That would be lovely. I have him busy helping me develop some photographic plates and prints."

Charlotte nodded. "And how are your little chickens?" she asked Amelie.

Amelie rolled her eyes. "No hair cutting, but a fair amount of mud bathing in the garden during last week's rain."

Charlotte laughed. "Scandalous little Hamptons, are they not?"

"So much so that I could swear they've been inhabited by the ghosts of our great-grandparents."

Charlotte thought of her mother, which reminded her of Alice's comments about the guest list. She glanced around and saw a few faces she recognized, but more she did not. In an undertone, she asked Eva, "Did Nathan mention the reason for his last-minute request to your mother-in-law?"

Eva nodded. "He told his mother he means to curry favor with them for their pending votes for police funding."

"Very clever," Amelie murmured. "I wish Sally could be here this evening. We must ask that she share her recollections of the friends."

Charlotte nodded. "Sally was the youngest, however; she may not remember much."

Amelie reached for Charlotte's hand and held it. "Michael and Nathan told us what you and John have learned thus far. I hope you do not mind."

Charlotte nudged Amelie's shoulder. "Of course I do not mind, silly. I'd have told you myself if I'd had the time. I confess, though, I do not know how to behave."

"What do you mean?" Eva asked.

"I mean around the . . . the . . . I don't know what to call them. My mother's friends."

Amelie patted Charlotte's hand and said, "We'll call them 'The Friends.' That way we'll know exactly who we mean without saying any names."

"As for your behavior," Eva added, "you just be Dr. Charlotte Duvall, proud daughter of David and Katherine Duvall."

"Also, I have some avenues of inquiry we might pursue independent of our husbands," Amelie said, looking at Eva. "They are busy, as is John, and may not have time to ask some questions."

Charlotte's lips twitched. "You always did insist Michael deputized you, so we're well within our rights to investigate on our own. What did you have in mind?"

Amelie opened her mouth to answer just as the supper bell sounded in the hall. "We'll discuss it later, in private," she said.

They rose and made their way to the door as soon as the crowd thinned. Two women at the door turned as they exited and looked at the three cousins. One of them must have belatedly realized she was staring, and she offered a strained smile as her companion turned away and said something to the group of people exiting in front of her.

They left the room, and Charlotte turned to her cousins. "Were those women part of the Friends?" she murmured.

"Yes, indeed, they were," Eva said. "I was introduced to them thirty minutes ago."

"Does your mother ever see them?"

Eva shook her head. "Mother doesn't venture far from the village." She smiled. "She speaks of your mother with a sense of awe, Charlotte, as though her elder sister Katherine was rather larger than life."

They made their way toward the dining room. Katherine *had* been larger than life, certainly in Charlotte's mind through the years. She felt a pang of longing she'd not experienced since childhood. It seemed unfair that she was in the company of her mother's associates, but Katherine wasn't there.

Near the dining room entrance, Charlotte spied a tall figure, and her heart tripped in grateful recognition. John had come, and suddenly she didn't feel so bereft.

"He's certainly a handsome one," Amelie remarked, glancing first at John and then at Charlotte. "Looks positively dashing tonight."

Charlotte thought to shrug it off and say something like "Does he? I hadn't noticed," but that would have been ridiculous. Every woman in the vicinity noticed him.

Eva nodded ahead at Nathan and said, "I must join my husband. My mother-in-law is about to tell everyone that seating is not assigned, much to the giddy delight of those among us who are untitled."

Charlotte chuckled as they neared the entrance and noted John's gaze on her. He smiled just a bit, as though the two of them shared a secret, and it sent a thrill through her.

"Ladies," he said and reached for Charlotte's hand. She placed it in his, and he kissed it very chastely. He threaded her hand through his arm, as though it was a foregone conclusion she would be his dinner companion. She had no complaints; indeed, she'd have been most put out had he paid attention to someone else. He looked over her head at someone down the hall and nodded; before long, Dirk passed them with a nod of acknowledgment as he made his way out.

They followed her cousins and their husbands into the glittering dining room and its enormous spread of tables with their silver, china, and crystal. Mrs. Winston had indeed given her instructions for the guests to choose their seating as they would, and as John led Charlotte behind Amelie and Michael, he leaned close to say, "There are people here you may not know. I was unaware they would be attending, but I am glad to observe any reactions."

Charlotte felt a stab of disappointment at the thought that perhaps the reason he singled her out was due to his desire to watch the Friends and their behavior. She nodded and tried to keep her voice light. "Fortuitous," she said.

John glanced at her, studying her face for a moment before pulling out her chair and seating her at the table next to Amelie. Nathan had masterfully maneuvered two of the Friends directly opposite them, and then he and Eva sat next to one of the gentlemen Charlotte assumed was named James.

As an experiment in human behavior, Charlotte had to admit

it was brilliant. Eight people sat across from or near Charlotte, and their faces were a mixture of stunned surprise and outright shock that they quickly did their best to hide. The first course was served, and Nathan effortlessly made introductions for everyone in their vicinity as if nothing unusual was in the air.

She remembered the names listed in her mother's journal and on the police report, and now, as Nathan pointed out each one, she wondered if she was looking at the face of her mother's killer.

Charlotte's earlier exhaustion was replaced with a humming sense of anticipation, a surge of blood flowing from her heart to her extremities. Her mouth had gone dry, and she took a sip of water, licking her lips and spreading her napkin on her lap to give her hands something to do.

John quietly reached over and took her hand. "Are you well?"

She looked at him with a smile. "Never better."

CHAPTER 18

Charlotte had certainly never looked better, of that much John was certain. He'd been searching to escort her to dinner with a warning that her mother's friends were in attendance. When he finally saw her, his breath had left his lungs in a whoosh.

She was stunning.

She wore a formal gown he'd never seen her in before. The beautiful shade of blue was the perfect complement to her complexion and hair. Her high cheekbones and green eyes were accentuated by an artful hair arrangement, and she was exquisite.

The only thing to give him pause was the ice-cold feel of her hands. She was a bundle of nerves, although he'd never have known it to look at her. It wasn't every day one sat across the table from a stranger who might have altered the course of one's life. He kept his hand wrapped around hers until the first course was served.

Silverware clinked, and conversation filled the room, but in their small area, he felt tension radiating off the diners around him. Some looked repeatedly at Charlotte, while others refused to even glance in her direction. Laughter became a touch too brittle and forced; food was either shoveled into mouths or pushed around on the plate.

One thing John knew for certain was that whether one of

Katherine's friends had caused her death or not, they clearly had a visceral reaction to her daughter. It must have been like dining with a ghost.

James Carter, the only one of the gentlemen who had not known Katherine in childhood finally addressed Charlotte directly. "My dear Miss Duvall, you'll think me forward, but I simply cannot comprehend your stunning resemblance to your late mother. She was a beautiful woman, and you are her very image."

Charlotte lifted her brows in surprise, but smiled and lightly cleared her throat. "How kind of you to say so, Mr. Carter. I remember your attendance at my father's funeral. My memories of my mother are few; she was taken from me much too soon."

John was impressed that she delivered the line without a hint of sharpness or implication.

"My wife knew Katherine in school, didn't you, Phillipa?" Mr. Carter said.

She glanced at her husband as though she'd rather fall through the floor than speak but nodded. "Before she was Mrs. Duvall, when she was Miss Hampton."

"My goodness, such a small world we live in." Charlotte smiled and gently piled a small amount of food on the back of her fork before then removing most of it, eating the tiniest morsel of food John had ever seen. Her hands were loose on the cutlery; she didn't clutch it or otherwise betray her nerves.

Eva sat next to Mr. Finebough. She leaned forward to encompass him and the other gentlemen in the group, saying, "I have it on good authority that several of you actually spent a fair amount of time with the Hampton brood." She smiled and explained to others, "The eldest was Amelie's father, Albert, and then Katherine, followed by my mother, Esther, and lastly our aunt Sally, who had a conflicting engagement this evening and is unable to join us. Perhaps I am speaking for my cousins out of turn, but being surrounded by people who knew our family is so comforting, especially for the two of us who've lost those we loved."

Murmured assent sounded from those addressed, and James Carter lifted his wineglass. "To friends, here and away."

They all followed suit, raising their glasses and drinking to friends. Some of them clearly would see the irony in it, and John wished he knew who they were. *Someone* on the boat that night had had a hand in Katherine's death, of that he was certain. With the exception of Charlotte's father, the boat captain, and crew, those people were now present at this very table.

"Mr. Worthingstone," a gentleman farther down the table called to the man seated directly across from John, "I do hope you'll give the others what for in the next round of voting. Enough of this Labor Party nonsense!"

Several people laughed, but the man's wife admonished, "Not at the table, Francis! Politics at mealtime?"

Others offered good-natured chastening, and Mr. Worthingstone, for his part, took the comment in stride. "I know I shall do my best," he answered. "My colleagues here are also of a mind. Never fear."

"It is quite remarkable," Amelie said during the following lull in the conversation, "that the three of you share the same Christian name and that you all grew up together! It must have been confusing, at times."

Mr. Paddleton smiled, and some of the color that had drained from his face when he sat down near Charlotte had returned. "As it happens, Kat was the one who helped us differentiate. She said Finebough should be 'James,' I could be 'Jim,' and Worthingstone should be called 'Jamie.' Wouldn't you know it, but the names stuck."

"Not by the time I met you, darling," Mrs. Winifred Paddleton said, looking at her husband with an arched brow. "I cannot imagine calling you Jim."

Finebough cleared his throat and dabbed at his mouth with a napkin. "Paddleton means the names stuck only until we finished school. After that, we all become James again." He glanced at Charlotte and managed a tight smile. He seemed to want to say something else but changed his mind and continued his meal.

"Mrs. Finebough, you also knew my mother?" Charlotte asked.

Gwendolyn Finebough nodded. "Oh, yes, but when we were in school. Anastacia and I are sisters, you see, so we both were acquainted with her. It wasn't until we were all married that we began to attend events and gatherings socially as couples. Naturally, it would have been wildly inappropriate for your mother to spend time with the gentlemen as a single woman. Childhood friendships aside." Her smile was frosty.

"And you, Mr. and Mrs. Carter? When did you join this esteemed group of friends?" Amelie asked.

"I knew the Jameses in school." Mr. Carter chuckled. "And as a James myself, I suppose it was inevitable we would eventually move in the same circles. My, but we were a young bunch then! I had yet to take my position with the company, and these three were still a few years away from their elections."

"It sounds as though you all achieved your dreams," Charlotte said. "If only my mother could see you now, I am certain she would be so proud. There is something special about childhood friendships, wouldn't you say? They become almost familial."

Charlotte smiled, and to a stranger, it might have seemed

innocent, but John noted the slight tightening of her eyes as she lifted her drink to her lips. She moved her gaze from one person to the next, smiling again as she set down her glass. If not for the fact that she'd barely touched her food, John might have thought she was as relaxed as she seemed.

John noted that Mrs. Anastacia Worthingstone had been silently observing Charlotte throughout the meal. His opinion was that she was the luckiest of the four wives in terms of maintaining her beauty as she had aged. Her dark hair accentuated a pretty face, but her ice-blue eyes were very much that.

She smiled at Charlotte as the second course was served. "And you, Miss Duvall. Am I to understand you are a medical doctor?"

"I am." Charlotte matched the woman's smile.

"Refreshing that single women have so many options from which to choose these days. Why, not even fifty years ago you'd have been relegated to governess service."

"Mmm," Charlotte agreed.

"Isn't it astonishing, Phillipa," Mrs. Worthingstone continued, "that Miss Duvall has not fallen far from her mother's tree? We often remarked in school that Kat made the most unconventional choices."

Mrs. Carter, decidedly more reserved and timid than her friends, laughed nervously but refrained from comment.

"But then, it should hardly have come as a surprise given her origins." Mrs. Worthingstone smiled, probably hoping to seem innocuous. "Those Hamptons were always unpredictable—sometimes shockingly so! Always dancing on the line of proper behavior. One never knows what to expect."

There was a beat of silence at the table, followed by a few strains of uncertain—or perhaps incredulous—laughter. Considering that three Hamptons currently dined with the woman and Sally Hampton was a prominent force in society, Anastacia Worthingstone was either incredibly dense or incredibly calculating.

"What an odd thing to actually say aloud," Eva said with a serene smile.

Charlotte's volley at Mrs. Worthingstone was more direct. She chuckled at Eva and said, "I was under the impression that only my mother's good friends were permitted to call her Kat."

There were a few sharp intakes of breath, and Mr. Carter laughed unapologetically. John tamped down a smile by putting food in his mouth, but even then was hard-pressed to hide his mirth.

Mrs. Worthingstone arched a brow at Charlotte but refrained from further comment.

"You should know, Miss Duvall," Mr. Carter said to Charlotte, "that your mother engendered a sense of envy in some of the female variety. Clearly even the ghost of her has the power to resurrect some of the old sentiment."

"I *do* beg your pardon, James Carter," Mrs. Finebough interjected with a broad smile that ventured nowhere near her eyes. "Present company especially were not among those who envied Katherine. She was our friend, first and foremost." She turned to Charlotte with a gentled expression. "She truly was lovely, Miss Duvall, and it was an honor to have known her."

"I am glad to hear it, Mrs. Finebough, thank you."

"Mrs. Carter," Eva said, "I hope you'll share the results of your most recent charity work with the new school near Whitechapel."

John suspected everyone within earshot was grateful to Eva for smoothly redirecting the conversation. For his part, though, he'd have loved to watch Charlotte go another round with the women. Mrs. Worthingstone's backhanded slights toward Katherine were insensitive, to say the least.

Conversation continued as the meal progressed, and John kept an eye on the four couples, observing the dynamics among them. He noticed Charlotte doing the same thing; she said little to anyone, barely ate anything, but was very much aware of everything around her.

John also took stock of the event as a whole. Mrs. Winston had assembled an eclectic mix of London's upper echelons, where business deals would be forged and alliances made. John noted a number of people whose secrets he knew because he had always listened when his father conducted business and because he knew the value of information to the right person.

He regretted he had no useful knowledge in his mental files about the people whose lives had entwined with Katherine's. He wanted to speak privately with Charlotte to compare notes on her initial impressions of the players involved, so he was relieved when dessert was served. In that time, the MPs' wives avoided speaking to Charlotte or referencing her mother again. Mrs. Carter asked polite questions about Charlotte's experiences in the United States, but otherwise all verbal communication with the young woman ceased.

John noted with interest, however, the number of times the MPs themselves stole glances at Charlotte. It happened frequently, often with an additional side glance at their wives. Clearly, not only had the gentlemen enjoyed a friendship with Katherine when they'd all been young, but just as clearly, the women the men would later pair with did not care for the competition they assumed she posed. Perhaps she had been a thorn in the side of one—or each—of the women present; John knew little of

Katherine's personality or character. He knew Charlotte, however, and his concerns lay with her.

Mrs. Winston rang a bell and announced that activities would commence. Dancing in the ballroom, followed by musical numbers in the conservatory and games in the drawing room. John escorted Charlotte from the room, her arm threaded through his, and he put his hand atop hers.

"Are you cold?" he asked.

She shook her head. "Just my hands. Case of the nerves, I hate to admit."

He held her back to allow the others to file into the ballroom, and to observe the people with whom they'd dined. "What do you think of your mother's friends?"

She laughed quietly. "A pit of vipers."

"I am certain the men liked your mother well enough."

Charlotte glanced at him. "Until their wives convinced them she was a threat."

Exactly what John had been thinking. "What is your opinion of the Carters?"

"Of the four couples, they seem the least likely to have caused harm to my mother." She lifted a shoulder, watching the couple in question mingle with the crowd. "Could simply be donning sheep's clothing, however."

"Well, they are in the textile business, after all."

Her reaction was worth his ridiculous quip. She gave him a sidelong look and her lips tilted in a wry smile. "I had hoped to escape after dinner, but if you ask me to dance, I might be convinced to stay longer."

"Then consider yourself invited. Shall we?" He led her to the ballroom and then paused just outside the door. "I was unaware until I arrived that these extra guests would be in attendance. I'd have liked to give you fair warning, but perhaps we've learned some useful things tonight."

She nodded. "It is probably better that I wasn't aware. I didn't have time to fret or practice any speeches ahead of time. This was a much more honest interaction." She smiled, and he saw in the tightening of her eyes that she was shoring herself up for what might come. "I've learned some things about my mother, and considering the nature of those women in there, I believe Kat and I would have gotten along together just fine."

"I believe you're correct. Come along, my darling. We must put you on display."

CHAPTER 19

Charlotte smiled at John as he swept her into his arms, and they began dancing to the string quartet seated at the other end of the large ballroom. He'd called her "my darling," and while it was a term of endearment he'd used with her before, she wistfully wondered how it would be if she truly was his darling, and he hers. His hand splayed on her back felt proprietary, confident. There was no hesitancy in his touch, nothing tentative in his possession of her. Had it been anyone else, the very thought would have set her teeth on edge.

He twirled her around the floor, managing to speak to her with an intimate smile even while occasionally glancing at others in the room. She knew he was watching the Friends, but she was hard-pressed to think about them as he led her seamlessly around the other couples.

Someday, John Ellis would marry, and his wife would find herself well cared for in every facet of life. He would converse with her about matters of importance, would seek out her opinion. He would value their time together, would see to her comfort because it was in his nature. It was what he did. He would look at her across the length of a dining room table and smile in a way that held the promise of cherished time spent together alone.

Her breath caught, and she told herself sternly to manage her thoughts, lest they manifest in her expression. John understood nuance, and he read people like books. One look at her face as she imagined how wonderful it would be to be loved by him and he'd know exactly what she was thinking.

She blinked and quietly exhaled, looking over his shoulder, avoiding the gaze that would see too much if she wasn't careful. She couldn't even be bothered to care about the horrible people they'd dined with just a short time ago. She wanted them to go away, wanted to forget about her mother's trunk and her father's sadness, wanted to forget everything but John.

"Is something the matter?" he asked quietly, leaning his head closer to hers. His lips were full, his hazel eyes observant, and he warmed her chilled nerves by several degrees.

She closed her eyes briefly and exhaled again, managing a smile and shaking her head. "Just tired."

"Shall we find somewhere for you to rest?"

Charlotte wondered if Mrs. Winston's library was vacant. "I do not think that is a very wise idea."

He tilted his head as though in question.

She laughed, mostly at herself. "I am in an odd mood, John. Forgive me."

"I would know more about this mood, if you're willing to share." His eyes met hers, and he seemed to lose all interest in anybody else in the room.

"I am envisioning scenarios I have no business conjuring."

His attention narrowed, his gaze on her face sharpening, and she could see as realization crystalized in his mind. "Now, you *must* share."

"Absolutely not."

He chuckled and pulled her closer. His arm more firmly encircled her body, and his long fingers extended fully around her waist. He pulled her hand in, and for a moment she wondered if he would kiss her fingers as they skimmed along the shadows at the edge of the room.

"John," she whispered unevenly.

"Yes?" His eyes caught and held hers.

"You . . . we . . ."

The corner of his mouth turned up. "Yes?" He spun her out in a gentle pirouette and then wrapped her close again.

"Your mother will be scandalized to hear that you've been dancing most intimately with 'that Hampton woman.'"

"I do not want to think about my mother right now."

She smiled even as her chest rose on a quickened breath. "What do you want to think about?"

"I'm wondering what *you* have been thinking of the last several minutes since we entered this room."

"I've a feeling you know what I've been thinking."

"I would rather hear it from your lips than rely on my own conjecture."

"Now *you* must share your conjecture. Perhaps you're miles away from the truth."

He raised a single brow, a slow smile spreading. "Oh, Dr. Duvall, I believe I am quite close to the truth."

She laughed. "Well, then, there is nothing more to discuss."

"Did you miss me, Charlotte, when you were away?"

Her smile faltered, not because she was sad, but with the realization at how much the distance had affected her. "So very much," she whispered.

"Good." His voice lowered. "Because I ached with it."

She looked at him, not trusting herself to speak. There were suddenly too many people in the room, the glittering light was too bright, and there was not enough space for them to speak freely instead of in riddles.

He must have been of a mind because he twirled her quietly through an exit at the end of the long ballroom into a sitting room whose muted light shone from turned down sconces and a banked fire in the hearth.

"We'll be missed," he whispered, "and no doubt the entire room just witnessed my very obvious seduction of the most beautiful woman in all of London."

"Is that what it was?"

"If clarification is necessary, then I wasn't doing a good job of it."

She laughed breathlessly as he walked her backward from the door to the darkest corner of the room. "Oh, you did a masterful job of it, and I daresay your ego does not need verification from me."

His smile held a thousand secrets, and she wanted to learn each one.

She put her hand on his chest, not to push away but hoping to pull him closer. She trailed her fingertips along the edge of his cravat.

"Little do you know, Miss Duvall, you could crush my ego thoroughly with a careless phrase."

She shook her head with a low chuckle. "You are the strongest person I know, John. I appreciate the sentiment, but it is a bit of a stretch."

"You're the only one . . ." His smile faded, and the look in his eyes caused her breath to catch. "The only one who ever . . . I adore you, Charlotte Elizabeth Duvall." He clasped her fingers in his and pressed them to his lips.

She closed her eyes and leaned her forehead against their

clasped hands. Feelings she'd not known existed swirled through her, threatening to carry her off into the clouds. "John," she whispered. "I . . ." But she couldn't think, couldn't even form words that made sense.

His fingertips trailed along her cheek, and she reveled in the sensation, her eyes still closed. He threaded his fingers around the back of her neck, cradling her head, and with his thumb along her jaw, turned her face just enough to feel the press of his lips against the corner of her mouth. As though testing, questioning, asking permission.

Yes . . .

She wasn't certain if she uttered the word aloud, but it seemed to hang in the air between them. She turned her head, and when their lips met, her knees threatened to give way.

He wrapped his arm around her, holding her securely against him. His caress was exactly as she suspected it would be, given the force of his personality. He was solid, assured, and as he held her head in his hand, fingers splayed in her hair, his lips found hers again and again.

She sighed, her breathing ragged against his, and she slid her arm around his shoulders as his lips found the sensitive spot just behind her ear. His breath was warm on her neck, and she found herself oddly pleased that she wasn't the only one winded.

"We must go back," he whispered as he kissed the tip of her ear. "I don't want to. I'd thought to further investigate, to see if one of those blasted members of Parliament would ask you to dance, but—" He lifted his head to look at her face. "I cannot stand the way they watch you."

Charlotte licked her lips, trying to steady her breath. "We must draw them out, see if someone tips a hand. Otherwise, we'll learn nothing."

He nuzzled her ear with the tip of his nose, brushing his mouth against her neck with the barest of kisses.

She closed her eyes, pushing her fingers through the soft hair just touching his collar. "You're distracting me."

She felt his smile against her skin. "Good." He lifted his head and brushed his fingertips across her forehead, tucking aside a tousled curl. A grim sense of wonder filled his expression as he said, "I pride my intuition as unmatched. How did I not see this?"

"I did not see it either, and frankly, am still a bit stunned. I came back from America, and you . . . you . . . I cannot even find words." Her brows pulled together, and she looked at him, perplexed. "What am I going to do?"

He inhaled and exhaled, finally loosening his hold. His hands moved to caress her upper arms, fingers flexing as though he couldn't decide whether to release her or pull her back in. Her hands rested on his chest, and she longed to reach underneath his coat, to wrap her arms around him and press her cheek to his heart.

"You two should sneak out that way and make an early evening of it," a voice murmured from the doorway.

Charlotte dropped her hands and gasped, and John's head whipped to the door.

Nathan shook his head, one corner of his mouth lifted in a bemused smile. "If you make an entrance now, looking like that . . . Well, you'd better have plans to announce an engagement."

"We'll take that door," John murmured, pointing to a far exit, "and you'll make our excuses?"

"Yes," Charlotte agreed, glad the shadows of the room hid the flames in her cheeks. She put a hand to her forehead, flushed enough to wonder if she had a temperature. "Will you say I was feeling unwell?"

Nathan looked at John. "You're lucky it was me who wandered back here first." He paused. "Well, it was Eva who sent me. She was so busy watching the two of you dance she nearly tripped me twice."

Charlotte laughed unsteadily. "Please tell Eva I will see her tomorrow—I'm coming by your home to check Sammy's arm."

Nathan's eyes softened. "Thank you, Charlotte. We'll look forward to your visit." He glanced back to the ballroom and then at John, jerking his head toward the other door. "Go."

John took Charlotte's hand, and they hurried across the room, dodging a chaise lounge and nearly crashing into a large potted plant. Once into the darkened corridor, the sounds from the ballroom grew louder, and John shook his head. "Too many people," he murmured.

He turned and, with hands at her waist, guided her quickly around the corner where he took her hand again and rushed her through a series of corridors until they arrived at a servants' entrance at the back of the house.

He opened the door against a gust of wind and looked belatedly at Charlotte's bare arms. "Blast," he muttered and removed his coat, draping it around her shoulders before she could protest.

They heard voices coming down the hall, and he pulled her outside, closing the door with a soft click. They ran through the shadows of the kitchen garden, which was fallow and tidied for the winter months, and found their way to the mews where groomsmen gathered with the horses and carriages.

"Fitzhume," John told an attendant, who left to locate John's driver.

"Will you wait at the front entrance?" another attendant asked.

"We'll wait here."

The attendant studiously avoided gawking at Charlotte, though she could imagine the picture she presented: a woman whose curls were decidedly looser than they had been and standing behind the main house in a gentleman's jacket. She was grateful for his discretion, feeling a bit like Alice and the rabbit hole.

What on earth had just happened? She'd gone from mooning over her friend in the ballroom to being kissed senseless by him in the shadows. If she were to awaken in the morning and find it had all been a dream, she might have made more sense of it.

Fitzhume eventually appeared with the carriage, and John ushered Charlotte inside, giving him Hampton House's address. He settled next to her, and as the carriage began to move, he looked at her as though assessing her reaction. To everything.

She slid closer to him and leaned in, and she noted a flicker of relief in his eyes. He wrapped his arm around her, and she rested her head against his shoulder, suddenly very, very tired.

"I seem to be destined to fall asleep in your carriage," she murmured. "Apologies."

"I only wish the ride were longer." He settled back against the cushioned bench and stretched his legs across the expanse to the other seat. He pulled her against his lounging form, wrapping both arms around her and resting his head on hers. "We're going to have to do something about this, you know."

She yawned. "What did you have in mind?"

"I'll think of something." She heard the smile in his voice. He paused and the carriage turned a corner and merged into traffic. "This was inevitable, of course."

She smiled against his shoulder. "Why is that?"

"We're the last two of the group. Stands to reason, doesn't it?"

"It does." Yet she couldn't stop the worry that crept in like an unwelcome guest. "To presuppose a happy ending is probably unwise, however. You have a position in society that demands certain constraints be followed. I have a career that doesn't allow for . . . relationships." She stopped just short of the word "marriage." He'd not said it, not even implied it, and she would not make assumptions.

He lifted his head and turned her face to his. "Charlotte Duvall, do you not know me at all?"

"Of course I do. Were I ignorant of your responsibilities, I could remain in a state of bliss for at least a day or two. As it stands, I feel as though we're racing to get me home before the clock strikes twelve and I turn into a pumpkin."

He smiled. "Cinderella does not turn into a pumpkin."

"I'm certain your family would be happier if I were. I saw your brother and his wife tonight. They did not smile at me."

His expression tightened. "My family can hang."

She sighed and settled again into his shoulder. "Life is never so simple, and you know it. Please don't insult me by suggesting this situation is . . . simple."

"But I love you."

The admission drifted quietly in the air like a feather and eventually settled onto Charlotte's heart. Her eyes burned, and she shut them tightly. "Please don't say that," she whispered.

"It's true. It's always been true. It was you before I even knew you existed." His voice was low and quiet, and his thumb traced a gentle pattern on her shoulder. "We will work this out, Charlotte. I'll never come between you and your career, but I am hopeful we can find an acceptable solution."

If ever there was a man who could will something into being,

Charlotte knew it was John Ellis. The sense of foreboding that had settled on her didn't lift, though, and remained with her for the rest of the ride home.

When she opened her bedroom door—after another prolonged kiss with John just outside it—she caught her breath and nearly cried out. Her armoire had been turned inside out, the bedding mussed, and the vanity lay tipped on its side, the mirror shattered.

John swore under his breath. She took a step inside, but John put his arm around her waist and pulled her back. "Don't touch anything yet." She felt the effects of his anger through the tremor in his arm. He pulled her back from the door and checked his pocket watch.

"What time did you and Dirk leave for the dinner?" he asked tersely.

She couldn't think. She closed her eyes and reviewed the day. "Six thirty, perhaps. Maybe seven o'clock. Dirk will remember. Where is he?"

"I told him if I was able to make it to the dinner, he was free to go. He mentioned that one of his employees needed assistance tonight at the docks."

An ugly suspicion rose in her mind. "You do trust him?"

His mouth tightened with determination. "With my life, which he's saved, more than once." He paused. "Has he done something to make you suspect—"

She shook her head. "No. I suppose I'm suspecting everyone now of nefarious intentions."

His jaw clenched. "It's a fair question—anyone could be

involved. If I were a betting man, though, I'd wager everything on his trustworthiness. We must speak immediately with Mrs. Burnette to see who has come and gone since supper." He looked at her for a moment. "Please do not go in your room yet—wait until I return. I must send word to the Winstons' to see if Michael can break away from the party. I want another pair of eyes."

She nodded and glanced back at her disorganized room. Her eye snagged on something sitting on her pillows—they looked like photographs. "John?" She pointed at the items. "Those aren't mine."

He rubbed his hand over his jaw, thinking. Then he took a handkerchief from his pocket and frowned, saying, "This will have to do. I'll get them—there may be fingermark evidence."

Charlotte didn't argue, but fingermark evidence was such a new concept in police work that she didn't know if the extra effort was worth the trouble. She waited by the door, arms held tightly across her middle, as he retrieved the items and returned. The look on his face sent her heart thudding in alarm.

"What? What is it?"

John held two photographs, both of which were a product of Eva's work. One was a picture of Sammy and Henry, and the other was of Amelie's two girls, Cassandra and Sophia. The images were recent—perhaps within a few months. The children had posed for Eva with cherubic expressions, and Charlotte's chest tightened as she stared at them.

"It's a reminder of what my attacker told me in the alley. He threatened my family." She looked up at John, stricken. "What am I going to do? I can't . . . I can't have this—"

He shook his head and then crouched down to look at the doorframe. The wood bore slight gauge marks where the lock had been forced.

"He didn't have a key," she said. She leaned against the wall for support, trying to take deep, even breaths. Someone had been in her room, destroyed her things, left threats. Her throat was thick, and she felt she might be ill.

John quickly went to his room, then returned, placing the photographs into a large envelope. "You hid the contents of your mother's trunk, correct?"

She nodded and whirled back to the doorway. The trunk had been tipped over on the far side of the room and was partially hidden behind her bed. "After the attack, I put them in a decorative tea tin on the top shelf in the pantry."

He nodded and leaned down to place a quick, hard kiss on her lips. "Come downstairs with me. We'll talk to Mrs. Burnette and rally the troops."

She held John's hand as they walked down the stairs to the ground floor. When the front door opened and Dirk stepped through, Charlotte unconsciously squeezed John's fingers. He glanced at her and placed his hand over hers.

Dirk shook off his outercoat and looked up, going still when he saw their faces. "What's happened?" he demanded without preamble.

Mrs. Burnette rounded the corner, buttoning her housecoat. "What is it?" she echoed.

"We'll be needing additional security for the house—and for Charlotte's family," John said.

Dirk looked at Charlotte, his expression tightening. "What's happened?" he repeated flatly.

"He's paid me another visit." Charlotte shook her head. "Heaven help him, because I will kill him if he harms my family."

CHAPTER 20

John installed two constables in the room adjoining Dirk's at Hampton House and set up a rotation of guards outside, day and night. The sight of them had a ring of familiarity to it; they'd been obliged to have Hampton House guarded years ago when Amelie had first met Michael.

Michael and Nathan made similar arrangements in their own homes, and none of the children were allowed outside without their mothers or nannies—and a constable. After Charlotte's attack, John had filed a formal report, which he now added to the growing case file about Katherine Duvall's death. The two were inextricably linked, and his superiors saw the wisdom in officially reopening the investigation. They were working against time, however; even rotating continually, he couldn't keep the constabulary working as security indefinitely.

Charlotte seemed comfortable with Dirk continuing as her personal guard, and there was still nobody else he'd have trusted with her life, and she seemed to have recognized Dirk's sincere regret about the break-in.

John interviewed Mrs. Burnette to see who might have been granted access to Hampton House that night. She confirmed a delivery had been made after Charlotte had left. An American, she said, with a parcel of eggs that should have been delivered earlier that morning. She'd directed him to the rear entrance, where the cook had accepted the package. How he'd slipped in afterward, John could only guess. At least they had a description of the assailant: light complexion, brown hair, green eyes, thin moustache, nearly six feet tall, and built "like a pugilist," Mrs. Burnette said.

Constable Clancy Silverton had been able to lift prints from the photographs the vandal had left in Charlotte's room. Silverton had been training on the "Bertillon" method of gathering fingerprints as identification, and although the science itself was still in its infancy, John believed wholeheartedly in its efficacy. The Chinese had used fingermarks as identifiers centuries earlier, and John was determined to use the tool.

The following week, John entered the club after work and accepted a fresh edition of *The London Times* from an attendant. He headed up the stairs and into one of the lounges where he knew some of the gentlemen enjoyed an aperitif before supper. He made himself comfortable in a chair and opened the paper, declining the offer of a cigar from the room attendant but accepting a glass of port.

Charlotte had left Town that morning, traveling with Sally and Dirk to the country to sort the last of her father's affairs at the family home. Her intention was to put both Sally and Dirk to work with her, searching high and low for the mysterious packet Mr. Duvall had collected. This week marked the first time she'd been able to get away. She'd been at the hospital day and night, dealing with an influenza outbreak that was spreading through the East End.

John had been busy hosting socials and arranging security detail for visiting dignitaries from Turkey.

He thought of her constantly.

He was concerned with her health and well-being, as her job exposed her to contagious illnesses, but more than that, he missed her. He missed the feel of her lips against his, her hands threaded through his hair. He sent messages to her at least twice a day and her short, to the point, humorous responses made him smile. She was the bright spot in a mountain of chaos.

Today, he hoped to gather more news about Katherine Duvall's associates—the ones Charlotte and her cousins had dubbed "The Friends"—and he knew that Mr. James Carter was a regular club member, often attending twice a week. John planned to entice the man with a drink and conversation. He didn't have long to wait before Carter entered and greeted a few acquaintances. He looked around the room, and his face broke into a smile when he saw John.

John returned the smile, brightening his expression as though surprised at seeing Carter. He indicated an empty chair, and when Carter approached, John signaled for the room attendant to bring over another drink.

"Director Ellis!" Carter said. "Don't know we've ever crossed paths here before."

John rose, and they shook hands before sitting together in the comfortable chairs. John folded the newspaper as though he'd finished reading. "Truthfully, I don't always take the time to enjoy supper at the clubs. I've made a vow to do so with more frequency. Life is short, and all that." He smiled and lifted his glass.

"Truer words were never spoken," Carter agreed and took an appreciative sip of his port. "I imagine you've memberships not only in this club but also that other one down the street."

John chuckled. "It's true. Members of both parties like to solicit my good favor. Of course, I must remain impartial."

"Of course." Carter nodded but smiled.

"I enjoyed conversing with you and Mrs. Carter last week at the Winstons' dinner."

"As did we! I must say, Miss Duvall's presence was a pleasant surprise. Rather bittersweet, I suppose, for those of us who enjoyed friendship with her mother."

Excellent. Carter had opened with the very thing John wanted to discuss.

"I've seen a photograph, and the resemblance is uncanny."

"Uncanny? Man, the girl is her mother incarnate. I tell you, there is not a bit of difference between the two." He shook his head. "It was the saddest thing, her untimely end. So very vibrant, and taken too soon."

John nodded in sympathy. "Were you there that evening? I understand her death was rather traumatic for her friends."

"Oh, yes. My wife and I were a month shy of our wedding, and the gathering that evening was partially in celebration of the event. We were in the salon, having a lovely time, and not thirty minutes into the trip down the river, we heard a commotion outside. By the time I reached the deck above the salon, it was crammed full with members of our party and the boat's crew. It was some time before I realized someone had gone over the side." He paused, frowning. "Never dawned on me it was one of us. Figured it must have been a crewman or server."

John set his glass down on the small round table at his elbow and creased his brow, hoping to extract information without seeming to be conducting an investigation. "What happened next?"

"The captain stalled the boat, and two people went into the water after her." Carter looked into the distance, thinking. "Her husband, of course, and Paddleton, if I'm not mistaken. Did surprise me, come to think of it. Paddleton was always the meekest among us. Worthingstone was a much stronger swimmer—stronger all the way around—but I assume Paddleton must have been on the scene first. They floated her to the side where she was pulled up onto the lower deck."

John had assumed that James Carter was the least likely of the group to have done harm to Katherine. He'd not been a childhood friend so any letters that had been sent to her at school would not have been from him. Also, the way he'd behaved at dinner—speaking of Katherine fondly and candidly—cast Carter in the light of one who had nothing to hide.

Of course, the man *had* propositioned Nathan Winston's mother in his younger years, but perhaps that spoke more of a young man with bad judgment. When taken as a whole—the open dialogue, the friendly demeanor—John was comfortable shifting at least one of the Jameses onto the "not a likely murder suspect" list.

"Miss Duvall was so young when her mother passed," John said, "that her memories are few. I wish she could have seen Katherine in her younger years when she was fond of the three young James's."

Carter smiled. "I wasn't there either, of course, but from what I understand, Katherine was quite a ringleader. Everyone wanted to be where she was, do what she did. I imagine she may have given her mother and governesses fits, given that she wasn't demure and one for feminine pursuits." He chuckled and added, "Finebough said once that if girls had been allowed to play cricket, she would have been the best in town. I remember that anecdote because the ladies in the group were quite disdainful of the idea."

Carter pointed at John, eyebrows raised, and added, "This is what I referred to at supper the other evening! The others may have shown disdain for Katherine, but especially with the sisters—Anastacia and Gwendolyn—the envy was clear." He shook his head. "Unwarranted, really. Kat was a kind woman. She was effusive, enthusiastic, always the center of attention, but she also did things in secret, acts of kindness that I'm sure few people saw. My wife, for example—she was quite in love with me before I realized it, and being shy, she was not someone who commanded attention. Kat went shopping with Phillipa, helped her choose flattering things that women have a way with and helped her think of discussion items that I may find interesting."

He smiled fondly. "Phillipa told me the story years later and said she may have never pulled together the nerve to speak with me had it not been for Kat's encouragement." His smile faltered then faded as he said, "Katherine's death was untimely and cruel. I cannot imagine God's reasoning in calling her home so young."

John let the comment sit for a moment before saying, "An odd accident, to be sure."

Carter looked at him sharply. "Why would you say so?"

John lifted a shoulder and picked up his drink, taking a sip. "Only that from what I understand reading the police report, Katherine was tipsy and fell overboard, hitting her head in the process. What confuses me is that her sister claims she did not drink alcohol. Odd that she would have chosen to imbibe, especially on a moving boat, when she was susceptible to illness as a result." John didn't add that the autopsy documents showed no evidence of alcohol in Katherine's system.

Carter frowned at the amber liquid in his glass. "I never saw her inebriated. Perhaps she sought to dull the senses that night," he said quietly. "There was a sadness about her that even I noted, and Phillipa tells me I notice very little beyond my own nose."

John forced himself to remain relaxed in his seat rather than leaning forward and pressing for details. Instead, he said softly, "Strange for a woman with so much good in her life to suffer from sadness."

Carter spun his glass around with his fingertips. "Sometimes life can be disappointing, I suppose. We do not always find gold at the end of the rainbow."

John nodded thoughtfully. "Did Katherine favor one of the James's over the others?"

Carter's eyes flicked to John's. "Surely you do not wish to sully her reputation. For her daughter's sake, I would think you might be more circumspect."

John held up a hand. "Katherine's reputation is the last thing I seek to harm. I wish to understand her life so that I might help her daughter also understand it."

"And what is her daughter to you, Director Ellis? She doesn't have a father here anymore to look after her interests." All traces of good humor had fled Carter's face. "As Katherine's friend, perhaps I ought to take the young doctor's brothers to task for not keeping her in better care."

John almost laughed. "Miss Duvall's brothers are to her as oil is to water. As her friend, I appreciate your concern for her welfare." He smiled. "I suspect her mother is pleased that you speak on her behalf in the interest of protecting her child." He paused, weighing his words, then said sincerely, "My intentions toward her are the most honorable. If anything, I wish to protect her from those whose old jealousies might resurrect, now that she is in Town and looking so very much like her mother."

Carter eyed John thoughtfully. "I do not know precisely what sort of information you seek, but I do know this: Worthingstone was besotted with Katherine. Her softness, her affections, however, leaned more toward Finebough." He might have said more, but he glanced at someone beyond John's shoulder and lifted a hand. "Ah, here is my supper companion."

Lord Tipton, a man advanced in years but quick of wit,

approached them with a cane. "Carter, let us talk business!" His voice boomed through the room.

John and Carter both stood, and Tipton clapped his hand hard on John's shoulder. "Ellis! I do hope that father of yours will come to his senses someday. I cannot depend on that man to vote the right way even once!"

John chuckled. "My lord, I would never presume to influence my father one way or another. You seem in excellent health if I may say so."

Tipton leaned closer as if taking him into his confidence but didn't lower his voice. "Whiskey at breakfast in place of tea." He thumped his cane for emphasis. "'Tis the secret to longevity."

John smiled. "Noted, sir."

"Come along, Carter, we must talk about my proposition. And bring your friend if you like."

Carter shook John's hand. "Would you like to join us for supper?"

John had finished at the office, had no pressing engagements for the evening, and the only person whose company he wished for was Charlotte, and she was away.

With no better plans, he nodded and followed Carter and Tipton to the dining room. Oddly grateful for the lively company and conversation, he didn't even mind being harangued about his father's voting practices. He'd never admit it aloud, but he agreed with the old man.

In fact, he wondered how long it would be before Edgar and Hortense informed his parents about his and Charlotte's dance and then disappearance from Mrs. Winston's home. It had been a week—surely the summons was not far off.

With a weary internal sigh, he placed his napkin on his lap and smiled at his dinner companions and tucked into his meal.

CHAPTER 21

Charlotte stood in her father's parlor, looking at the organized stacks of paperwork and feeling a bittersweet sense of accomplishment. She'd sorted through mountains of receipts, old newspaper articles, scraps of lists and letters, and correspondence with clients in his role as their solicitor. The sight of his familiar script had caused a lump to form in her throat, which hadn't abated. At least the herculean task had been completed; she was grateful for that. But even after spending the bulk of the morning in his study, looking in every possible box and closet for something her father might have considered "evidence" of her mother's murder, she had found nothing important. She was beginning to wonder if he'd not been in his right mind, after all.

She joined Sally and Dirk in the library, where Dirk was examining the books on her father's shelves. "What did your father say in his letter to you? The one you received in New York?"

"The one that turned my whole world on its head?"

He smiled, and although she wouldn't call it a "grin," it was the biggest she'd seen so far. "That would be the one, lass."

"What are you thinking of, specifically?"

"Something about reading to you in the library."

She smiled. "There was a large book of fairy tales that I read so much it nearly came apart at the seams."

He nodded and turned back to the shelves. Sally was sorting through a stack of papers she'd found beneath a side table.

Her eldest brother, Thomas, and his family were to take possession of the home and property, with monies and other assets having been divided evenly among the rest of the siblings. The money didn't mean Charlotte was suddenly independently wealthy, but it was enough to provide security, peace of mind.

Joan, her sister-in-law, had briskly taken hold of the house and everything in it, and anything that would logically go to Charlotte was given with reluctant, tight fists. Holding a small hatbox, Joan entered the library. She surveyed the progress they'd made and nodded, once.

"This is a collection of the letters you sent to Father from America," Joan said and held out the box to Charlotte. "I thought you might like to have them returned. Thomas said we should simply toss them out, but men don't always appreciate sentiment, do they?"

The comment was the most pleasant Joan had ever offered, and Charlotte did her best to keep her mouth from falling open. She took the box with a smile, still feeling a bit raw from sorting through dozens of papers bearing her father's script.

"Thank you, Joan."

"There is a letter on top from your father to you. I believe he wrote it after you were already on your way home."

Charlotte's heart thudded as she opened the box and removed the envelope on top. "Oh, goodness," she said, noting her name written in a shaky version of her father's usual strong handwriting. "I'll read it later this evening." She turned it over, noting a clearly broken seal. She looked at Joan, puzzled. "Did you open the letter?"

Joan looked uncomfortable. She didn't meet Charlotte's eyes

but examined the hatbox. Finally, lips pursed, she said, "He wasn't fully in his right mind, you see." She looked up at Charlotte. "But, no, you wouldn't have seen because you weren't here."

Charlotte stared at the woman, her irritation rising. "You opened a letter my father had written to me?"

Joan folded her arms, lifting her chin a notch. "I wasn't certain what was inside."

Charlotte's mouth slackened. "It was not your business what was inside!"

"It most certainly was!" She glanced at Sally and Dirk, who were studiously avoiding the conversation. Joan continued, lowering her voice as though she could keep them from overhearing. "We were here, looking after him while you were off chasing ridiculous notions instead of caring for him, and for all we knew he could have put . . . put money in there! Or a deed, or something that needed to be put in the bank or the safe!" Color rose high in the woman's face, and she waved a hand in irritation. "I'll thank you not to take a superior attitude with me!"

Charlotte saw spots in front of her eyes, and the box trembled in her hands. She set it down but clutched the letter tightly. "Joan, you had no right!" Her eyes burned, and tears threatened to fall as her temper climbed. "You had no right to read a letter Papa wrote to *me*."

"Oh! *You* have no right to return like the prodigal son, believing you are owed the world!"

Charlotte's voice rose with her outrage. "I don't want the world! I want a letter from my father, intended for my eyes, to *not* have been opened by anyone else!"

Footsteps sounded in the hall, but Charlotte barely registered Thomas's entrance.

"You have never liked me, Joan, although for the life of me I cannot determine what I have done to cause it!"

"You were born! Tell her, Thomas! Tell her how your father's whole devotion shifted from you and your brothers—*his sons*—to his new wife and then their darling two children they had together. A whole new family, with no time or attention left for the ones who came first!"

Charlotte felt dizzy. Her hands were cold. Her brothers had barely tolerated her, had never seemed to care for her, and she had assumed that was the way of most siblings. She licked her dry lips as she looked at Thomas.

"Is this true, Thomas? Is this why you've had no use for me these long years? Robert was a boy like the rest of you, so I suppose you tolerated him well enough, but you never hid the fact that you had no use for a sister." She swallowed as tears slipped free. "Did you hate me because I look so much like her?"

Thomas shook his head impatiently. "This is nonsense. Joan, go to the gardens and see what needs to be done to winterize."

Joan glared at Charlotte and then her husband and spun on her heel. Thomas moved to follow her from the room.

"Tell me!" Charlotte cried out. "You ought to at least be man enough to tell me the truth!"

Thomas froze and turned around. His face was as calm and implacable as ever. At his age, he resembled their father, and for a moment her heart ached.

"Charlotte, we've already discussed this." He looked uncomfortably at the other two in the room but continued. "I was a teenaged boy when Father married your mother. Everything changed, that much is true. What was worse, though, was the fighting that came after you were born." His jaw clenched. "They spoke harsh words to each other behind closed doors, hurled accusations—unthinkable accusations—at each other."

Charlotte's breath caught in her throat.

Thomas's face leeched of all color as he continued. "He had been happy, before, and then he was spent." His shoulders slumped. "He had nothing left after her death. He was a different person. My father died with Katherine, and she was the cause."

"How *dare* you?" Charlotte whispered.

"He was nothing but a shell all these years since. He moved through the motions of life like a ghost." Thomas looked tired. "Of course it was her fault. Father knew it; we all knew it."

Sally spoke into the silence that followed. "My sister was a mother to you from the first day, Thomas." She spoke quietly, firmly. "She stepped into a home of five motherless boys and loved each of you as her own. She was young herself, yet she rose to the occasion. Perhaps you've forgotten."

Thomas had the grace to look chagrined as he regarded Sally. "She was good to us. But she married my father because the man she loved married another. I do not know his identity, but I know he was in their social circle. That was the truth of it. I heard them fighting about it with my own ears." He swallowed. "What sort of husband can be expected to live with such a thing, knowing his wife's heart belongs to another?"

Charlotte sank onto a sofa, still clutching the letter from her father. Katherine's journal had been true—and her father had known? She closed her eyes.

"Be that as it may," Sally said quietly, "it does not change the love she felt for you. All of you, her children. And you're wrong, Thomas, if you believe she did not love your father. She did. She loved him very much."

Thomas's smile was bitter. "He was as much her father as he

was ours. She may have loved him, but it was not the sort of affection he had every right to expect from a wife."

"I remember them together," Charlotte protested. "I remember them laughing, I remember picnics . . . I—" The words caught in her throat. She wiped her eyes, frustrated. "Thomas, I *remember*!"

"You remember moments, Charlotte," he said, sounding weary. "Toward the end, it was stilted. Awkward. And then it was over. He hadn't wanted to go to London, but it was in celebration of James Carter's engagement. Katherine took you and Robert, and he followed later." He cleared his throat and straightened. "Whatever occurred that night, I do not blame Father."

Her heart pounded. "What are you saying? What *did* happen that night, Thomas?"

"I do not know. I do not want to know. I never asked that he elaborate or explain. I only know he pulled her from the water, but she was gone. If you bear any love for his memory, perhaps you'll leave the past where it belongs and allow him to rest in peace." He paused, then nodded toward the letter in Charlotte's hand. "I apologize for my wife's interference in your correspondence. Please feel free to remain here at the house if you wish—your bedchamber is yours for two more months."

He left the room, and the silence was deafening.

Sally moved some papers aside and sat down near Charlotte with a sigh. "They're going to turn your room into a solarium," she said drily.

Charlotte looked at her aunt and in spite of herself, laughed. She sniffled and said, "How, pray tell, are they going to accomplish that? Remove a portion of the third floor and put in glass?"

Sally chuckled and rolled her eyes. "Joan claims that since

your room faces south, it consistently receives the best light and that your windows are the largest."

Charlotte sat back and shook her head. "My windows are no larger than any of the other bedchambers." She retrieved a handkerchief from her pocket. She dabbed her eyes and nose, feeling very much like the little girl who had sat in that very room for hours on end, reading stories, drawing pictures, sometimes hiding from her brothers who seemed to find entertainment in teasing her.

I suppose I should thank them for it. It made me resilient.

She opened the letter, but to her disappointment, it was little more than an apology for throwing her into the middle of his "mess." He said nothing else that explained the mystery he'd given to her. She told Sally and Dirk, knowing they'd be curious.

Silence stretched, the only sounds the ticking clock and the crackling fire.

Eventually, Sally clapped her hands once. "Charlotte, I know you have a few days' leave from the hospital, and I know Eva is taking Sammy, Henry, and a constable to visit her mother this weekend. It's been ever so long since I visited my sister. We'll finish our business here and join them for a lovely Hampton ladies' reunion. Mr. Dirk?"

Dirk cleared his throat. "That does sound lovely."

Charlotte looked at Sally in surprise. "Visit Aunt Esther?"

"I propose we enjoy some very pleasant company and reminisce about time spent at the Hampton country estate when your mother was young and her friends were frequent visitors. Esther was closer in age to Katherine; she may have perspective that I lack."

Charlotte nodded, feeling raw.

"Unless you'd rather we not speak of those times and entertain ourselves instead with other conversation." Sally paused.

"There is certainly no shame in postponing your quest in order to gain some distance from it. Well," she paused, acknowledging the large Scotsman in the room, "perhaps time is not on your side. Your irritating assailant seems determined to continue the ruckus."

"I still want to know the truth, now more than ever. Perhaps then I can let it rest." She looked at Sally, her closest link to her mother. "Papa loved me, was good to me as I grew older. He was distant, but I—" Her voice broke. "I do not think he resented me. Even looking like her, I think he still loved me."

"Dearest girl, of course he did. *Of course*, he did. I visited you in those years, and I saw it with my own eyes." She paused and smiled gently. "You resemble Katherine, but you are not Katherine. Your father knew that. I think he felt guilty that he could not offer the same presence for you that a mother would."

And that, Charlotte thought, was the problem. "What was the source of that guilt?" she whispered and looked at Sally, stricken.

Sally exhaled, watching Charlotte. "Do you truly want answers? What if you learn things you wish you hadn't?"

"It will be better than wondering."

"Then we shall keep asking."

"I've found something," Dirk announced.

Charlotte looked over her shoulder at him. "What is it?"

He held up a large book, and she smiled. "The fairy tales!" She felt a lump in her throat as he approached. She moved a pile of books off the sofa so he could sit down next to her.

"I believe it contains more than just fairy tales." He handed the book to her, encouraging her to open the cover.

When she did, she saw a lovely inscription from her mother that she'd completely forgotten: "For my dearest princess. Love eternally, Mama." Tears gathered again, hot in her eyes, and she shook her head. "I do grow weary of so many emotions," she muttered.

Dirk handed her his handkerchief. "It is not only that, lass. Flip through the pages."

She did as he suggested, and her mouth dropped open. Sandwiched between the pages of the book were separate pieces of paper: newspaper articles—one detailing the accident and another of Katherine's funeral—notes her father had scrawled, invitations to events, a list of those questioned by police after the death, and eventually, a small, crumpled letter written in a feminine hand.

Curious, she lifted it.

> *Katherine, you would do well to leave James alone. Your continued advances toward him only engender false hopes. We've talked, and the ladies all agree it is time to restructure our social circle. I do hope you've integrity enough to gracefully remove yourself. The Carters' engagement celebration is meant to include you and David, but perhaps it would be easier for all involved if you tastefully make your apologies and remain in the country.*
>
> *—Anastacia Worthingstone*

Cold spread through Charlotte's limbs. She read the letter aloud to Sally and Dirk, the latter of whom whistled low when she finished.

"Perhaps not damning evidence," Dirk said, "but certainly doesn't cast the lady in a good light."

"Which lady?" Charlotte asked, bitter. "My mother and her 'advances' or the supercilious Mrs. Worthingstone?"

"I did not mean your mother," he said quietly.

"Charlotte," Sally said firmly. "Kat did not ever have to seek for attention or approval. If not her morals, her pride alone would have prevented her from pursuing a married man." She shook her head. "Do not ever doubt her integrity. Kat had loads of it with plenty to spare."

Charlotte nodded. She tucked the paper back in the book and returned to the first page. She ran her fingertip over her mother's words, frustrated at the inequity, the unfairness of it all.

"Are there large items to be shipped away or perhaps packed in the carriage?" Dirk asked Charlotte. "We needn't remain here any longer, unless you wish it."

Charlotte nodded and closed the book. "I'll show you which boxes."

Sally spoke up. "Mr. Dirk, one might assume you are looking forward to our Hampton ladies' tea party."

"I am looking forward to getting away from that woman."

"Joan?" Charlotte said.

"Yes. I find her face offensive."

CHAPTER 22

Esther Hampton Caldwell was the pattern from which Eva had been drawn. Eva was the mirror image of her mother every bit as much as Charlotte was of Katherine. Lovely, polished, well-spoken, and intelligent, Charlotte had forgotten how calming Esther was. After a few moments in her company, she began to relax.

Eva had arrived the night before with Constable Denton, Sammy, and Henry, and now the two children and Dirk were playing with the ponies on the small farm. As the women settled into the parlor with a fresh pot of tea and sandwiches, Charlotte nodded to the window where the children were visible in the distance.

"Sammy is still healing well, Eva?" she asked her cousin.

"He is. Also seems to be returning to his old self. He's been bright since your visit."

Dirk lifted Henry into the air and settled him carefully on the small saddle, holding him in place as Sammy led the pony slowly around the paddock.

"Henry's growing so big, Eva," Charlotte said. "Even in the short time since I've been home, I believe he's added at least another inch."

"He changes daily," Eva agreed. She patted the seat next to

her and then poured a cup of tea. "Drink this, Charlotte. You look pale."

Charlotte obediently sat next to Eva and took the saucer and cup. "Yes, Mrs. Winston, right away."

"What ails you?" Eva asked as Esther and Sally made themselves comfortable near the younger women.

Charlotte sighed. "Where to begin? You already know some of it, Eva." As she recounted the events that had occurred since her return to London, she felt overwhelmed by how quickly her life had been overturned.

When she finished, Sally was the first to speak. "Esther, I was wondering what you remember about the time we spent with the Jameses. You were closer in age to Katherine, whereas I was quite small."

Esther nodded and set down her tea. She folded her hands in her lap and looked at Charlotte, nodding absently. "I suppose what I remember most was how devoted they were to your mother." She smiled. "But then, weren't we all? Kat was—" Esther paused, searching for the words. "She was larger than life. Everything was twice as exciting if she was there. She was inventive and clever, and she made certain to include everyone—even me and Sally, the pesky younger sisters."

Sally chuckled. "I was pesky, no question. You were fun also, Esther. I think if Kat had a confidante, it was you."

"I suppose so, although she was also full of secrets." Esther smiled gently at Charlotte. "The diary you found is something she must have hidden from everyone. And you said there are letters from 'James' while they were away at school?"

Charlotte nodded. "Not a surname anywhere. Some of them were folded and sealed with my mother's address written on them. Other times, they must have come in envelopes, but there weren't any of those to be found. I believe my biggest question now is this: which James did she favor the most?"

"I'm afraid that is a hard one to answer. There were times when I believe she felt an extra measure of fondness for each of them. One at a time, of course. Their families were well connected, and expectations for their futures were set from the cradle. As for which of them she would have been in love with just before she married your father, I couldn't say." She spread her hands. "It might have been any of them."

Charlotte nodded, disappointed. "If I could only narrow down that one thing, I believe it would lead to more answers. My supposition, after chatting about it with John, is that either James or his wife wanted my mother out of the way, so they hit her on the head and shoved her overboard. So which James? Which wife? Or fiancée? James and Phillipa Carter had yet to be married."

She paused as the others considered what she'd said and reluctantly added, "Or it could have been my father. I must be objective, but it is difficult."

"Oh, no," Esther said. "I find that highly unlikely. Your father was a gentle person, and he adored your mother."

"What was your impression of each of the Jameses?" Eva asked Esther.

Esther picked up her teacup and tilted her head in thought. "Worthingstone was a leader. Handsome, full of charisma, girls in Town always sought his favor. Finebough was introspective, very much a thinker. Paddleton was almost like a 'younger brother' sort of friend. He was quiet, tagged along in the beginning because our parents were all friends, but he eventually found his own place. The Jameses each had distinctly different personalities, that is for certain."

"And the women came later, of course," Sally said. "Kat knew them from school, and again, our parents knew their parents, so the circle enlarged."

Charlotte frowned. "Which James would have been in love with her?"

Eva interjected, "Or rather, which woman disliked Aunt Katherine the most?"

Esther pursed her lips and shook her head, thinking. "Hard to say. Many women envied Kat, but few outright disliked her." Her eyes narrowed. "We might assume from Anastacia's letter to your mother that she was protecting her own husband. However, she does state that 'the ladies' had *all* decided your mother should stay away." She took a breath. "I will say that Anastacia Worthingstone and Gwendolyn Finebough were often unkind girls at school. They're sisters, and thick as thieves." She glanced at Eva. "My own sweet daughter knew her share of that kind."

Eva nodded and looked at Charlotte. "I did notice more bite in those two the other night at supper, whereas Mrs. Carter said hardly two words until I asked about her charity, and Mrs. Paddleton even fewer." She shrugged and added, "Quiet doesn't always mean a lack of vitriol, however."

"If I'm not mistaken," Sally mused, "Anastacia and Gwendolyn had feathers in their caps for their future husbands from their first Seasons. Both sisters and their parents were instrumental in helping the men get elected."

Charlotte chewed on her lip. She tried to imagine someone accosting a person the way she suspected her mother had been. She examined her thoughts critically, objectively. "If my mother was struck from behind and then shoved over the side of the boat, I imagine it would have taken a fair amount of strength."

Eva nodded thoughtfully. "Or two people might manage it.

One to distract, the other to strike the blow, then both to maneuver the victim over the railing."

"That could work," Charlotte said. "I fear the weapon used may resemble a small tool—something like a pickax, but I cannot be certain from the autopsy photos alone."

"Would someone have access to a pickax on a river ferry?" Eva frowned.

Esther looked at Sally. "I'm fairly alarmed. Do they always speak like this?"

Sally nodded. "They've both seen plenty of corpses, I'm afraid, and spending so much time in the company of detectives has a way of hardening the most delicate of women." She smiled at Charlotte and Eva, who chuckled.

"I don't know I've ever been considered 'delicate,'" Charlotte said. "And Eva is beautiful, but I've seen her hefting photography equipment like a sailor."

"That leaves Amelie." Esther laughed.

Eva's eyes widened in mock innocence. "You mean the girl who stabbed a man in the neck with a hatpin?"

Charlotte's laughter grew, and as the conversation continued, her spirits began to rise. By the time supper came around, she was feeling more like herself.

Esther and Sally left first to prepare for the meal, but before Charlotte could leave, Eva held up her hand. "One moment, if you please. Sammy and Henry will be barging in here any moment, so you must be brief."

Charlotte frowned. "About what?"

Eva looked over her shoulder and lowered her voice. "You and John! Nathan was useless with the details, and Amelie and I are at our wits' end! One moment you were dancing like two clinging vines and the next you disappeared."

Charlotte hadn't been expecting the question and heat rose in her face. "We . . . nothing. We just talked and then went home." She grimaced. "And found my room in shambles."

"Your coat was left in the cloakroom at my mother-in-law's house. What did you wear outside?" Eva's attention was riveted to Charlotte's face.

"His coat," Charlotte mumbled.

"His coat! And which door did you use to leave?"

Charlotte paused before admitting, "The servant's entrance."

"Ah!" Eva sat back against the couch, her eyes huge. "The two of you, grown, professional adults, sneaking about like bandits!"

"You know how people will talk," Charlotte protested, "and once we'd gone into the other room, we couldn't very well just waltz back in."

"Why not?"

"My hair was mussed."

Eva's mouth dropped open and a smile formed. "He kissed you!"

"What did you think we were doing in there?" Charlotte hissed. "Of course he did!" She also sank back against the couch. "We were quite compromised."

"So," Eva said, eyes bright, "when will you marry?"

"Marry?" Charlotte felt a measure of alarm. "One kiss, Eva, that was all it was. Anything beyond a kiss near a ballroom is impractical. He is tied to his career, and I cannot have one if I marry."

"The heart frequently makes decisions for the brain," Eva muttered, shooting a dark look at Charlotte. "Your practicality might just find itself out the window."

"Then I shall climb out the window and retrieve it. Come now, Eva, examine it through my eyes."

"Do you love him?"

"Of course I love him!" She paused, frowned, and shook her head. "I love him dearly, as you do, as Amelie does, as Michael and Nathan do. We all love each other as does one big happy family of friends."

"Some of us love certain members of our family of friends a bit differently than others," Eva told her drily.

"I cannot, I do *not*, have time or energy, I simply—" She shook her head again. "Eva, I do not trust love as far as I can throw it, and as I'm learning, love is ridiculously heavy and cumbersome. My own mother may have been fickle, at best, and I'm very much like her. I have her temperament; I do things unconventionally. I pursued medicine, for heaven's sake." She shook her head. "I will not repeat her history."

"Of course you will not repeat her history." Eva reached for Charlotte's hand and clasped her fingers. "You are not her, Charlotte."

Charlotte sighed. "My mother fell in love with a man whose familial expectations for his marriage were clearly set in stone. I will not do the same."

"John's life has already deviated from the course his parents would have set for him."

"My career demands I remain single. John's career depends on maintaining a relationship with his father." Charlotte lifted the corner of her mouth in an almost-smile. "I am one of 'those Hamptons,' Eva. Perhaps more so than any of us. I will not put him in a place where he must choose."

CHAPTER 23

A knock sounded at John's office door early in the morning, and he sighed, irritated by the interruption. He straightened his jacket lapels and opened the door to see his father, the Earl of Ashby, standing on the other side. "I could not be more surprised if you'd been a kangaroo," John told him. "Please, come in. To what do I owe the honor?"

His frown lines were incredibly deep, which meant his father had serious business on his mind.

John indicated a chair. "Will you have a seat?"

"No, thank you. I shall come to the point," Ashby said. "Edgar and Hortense have said they observed you at a social function with that Hampton woman enacting in behavior lacking decorum."

John waited for his father to continue. When he did not, John said, "Forgive me, my lord, but I fail to see how this concerns anyone but me. And to be clear, I was not behaving with a lack of decorum." He only ever called his father "my lord" when he was perturbed with the man.

"I also have it on good authority that at supper, you participated in a scandalous conversation, again involving that woman and her mother's short, unfortunate life. I hold Worthingstone, Finebough, and Paddleton blameless—they can hardly be expected to know in advance if remnants of poor associations from the past will surface, but—" Ashby paused, his hand tightening in a fist, evidence of the depth of his agitation. "Your proximity to that family is entirely unacceptable. Your subordinates may have married into it, but they are just that—your subordinates. That you blur those lines outside this office is but another mark against you that I cannot comprehend."

"By all means, please continue down the list of complaints. We may as well air it now."

Ashby's nostrils flared. "This is not a joke!"

"And I am not laughing!" John leaned forward and lowered his voice. "Contrary to what you may tell yourself and your colleagues, I earned my position on my merits alone. How I conduct my affairs here and outside these walls is no business of yours, sir, and I will not defend it or explain it to you."

"How do you think your colleagues, your superiors here at the Yard, will react if all legislation for additional funding suddenly disappears? The vote approaches soon, and you forget who I am!"

John wondered how much of his father's anger was because of Charlotte and how much was because John was pushing back rather than diplomatically brushing his complaints aside. Though John often used his father's position to curry favor with those in power, he wasn't dependent upon it. Ashby wasn't the king, and John was tired of acting as though he were.

His frustration rose to new heights, and it sounded in his voice. "If your intent is to sabotage the success of an entire law enforcement agency merely because you do not like my choice of friends or dance partners, then I assert it is *you* who casts aspersions on the Ashby name, not I."

His father's face turned white with anger as he searched for a response.

John pushed forward. "A good reputation is based on more than conversation at a social event. It is built in the good we provide for others, and heaven knows I see little enough of that day to day. You pride yourself on your standing with God, and yet you will ride past the suffering clogging these streets without blinking an eye. You would use your influence and status—your own *good name*—to sway members of Parliament to deny people the resources they require to keep you safe? For what?" John spread his arms wide. "Because of me?"

He took a deep breath and ran a hand through his hair, stepping back, searching for calm. "I defy you to speak with anyone in this town who would suggest I am anything but circumspect and dedicated to my profession. The only people who might have cause to complain about me are those I've arrested or imprisoned."

"Perhaps," Ashby snapped, "not everyone has as high an opinion of you as you claim. You ought to think before you begin gossiping about government officials. Tipton caught me at the club the other night, mentioned your supper together. He is impressed with the thorough way you follow politics and said you had questions about three men in particular—coincidentally the same three who sat through an extremely uncomfortable meal with you just days before."

"I make no apologies for following inquiries. That is my job."

"You find yourself on shaky ground, John, but at least I will rest easy knowing I have cautioned you. Your hubris will be your downfall."

John looked at the man who had never before entered his office, never asked about his work, never expressed the slightest bit of pride in his son. He sighed, realizing what he ought to have known years earlier. Such pride would never come.

"Father, I have worked tirelessly to garner your good opinion. I have struggled and dealt with prejudice from those who suggest I arrived at my position because it was given to me. Those who know me well are aware of my constant drive to do the work and do it well. I would like you to trust my judgment in those with whom I associate. I do not waste my time with people who do not deserve it."

Ashby's expression remained stony. Without saying another word, he turned on his heel and left, shutting the door firmly behind him.

John exhaled and sank into his chair, putting his head in his hands. He was glad he'd finally said aloud to his father all the things he'd been thinking. He wondered, though, how far Ashby would go to prove a point. John couldn't expect any support from his brother or his mother.

It was interesting Tipton had brought up John's questions about the Jameses. John wasn't concerned about the MPs' politics as they were not the sort who regularly supported causes John championed, and from what he'd heard, James Carter wielded more power over both houses than Katherine's former friends did. Ashby was right about one thing, though—John needed to watch his step. Just because the three men didn't have great influence now did not mean that one or all of them wouldn't at a later date. As he'd seen during the supper at Mrs. Winston's, memories didn't always fade.

He sighed and rubbed his face. The day hadn't even begun, and it was already sour. Perhaps some fresh air would clear his head. When he opened his office door, he saw Dirk and Charlotte approaching. He felt a flash of concern. It hadn't been that long since he'd seen them at breakfast.

"Is something wrong?"

Dirk took a seat at Amelie's desk as John ushered Charlotte into his office before anyone else arrived.

"No, it's just that I've received word that the hospital is swamped. I have a couple hours before going in, because I'll probably need to stay through the night. I wanted to come by and say hello."

"I am very glad you did. This day has gotten off to a horrid start." He sat against the edge of his desk and pulled her to him. She only allowed him so much, though, and then resisted moving any closer. "What's the matter?"

She shook her head. "I wasn't trying to eavesdrop, but I overheard everything." She bit her lip and frowned. "It only underscores what I was trying to explain to Eva. She has grand notions that are little more than fairy tales."

He raised his hand to her cheek and, when she didn't stop him, cradled it in his hand. "What sort of fairy tales? Involving whom?"

"I'd rather not say."

He chuckled and rubbed his thumb along her skin. "I am sorry you overheard the conversation with my father. It was incredibly insulting."

"I shall keep my distance, John, and most definitely in public. We are good friends, and there is no reason for that to change, but I'll not be the reason others suffer."

He tightened his jaw, tamping down his worry that he wouldn't be able to talk her out of her decision. "Others will not suffer because you and I are good friends—exceptionally good friends."

She closed her eyes, her lashes creating fans on her cheeks. He put his hands on her arms, and when she didn't resist, pulled her close to him. She kept her arms folded, so he wrapped his around her back and rested his chin on her head. He rubbed his hand up and down her back, gently kneading the muscles on her neck that were tighter than a drum.

She exhaled softly, and he smiled, putting "massage" on the list of "things Charlotte liked." If she did not care for him, he would have left her alone. If she planned to keep her distance because of her job, he would have left her alone because of that as well. But if she put distance between them simply out of concern for what others may threaten, he would fight that tooth and nail.

"Perhaps we can just steal a few moments here and there," she mumbled into his jacket. "It is not as though we've made declarations of love and devotion. We can continue as we always have."

"Hmm. Well, Miss Duvall, what we have always done did not include this."

"I know." If he didn't know her better, he'd have sworn she was whining.

As for declarations of love and devotion, he'd already declared his feelings for Charlotte to Michael and Nathan. As long as they kept their lips closed, he could buy some time to ease her into the idea that they should be together every minute of every day.

He did want it, he realized. He wanted to marry her. Perhaps they could locate a hospital with relaxed rules concerning a woman's marital status. He would bend anything and everything to make it work, because he loved her and wanted to be her husband. He'd always assumed the decision to marry would feel like a burden. Instead, he felt lighter. Happier.

She lifted her head as he continued the slow assault on her

tight muscles, her beautiful green eyes inches from his. "Friends?" she whispered.

"Oh, yes." His eyes flicked down to her lips. "Very good friends."

With a sigh that sounded suspiciously resigned, she put her arms around his neck and kissed him.

Had his father returned at that very moment, John wouldn't have cared one bit. Amelie, Michael, Nathan—anyone could have opened the door and though Charlotte might be embarrassed, he'd not have an ounce of regret. *She* had kissed *him* this time, and he hoped she would never stop.

Regrettably, she finally pulled back, but he followed her with another small kiss, and then another. She put her hands on either side of his face and breathlessly laughed. "We must stop. My hair will be mussed, and everyone will talk."

"There's nobody out there yet but Dirk, and he is delightfully nonjudgmental."

"There will be! And what if your father returns?"

"I'll introduce you to him."

She shook her head, exasperated. "This is not going to work."

"What isn't? We're just good friends, after all."

"John."

"Charlotte."

"What is this? I cannot simply call it 'friendship.' Suppose I see you at an event, dancing with someone else. Am I to assume you will also spin her into an adjoining room and kiss her senseless because she is another of your friends?"

He chuckled and touched his forehead to hers. "Darling, I can assure you I do not go around town kissing my friends." He lifted his head and looked into her eyes. "My kisses are reserved for one friend only."

Her eyelashes dropped, and her mouth quirked into a smile. "I suppose that is acceptable."

"I would hope for the same from you."

"I can also assure you that I do not go around town kissing my friends."

"Very good. Then we have an accord."

Her brow wrinkled. "But we are not . . . I have not committed to anything . . ."

"Have you proposed to me?"

"No, I have not."

He smiled. "Then I see no reason for concern."

She sighed and dropped her hands to his shoulders. "I must go. You have work to do, and I should slip out unnoticed while I still can. We missed crossing paths last night, but I should like to discuss our progress on my mother's case and the information I learned from Aunt Esther."

"When do you next have a decent swath of time?" Unable to keep from touching her, he traced her ear, her neck, her jaw, and her eyes drifted closed.

"I must go," she whispered.

He cradled her head in his hands and kissed her again, relishing every breath, losing himself in it.

Contrary to his earlier thoughts, a knock on the door was as effective in cooling his ardor as a bucket of cold water.

Charlotte jumped back. She smoothed her dress and rushed to the small mirror on his wall and stood on tiptoe to check her hair. "I told you this would happen," she hissed at him. "Trust my own judgment," she muttered. "I forget that at my peril!"

"One moment," he called to the door and then stood behind Charlotte, putting his arms around her waist and lifting her higher to the mirror. Meeting her eyes in it, he placed the softest of kisses on her neck. "If you wish, the wardrobe to your right is just big enough to hide you."

Her eyes widened, and she whispered, "Do you hide women in there often, Director? Perhaps you have more friends than you admit!"

He fought a smile and carried her to the wardrobe door. "It would bother you, then?"

She climbed inside and shoved his great coat aside, glaring at him. "You, hiding women in here regularly? Yes!"

He grinned. "Good." He closed the door on her muffled curse and went to answer the office door. His day had gone from bad to wonderful, and he only hoped this latest visitor would at least fall somewhere in the middle.

"John?" Amelie asked, perplexed. Her expression bordered on worried. "Are you all right?"

He sighed in relief and opened the door wider. She entered, and when he closed the door, he called to Charlotte, "The coast is clear. Relatively."

The wardrobe door creaked open, and when Charlotte saw Amelie, she flung it wide. "Thank goodness." She stepped out, brushing at her dress and hair. "I might have been stuck in there for hours."

John smiled at her. "Only if I'd been feeling vindictive."

Amelie stared. "What are you doing in there, Charlotte?"

"Inspecting the Director's outerwear. Coat seems good, John, as do the galoshes. Ready for the next rainstorm."

"Excellent." He looked at Amelie, who was eyeing her cousin in dawning awareness. "Are those files for me?" he asked.

"Oh." Amelie looked at the documents she held in her arms. "Yes. This is the one I copied, and as there is no way to reproduce the photos, perhaps you might find a safe place to store them? Something under lock and key?"

He nodded and took the files from her. "The cabinets here do lock, but locks can be picked. I'll store them elsewhere."

"I wonder if Eva could take a photograph of the photographs? If the original plates are unavailable, as you suspect, it might be an option. Would it even produce a useful result?"

John nodded. "Worth a try. Good idea. I'll check with the coroner's office first for the name of the company. It wasn't stamped on the photos themselves."

Charlotte's attention perked up. "Which file are you discussing?"

Amelie looked at John, and he appreciated her professionalism. She wouldn't tell Charlotte if the matter were confidential, and it said much for her character. He nodded, and Amelie said, "Your mother's, Charlotte. John asked me to make a typed copy of each document so that we are not reliant on only the originals."

Charlotte looked at John. "Why would that be necessary?"

"It probably isn't, but I do not trust the scruples of some of the people at play in this. There is much to be lost if accusations are thrown about. An extra copy of the file provides insurance."

Voices sounded in the outer area, and Charlotte donned the hat and gloves that had been discarded sometime between her entry and the neck massage. John watched her prepare to leave and finally understood the word "longing."

"Please notify me when we can discuss the case, Charlotte," he said as he walked the cousins to the door.

"Is that what we are calling it?" Amelie murmured, one brow raised.

"Amelie, I shall dock your pay," he said.

"No, you shall not. In fact, I demand a raise to keep quiet about everything I witnessed here today."

"If you do not keep quiet, I shall be forced to arrest you for impersonating a deputy, which I have on good authority you've done more than once."

"John!" Amelie's eyes flashed, and for a moment he wondered if she were truly irritated. "Michael did deputize me!"

"Amelie, that is not how it works."

"Come along," Charlotte said, ushering her cousin from the room. "We have some time before I must leave for the hospital, and I'm sure Director Ellis will allow you a short visit with me."

"Very smooth," John said to Charlotte as they stood near Amelie's desk. "Robbing me of both your company and my employee. Now what am I to do?"

Dirk moved out of the way as Amelie reached into a desk drawer and withdrew a stack of papers. "You need to review and sign each of these, and when I return, I'll give you the rest. I saw in your appointment book that you have tea with the Turkish dignitaries before they return home, so now is a good time for you to do this." She handed him the stack with a brisk smile. "And you," Amelie said to Charlotte, "come with me. Mr. Dirk, I presume you will follow."

"Yes, he most certainly will," John said. Dirk shot him a look that said he could speak for himself.

"Where are we going?" Charlotte asked Amelie, casting a bewildered look back at John.

"Investigating."

"Do not tell people you are a deputy!" John called after them.

"Only in a pinch," Amelie responded as they disappeared around the corner and out of sight. Dirk walked behind them, and John didn't know if he pitied the man or envied the fact that he was leaving the building.

John hefted the stack of documents in his arms and returned to his desk, wondering when he'd lost command of his own ship. If only Amelie had been present when his father had arrived, she'd have given him a good dressing down and sent him on his way.

It was only after he'd signed a dozen papers that he remembered what Amelie had said to Charlotte. They were going "investigating." Since Amelie had just read Katherine Duvall's entire police file, he had to wonder what she meant. An uneasy feeling settled in his gut, and if not for his pending appointment with the Turks, he'd have gone after the cousins.

"Charlotte, be smart," he muttered. He couldn't be certain how people would react when a ghost came around asking questions.

CHAPTER 24

Charlotte looked at Amelie as they neared a busy warehouse district. The cab slowed, and Amelie nodded. "I believe it's just along here." She pointed out the window, and when the vehicle came to a stop, she stepped quickly outside.

"*Now* will you tell me what we're doing?" Charlotte asked.

Amelie paid the driver and turned to Charlotte. "As I was transcribing your mother's police file, I noticed something that sounded familiar. Fairmont Riverboats."

Charlotte waited, expecting more.

"You know? Fairmont? They're the ferries that take passengers into London and back for work or errands and the like."

"I know what they do, Amelie," Charlotte said, exasperated. "There are dozens of companies though—more ferries on the waterways than is probably safe. I don't remember all of their names."

"I do." Amelie linked arms with Charlotte. "And this is the docking warehouse where they maintain their fleet." They approached the large structure that housed ferries in various states of repair. Clanking machinery echoed through the building, along with shouts and conversation.

"Pardon me," Amelie said, catching a young dockworker's attention. "Where are the Fairmont offices?"

The worker pointed toward the back of the building where a door was just visible behind a grease-smudged engine. Charlotte followed her cousin, wondering if it was wise to put so much blind faith in her. Amelie expected certain things from people, and she usually got them. Sometimes, however, her judgment was off. Dirk's presence was a comfort, at least.

Amelie knocked on the door, and a gruff voice answered. She opened the door a crack and said, "Mr. Fairmont?"

"No, I ain't Fairmont. If ya got a problem, see management." His eyes widened as he spied the large Scot standing behind them.

"And where might I find management?" Amelie asked with a smile.

"Offices in Central London."

Amelie waited expectantly, and with a huff, the man scribbled something on a piece of paper and handed it over. "Tha's the address."

"Thank you, sir!" She smiled again, and the man answered with an impatient grunt.

Before Charlotte knew what was happening, Amelie had them back in another cab and headed toward the new address. By now, the not-knowing had become a game Charlotte was willing to play, and when Amelie looked at her with a bright smile, she didn't ask any more questions. Even Dirk was willing to go, no questions asked.

In truth, her mind was still back in John's office with her lips pressed against his. She didn't think she would ever get over the wonder of kissing him. She'd wanted to kiss him in the Fulbrights' library, and had she known what she was missing, she'd have indulged. She looked out the window at the passing carriages, horses, and bustling pedestrians, but saw none of it.

"And what are you thinking about, that has you smiling so?" Amelie asked.

"Nothing, just—" Charlotte shrugged. "Usual sorts of things."

"John sorts of things?"

"Well, no, I'm only—"

Amelie held up a hand. "I can read it in your face." She smiled, and her eyes softened. "I am so glad, Charlotte! We've all waited for so long!"

"Amelie," Charlotte said, growing increasingly uncomfortable, "we've declared nothing. We are not engaged; we are still just very good friends."

"Mmm."

"Please, I cannot have rumors spreading."

"I, madam, am more secure with secrets than a steel trap." Amelie looked affronted.

"You would tell Eva."

"Eva does not count." Amelie sniffed. "Nor do you. The three of us are as one."

"I am not a potted plant," Dirk said.

Charlotte gaped at him and then laughed. "That was very funny!"

His answering expression was flat. "I can hear everything you're saying."

"Dirk, you don't gossip with *me*, and we've spent weeks together. I cannot imagine you gossiping with anyone else."

"Fair enough."

Amelie smiled. "I wager he would loosen his tongue if plied with enough whiskey."

"That is why I do not drink." He didn't laugh along with them, but Eva nearly fell from the seat when he gave her a barely perceptible wink.

Charlotte looked at Amelie and let out a frustrated sigh. "It is not as though I am hiding anything, it is only that I do not know what is happening."

"I am glad you've finally joined our ranks. I fell in love with a grumpy detective quite against my will, and Eva denied her feelings for Nathan from the beginning." Amelie paused. "Rather like you and John. They were convinced they were just friends, and you are following suit."

"I have nothing to say about the matter, except that I do not want anyone to say anything about the matter."

Amelie nodded and mimed locking her lips with a key and then throwing it over her shoulder. She pointed at Dirk, who blinked deliberately, once, in response.

They came to a stop outside a tall building with a light gray façade, and, after paying the driver, Amelie led the way to the broad front door.

Inside they found a reception area and long hallway. Different names were printed on nameplates, and lack of a receptionist required them to wander the corridor until they saw one labeled Fairmont Riverboats. Amelie looked at Charlotte with a shrug and cracked open the door.

Inside was a young woman sitting at a typewriter. She looked up as they entered. "Yes?"

Amelie gamely stepped forward. "Miss . . ."

"Streatfield."

"Miss Streatfield, I am Mrs. Baker, this is Miss Duvall, and accompanying us is Mr. Dirk. We are on a rather . . . odd journey. Do you know much about the history of Fairmont Riverboats?"

Miss Streatfield's brow wrinkled. "I know some of the history, I suppose."

Amelie looked at Charlotte and then tried again. "For example, do you who might have been managing the company in roughly 1869?"

"The old Mr. Fairmont was the original owner. I suppose that would have been him. It was a much smaller company then. I can ask our current president. He is the owner's son."

"Is he here today, by chance?" Amelie asked.

"Yes, he is. I'll see if he has time to answer your questions."

Charlotte glanced at Amelie. Was she looking for the captain who had piloted the boat the night Katherine died?

Miss Streatfield disappeared into a side office and then reappeared, motioning to the cousins. "Mr. Fairmont will see you now." She smiled and stepped away from the door.

The man was in his early forties, and his face bore a pleasant, if bemused expression as he stood from behind his desk to greet Amelie. He then turned to Charlotte and his demeanor changed. His face slackened, paled, and he sat down hard in his chair. "Miss Streatfield," he managed, "close the door."

Dirk stepped inside and took up his post before the secretary could follow the command.

Amelie looked at Charlotte. "I believe we are in the right place, Miss Duvall." She took a seat, and Charlotte followed.

Once Mr. Fairmont recovered from his initial shock, he cleared his throat. "Duvall. Are you kin, then?"

Charlotte nodded. "Daughter."

The door clicked quietly closed.

"Uncanny." He reached inside his desk and withdrew a cigarette that he lit with shaking hands. He took a long drag and blew smoke to the side, watching Charlotte the entire time.

"Were you there the night of the accident?" Charlotte asked. She didn't see any need to delay the conversation with small talk. "You would have been close to twenty, I suspect?"

"Twenty-one. I was helping my pa. Carter Textiles—the son, in fact—had hired the boat for the weekend. We were to sail up and down the river, wherever the party wanted. We had just the one ferry, and a job like that was big business for us. My pa took special care of the boat—polished her until she shined."

Charlotte's heart beat faster. "Your father was questioned by police, and his statement was that his back was to the people on the deck. Did you witness the accident?"

He shook his head. "The boat, you see—" He pointed to a framed photo behind his desk. "The wheel is down here in the middle, covered. The deck is behind, above the salon. We didn't see anything."

"But you heard something?" Amelie asked.

"Screaming."

Charlotte swallowed.

"Duvall," Mr. Fairmont said. "Never will forget that name. Or her face." He looked at Charlotte and shook his head. "I wish my pa was here. He felt responsible, you know. Happened on his watch, he said."

"It wasn't his fault," Charlotte said. "I would like to know exactly what happened that night, though."

"You read the police report, you said."

Charlotte nodded, trying to decide how much to divulge. While she was thinking, Amelie interjected. "Mr. Fairmont, it is a credit to your father that he built the business from one ferry into such a successful endeavor." She smiled. "Or perhaps it happened while under your management?"

He shook his head. His eyes flicked to Charlotte and back to Amelie. He seemed most comfortable leaving his attention anywhere that wasn't on Charlotte. "Wasn't too long after the accident that my father inherited some money. He put it into the business, bought a whole fleet. He worked hard," he said, taking another drag on the cigarette, "even with the inheritance. It wasn't like we got everything just handed to us."

He sounded defensive. Charlotte decided to risk a guess. "Perhaps Carter Textile felt responsible for your father's trouble? Maybe the 'inheritance' came from them?"

"I don't know where it came from." Mr. Fairmont's voice was sharp. "My pa said good things happen to good people, and that's that."

"Mr. Fairmont," Amelie said in a voice that successfully soothed toddlers, "nobody is questioning your father's hard work, and I'm certain he was a good man. You seem like a very good man too. I'm sure the money your family received was given in gratitude."

Mr. Fairmont nodded, but he seemed increasingly nervous. Agitated. Had the money actually been given to the Fairmonts to ensure their silence?

"Are you certain you didn't see anything?" Charlotte asked. "My mother wasn't a drinker, and she was comfortable in and on the water. With so many people there, I simply can't believe nobody saw anything."

"It was crowded," Fairmont agreed. "By the time I reached the deck, it was swarming with people."

Amelie tipped her head. "How long do you believe it took you to run from the wheel to the deck?"

He lifted a shoulder. "I don't know—by the time I heard screaming, I'd guess about ten seconds."

"Did you hear one scream at first? Several?" Charlotte pressed.

"I don't know, it was chaos! It's a blur in my mind. Anything I saw would be in the police report."

"Your witness statement isn't in the police files," Amelie said, frowning. "You're certain they took one from you?"

"Yes. Wrote it all down."

"What, exactly, did you tell the officer?" Charlotte asked.

"I can't remember, I tell you! I've tried to forget it. I had never seen a dead body before." He glanced at Charlotte. "Apologies," he mumbled.

"Not necessary," Charlotte said quietly. "You saw them pull her out of the water?"

He nodded. "They did try to save her, push out the water and such." He shook his head. "There were so many people everywhere and screaming and crying. It was all my pa could do to get the boat to shore. Glasses full of liquor spilled, one of our crew lost consciousness. I slipped and fell on someone's walking cane, bruised my . . . myself something good."

Charlotte smiled. "I trust your bruises healed."

He nodded, releasing a shaky breath. "Miss Duvall, I am so sorry about your mother. There was nothing anyone could have done."

"And you believe in your heart that it was an accident?" Charlotte asked, sliding forward in her seat as though to rise and leave. She wanted the question to sound like an afterthought, when in reality, it was the most crucial one of all.

"Police said it was. Guests said it was. So, yes, it was."

Charlotte nodded. She suspected it was the most they would pry from the man. She wasn't without sympathy—he seemed to have been genuinely traumatized. They thanked him for his time, and he moved to stand.

"We'll see ourselves out," Amelie reassured him and waved him back down.

He sank into his seat again, likely in relief.

The cousins were quiet as they left the offices and hailed a cab. "We may never learn what he told police," Amelie finally said, frowning in thought, "but if they really took his statement, where is it? And secondly . . ." Amelie looked at Charlotte and Dirk. "Who paid the Fairmonts off?"

Later that night, Charlotte sat in her office at the hospital with Dirk. She was exhausted, but the hustle of the hospital was a mirror of her own training while she'd been in school. She'd learned how to eat and sleep when she could afford the snatches of time. The influenza outbreak seemed to be tapering, thankfully, and they'd lost only one child that day rather than three the day before.

Charlotte's hands were raw from constant washing in a carbolic solution, and she was grateful to see the nurses' quick efficiency in the patient wards and that they kept themselves to impeccably clean standards. With luck, the caregivers would avoid contracting the illnesses themselves.

She was grateful to finally have a few moments to stop working and eat a quick supper. The morning seemed an eternity away. Had it really been the same day that she'd visited John in his office and gone with Amelie to question Mr. Fairmont?

She poured some tea and flicked the napkin open, murmuring thanks to the staff who worked tirelessly in the third-floor kitchen. Many of the patients Delaney served ate better in the hospital than they did at home. She dove into the stew meat and potatoes with relish.

Dirk was as quiet as ever, but she knew he absorbed everything around him. Charlotte suspected his unwillingness to babble—or engage in long conversation, even—might have contributed to his legendary mystique. She'd gotten one thing out of him, however; he had a sister and a seven-year-old niece.

"Will you go home for the holidays to visit your family?" she asked.

He nodded.

"And what gift will you take to your niece?" Charlotte smiled, picturing a redheaded little girl, perhaps not so unlike herself.

"She enjoys rugby."

Charlotte choked on her sip of tea, then laughed. "A girl after my own heart. I would have loved a friend to play rugby with. You've seen an example of what my brothers were like—useless."

His smile looked almost bashful. "If I'd been your brother, lass, I would have played rugby with you."

She sobered, and her eyes filled with tears that she didn't bother to stop. She couldn't have been more stunned if he'd stood up and danced. He seemed moved by her emotion because his own eyes looked suspiciously bright.

"I believe your mother was a lovely person," he added, "and you've every right to be proud to be her daughter."

She sat back in her chair and put a hand to her chest. She swallowed, trying to find her voice. "I believe that's the kindest thing anyone has ever said to me. Thank you, Dirk."

He nodded and straightened, clearing his throat. They finished their dinner in comfortable silence.

A knock sounded at the door, and it was opened before Charlotte could say a word. Dirk stood as Mr. Stanley stepped across the threshold even though she hadn't invited him in. He hadn't liked her from the beginning, and her criticism over his lack of anesthetic knowledge had not endeared her to him.

"Are you lost?" Dirk asked the man.

Stanley looked Dirk up and down but failed to hold his eyes for long. He looked at Charlotte, who had an idea of the reason for his visit.

"Mr. Stanley," she began, "as we have no designated anesthetist, we all must take our turns. I didn't have an issue with you today, but I stand by my statement from last week—"

He held up his hand. "I am not here about that, nor do I give a fig about any issue you have with me today or any day. It has come to my attention that one of the hospital's benefactors is withdrawing his annual donation."

The world seemed to freeze in place. Charlotte's stomach sank. The hospital depended on the city's wealthiest donors for its daily survival. They could not afford to lose even one.

"Why are you telling me?" Charlotte asked.

"I believe you might know the name. The gentleman's wife is a private patient of mine from my time at Mt. Vernon. Mrs. Worthingstone?" His face was smug. "I do not believe it is common knowledge that you have a once-removed association with her husband, an esteemed member of Parliament, but I do find it odd that so soon after your arrival here, we lose funding from one of our largest benefactors."

Charlotte's mouth had gone dry, and she struggled to swallow. She took a sip of her tea, but when she set down the cup, it rattled against the saucer. "I shall speak with Mr. Corbin and Matron Halcomb. Perhaps there has been a misunderstanding."

He smiled. "I do not believe there is."

Her frustration flared. "I should think you would not be happy at this turn of events, Mr. Stanley. If the hospital closes, your job also ends."

"I'll find work at another hospital. Mt. Vernon has wanted

me to return for an age. Unfortunate for you, I imagine. This was one of very few hospitals willing to hire a woman doctor."

Dirk tensed and moved fractionally closer to Mr. Stanley.

Charlotte stood, folding her napkin. "I did not invite you to enter my office. You've delivered your message, and now you may go."

He lingered for a few insolent moments before narrowing his eyes at her and leaving.

"Perhaps he's lying." Dirk's eyes narrowed as he watched the man retreat.

"If we are fortunate," she murmured. "I need to ask the matron." Her heart was beating quickly, and she felt the weight of the world settle on her shoulders.

Dirk walked with her as she left her office and made her way down to Matron Halcomb's office. When she found it empty, they turned and climbed the stairs to Mr. Corbin's office.

At her knock, a voice beckoned, and she entered to find Mr. Corbin and Matron Halcomb seated at a table, reviewing accounting books. The head administrator looked exhausted, and Charlotte felt sick.

"Please, come in," Mr. Corbin said.

She entered but did not sit. "Sir, Matron, I've heard distressing news. Is it true we're losing funding?"

They nodded, and Mr. Corbin rubbed his eyes. "Our annual contribution gala is coming, and we received notice today that the Worthingstones will not be renewing their donation." He shook his head, his eyes troubled. "I do not understand it, for the life of me. Not only did the Worthingstone family establish this hospital, but they have supported it for two generations."

Matron Halcomb shook her head. "I do not know if we can cut costs enough to offset the loss." She paused. "Oh, Charlotte, you look stricken. I am so sorry that you are facing the possibility of employment loss so soon after gaining it."

"No, I—"

"Miss Duvall," Mr. Corbin said, "I shall provide the best of references for you, should it come to that. I am well acquainted with several other hospital administrators."

This is my fault. This is all my fault.

The phrase repeated in her mind. She pulled herself together and nodded. "Thank you, Mr. Corbin. Perhaps a miracle will happen, and the necessary funding will come through."

"That's the spirit," Mr. Corbin said. "We're not beaten yet." He smiled at Charlotte, and she did her best to return it. "Besides, we still have monies pledged from the Paddletons and Fineboughs, among others. Our members of Parliament do take care of us."

Her heart sank further.

"Go home, my girl," Matron Halcomb said. "Morning comes early, and our doors are still open."

Charlotte nodded and left the room, numbly returning to her office where she removed her doctor's coat and gathered her things.

"We have a visit to make on the way home," she told Dirk, who frowned, but didn't argue.

She stopped in the main office, and on a whim, checked the files under "W." Of course, she chastised herself, the Worthingstones would never have been patients at the hospital, so she would find no information there.

She turned instead to the rows of volumes that lined the shelves—hospital records dating back decades. Tracing her finger along the spines, she located one labeled "Benefactors" and pulled it down. She flipped through the pages until she found the one she sought. Making a note of the address in her small notebook, she replaced the book and left the hospital.

With Dirk by her side, she made her way to the train station and boarded the train that would take them across town. They then took a hansom cab to the stylish square where the Worthingstone mansion stood.

"I'll pay you double to wait here," she said to the driver. Pulling her coat against the cold, she resolutely made her way to the entrance and knocked before she could think twice about what she was doing.

"You can wait here with the driver," she said to Dirk.

His flat, answering expression brooked no argument.

She exhaled, her breath forming a cloud. "I do not know if they'll be straightforward with me if someone else is listening."

"I'll wait just outside the parlor door, then."

She nodded. She knew how bedraggled she must look. She was tired, had worked all day, had dealt with two stabbings, one oil burn, and one gunshot in the thigh that had required immediate surgery. Her hair was no longer freshly coiffed, but instead had been muscled back into submission with pins as the day had progressed. She looked as plain as a woman could possibly look, and her sense of defeat likely exacerbated it.

She swallowed as the door opened.

"Servants' entrance is in the rear," the butler told her.

"No," she interrupted before he could close the door. "I am here to see Mr. Worthingstone."

"He is not in residence this evening."

"Mrs. Worthingstone?"

"My lady is extremely busy."

Charlotte closed her eyes, fighting defeat. "Will you tell her that Katherine Duvall's daughter is here to see her? Please."

The butler sighed and looked at Dirk as though he'd dragged in something unpleasant on his shoes, but then instructed them to wait just inside the door as he left the large front hall. He returned quickly enough that Charlotte figured her request had worked.

"This way," the butler said and led them up a flight of stairs. Just to the left, with a lovely view of the square, was a large parlor. Dirk stood outside the door and stared at the butler as though daring him to protest. The butler sniffed, but gestured Charlotte inside and waited as a maid and two other guests exited the room, the latter looking at Charlotte in undisguised distaste. The door closed behind her with a quiet click.

Anastacia Worthingstone sat in a regal chair by the hearth, her dark hair gleaming in the lamplight. "Of all the sights I thought never to see darkening my door."

"A word, if you will?" Charlotte asked, keeping her voice mild.

"Please." Mrs. Worthingstone gestured to a chair near hers. As Charlotte sat, the woman continued, "May I have the butler take your coat? Would you care for tea?"

Charlotte heard sarcasm in every word, whether it was intended or not.

"No, thank you. I only need a moment of your time. I believe you know I am a physician at Delaney Hospital, and I fear the administration received distressing news today."

"Oh?"

Charlotte took a calming breath. Mrs. Worthingstone would make her say every last word. "We were informed that the Worthingstone foundation will no longer be a benefactor for Delaney. Perhaps you were unaware? I did hope to speak with your husband but was informed he is not here."

"I am aware, of course. I have a hand in all foundation affairs."

"Mrs. Worthingstone." Charlotte searched for the right words. "Why? Why would you do this? The family foundation has sponsored the hospital since its inception."

"The family foundation has a responsibility to sponsor appropriate organizations. Not those that support unsavory populations."

Charlotte shook her head. "The population the hospital serves has never changed. It has always cared for the poor and destitute in the East End."

"I am not speaking of the patients."

It is *about me.* Silence echoed through the room. The ticking of the mantel clock was an accompaniment to the phrase that repeated itself in her mind: *This is my fault. This is my fault.*

Feeling her eyes burn but unwilling to shed even one tear in the woman's presence, Charlotte straightened her spine. "What do you suppose would encourage the family foundation to change its mind about the donation?"

"I suppose the foundation might be encouraged to reconsider if the hospital cut all ties with current unsavory elements." The woman's ice-blue stare regarded her in triumph.

Charlotte quietly exhaled. "What guarantee would a person have that the decision would be reversed?"

"If Delaney Hospital no longer supports the objectionable party, the decision will be immediately reversed. The objectionable party may then return from whence they came."

Charlotte nodded slowly and pursed her lips. "And the foundation will not encourage other charitable organizations or families to abandon Delaney Hospital?"

"That seems a reasonable assumption." Mrs. Worthingstone

relaxed in her chair, her hands placed lightly in her lap. There was nothing in her demeanor to indicate discomfort or unease. It was as though she destroyed careers on a daily basis.

"It isn't enough that my mother is dead," Charlotte said quietly.

"This has nothing to do with *Kat*, Dr. Duvall."

And there it was. Charlotte had embarrassed the woman at supper. She was unable to hold back a laugh that escaped quietly through her nose. "I see." She met Mrs. Worthingstone's bland smile and bit back a dozen retorts that would have assuaged her personal pain but also nullified the positive results of her visit. Instead, she said, "Delaney Hospital's unsavory element will draft a letter of resignation to be handed in tomorrow morning."

"The element might then send a message here that it is finished. Once that has happened, I am certain the family foundation will renew its devoted efforts to the worthy cause. Otherwise, the morning papers might be forced to share the unfortunate news."

"Ma'am." Charlotte stood and bobbed a curtsey, wanting to wipe the serene expression from the woman's face with her fingernails.

She left the room on legs that shook and made her way carefully down the stairs so she wouldn't tumble to the bottom. Once outside, Dirk promised the cab driver a healthy fare to take them all the way to Bloomsbury and the warm security of Hampton House.

To Charlotte's dismay, the sobs she had been able to keep at bay while facing off against Mrs. Worthingstone overtook her in the cab. She relayed the conversation to Dirk, who sat across from her, elbows braced on his knees. His expression grew darker with each detail.

"I don't want John to know, not yet," she said. "He'll try to talk me out of resigning, but the hospital can't afford even the smallest lapse in funding."

Dirk eyed her as if he'd argue, but then nodded. "He is at a police commissioner function until at least midnight. You can go to bed and tell him in the morning."

She shook her head. "I'll leave before he's awake." She looked out the window. "He will be so upset for me."

"He is a grown man," Dirk said, coming as close to exasperation as she'd ever heard from him. "You're not giving him any credit for mature behavior."

"It isn't that. He will be sympathetic and loving, and *that* will be my undoing. I won't be able to fulfill my responsibility."

"*You* are a grown woman," he said. "I can't imagine you shirking any responsibility."

She wiped her cheeks. "I can't explain it." Her breath hitched.

He watched her for another moment and then sat back. "Very well," he said quietly. "But you must tell him by tomorrow noon. The Worthingstones appear in the middle of this case at every turn—this may be crucial information for him to have."

She nodded and blew out a quiet breath. "Tomorrow at noon. Thank you."

He acknowledged her thanks with a nod but kept any further thoughts to himself. The rest of the ride home was silent and cold.

CHAPTER 25

John was surprised the next morning to learn Charlotte and Dirk had already left for the hospital. She was burning the candle at both ends, and he worried she'd run herself ragged. Mrs. Burnette and the maids had quietly straightened Charlotte's room after the break-in, and he noticed Sarah checking on Charlotte more frequently. She offered to bring her tea, to style her hair, to gather clothes to be laundered. Hampton House as a whole seemed concerned for her. The stress still showed on Charlotte's face, although her bruises had faded.

His morning was busy, but he stopped by his office between appointments to see Amelie at her desk. He was glad she'd been able to return for a second day after the mysterious investigation with Charlotte ended with her heading to work and Amelie rushing home to nurse an ill toddler.

"Sophia is well, I hope?" he asked, accepting another stack of papers requiring his signature.

"She is." Amelie blew out a relieved breath. "I worried it might be influenza, but she was right as rain by bedtime. I do apologize for my hasty exit. As it happens, I have information for you."

John glanced at his timepiece and muttered a curse under his breath. He had less than thirty minutes to travel across town to meet with his Paris police liaison. He motioned toward his office with his head and took the cup of tea his desk sergeant handed him. He fumbled with the door handle, and Amelie opened it for him.

John dropped the papers on his cluttered desk, looking for a pen. His workspace was ordinarily neat as a pin, so the mess was a testament to the chaos his day had become.

Amelie handed him a pen, and when he fumbled with the cap because he still held his tea in his other hand, she shot him a flat look and removed the cap for him. "You might take a breath," she said.

"I do not have time for a breath," he muttered. Worried he would spill the blasted tea, he handed it to Amelie with a frown. He hastily scrawled his signature on the documents he could read at a glance, setting aside those that would require more time. He gathered the notes he needed for the meeting, and Amelie handed him the late-morning newspaper to read in the carriage.

He nodded his thanks and moved to tuck it under his arm when a headline caught his eye: *Worthingstone Family Foundation to Continue Annual Donation Despite Rumors to the Contrary.*

He scanned the article as he walked but stopped cold at the door. Amelie bumped into him from behind. His blood froze in his veins as he read the piece, which included an interview with Mr. Stanley, the surgeon who did not care for Charlotte.

> Mr. Corbin was unavailable for comment at the time this article went to press, but Mr. Stanley, head surgeon, was quoted as saying, "The Worthingstone family has been integral to the success of Delaney Hospital for decades. Their desire that the institution hold

> the highest standards with doctors and staff has always been a measuring stick, and although a recent, controversial hire fell short of that standard, the matter has been rectified, and the person in question tendered her resignation this morning. Delaney Hospital looks forward to continuing our relationship with the Worthingstone family with gratitude and an eye toward the future.

"What is it?" Amelie moved around to face him, and when he looked up, she must have seen his fury. Her eyes widened as he thrust the paper at her and walked slowly back to his desk, seeing nothing but a red haze.

He knew when she'd reached Stanley's quote by her outraged gasp. "Something must have happened last night. She said nothing about this yesterday. Everything was fine." She sank into the chair opposite his desk and stared at the paper.

John gripped the back of his chair until his knuckles turned white. He wanted to hurl it through the wall. The Worthingstones did not like his and Charlotte's questions, or perhaps just *her*, so they'd threatened to withhold funding unless she resigned.

Amelie placed her hand to her forehead. "She must be devastated. I should go to her." She paused. "If she handed in her resignation this morning, she might still be in Town. I don't know what to do."

"Ruin them," John bit out. "That is what we should do."

Amelie looked over her shoulder and quickly closed his office door. "John, you cannot say such things aloud. Not in your position."

She was right, of course. He felt the same sense of helplessness and anger he saw on her face. "Where would she go? Home? To your Aunt Sally?"

Amelie sighed. "Possibly. I'd have said to me or Eva, but she knew I'd be here this morning, and I've not seen her." She shook her head and then looked at John. "You must go to your appointment. I will telegram Sally at the *Gazette* and see if she's heard from Charlotte."

Thankfully, Amelie was thinking logically, because for the first time in his life, John could not. His logic had fled in the face of his rage. He took a deep breath, flexing his fingers. He was surprised he'd not left grooves in the chair.

"I will see her reinstated at that hospital." John wondered where Charlotte was, frustrated that he wasn't with her.

A sharp knock on the door caused Amelie to jump. She opened it, and the sergeant entered, his face flushed. "There's been a murder, guv, a bad one."

John frowned. "Where?"

"Central London. Their division is on another call." He rattled off an address from a piece of paper.

Amelie stared at the sergeant, mouth going slack. "Isn't that the office of Fairmont Riverboats?"

He nodded. "That's the one. Mr. Fairmont."

John looked at Amelie. "How do you know that?"

"Fairmont Riverboats—that was the ferry where Aunt Katherine died. Charlotte and I visited the owner of the establishment yesterday. With Dirk."

"You did *what*?"

"I haven't had the chance to tell you. Sophia was ill, and then you arrived here now all willy-nilly, and then this . . ." She pointed at the newspaper.

John closed his eyes. "Amelie, what did the man tell you?"

"He remembers the night." She paused. "*Remembered* the night. He also claimed he gave a witness statement to an officer who wrote it down, but it's missing from the file."

A sense of foreboding settled into the room, and John wished more than ever he knew exactly where Charlotte was. "Come with me," he said. "You can tell me everything on the way. Sergeant, send word to Mr. Francois at the Bistro that I will reschedule our luncheon. Locate Detectives Baker and Winston and send them to that address as quickly as possible."

The sergeant nodded. "Where . . . where are they?"

John took a measured breath.

Amelie took the man by the arm and grabbed her coat from her desk. "Look in the appointment book at the main desk. I believe they are conducting interviews today near Piccadilly regarding the missing children case."

Amelie kept stride with John as he left the office, struggling to shove her arms into her coat while trotting alongside him. He belatedly realized he was acting the cad and stopped to help her. Then he took her arm and rushed her down the stairs and out to the carriages.

He told the driver the address, and then followed Amelie into the conveyance. "Why on earth didn't Dirk tell me?"

"You were out late last night, yes?"

"Yes," he admitted. "Not so late that—" He brushed it aside. "Never mind. I want every detail. Dare I hope you wrote it down?"

She reached into her reticule and pulled out a small, black book not unlike the ones his detectives used. He felt the hint of a smile turn the corner of his mouth in spite of himself.

"Shall I read it to you?"

He nodded. "Please." When she finished a very comprehensive

recitation, which included details about the assistant's clothing and Mr. Fairmont's office, he began organizing his thoughts in order of importance. Underlying it all was a sense that something was building. "No more solitary investigations. And bring everything you learn directly to me."

"Of course." She looked troubled. "The poor man. Did we do something that got him killed?"

"It isn't your fault. This may be one thing in a series of events that were bound to happen. When we arrive, stay back from the activity but please make note of anything that seems off or catches your eye."

"I will." She nodded.

Her attention to detail was unmatched, and she'd have made an excellent detective, though in most circles, he'd have been considered a heretic to employ a married woman with two small children. The inequity at Charlotte's situation—the Worthingstones notwithstanding—and the general prohibition against hiring married women for professional work grated the more he thought of it.

He forced himself to unclench his jaw. He'd be facing a blinding headache if he didn't relax. It would be a long day that he'd be best advised to take in stride. "Who is caring for your children today?"

She looked at him in surprise, and he realized that as a friend, he probably ought to pay more attention to her and Michael's lives away from work. "Inez Shelton's niece, Madeline. She's young, but competent and excellent with the girls." She smiled. "Doesn't allow Sophia to run amok."

"If you need to return home, I'll arrange a cab—"

She shook her head. "I made certain all was well before I left, and Madeline knows how to use the telegraph machine to contact me or Michael at the office." She smiled. "This one day a week away does me a world of good, John; it's more a favor to me than you."

He couldn't help but be troubled. "It was only a few years ago that you were caught up in something very messy. You have even more to lose, now. Please, be careful."

"I will." She smiled. "I am not that same naïve girl. The rose-colored glasses slipped a bit."

"Not too much, I hope. The world has enough cynics." He looked out the window as the carriage rocked to a stop. "On that happy note, let us step into a grisly crime scene."

She grinned. "After you."

The building was abuzz with activity. Constables threaded up and down the hallway leading to Fairmont's offices, and as John neared the door, he heard a woman sobbing.

Amelie peeked around him into the room and said, "That is Miss Streatfield. Perhaps she might be more comfortable speaking to a woman."

John motioned to the constable who was trying to question the woman and quickly introduced himself.

"Can't get her to stop crying for two minutes," the exasperated man told John. "Don't have the foggiest idea what she's saying."

John nodded and then turned to the woman. "Miss Streatfield, is it? Mrs. Baker is going to take you to the reception area down the hall for a cup of tea. The police officer will have some more questions for you, but Mrs. Baker will stay by your side. Will that help?"

Miss Streatfield looked at Amelie with wide eyes. "You were here yesterday. He was alive only yesterday!"

Amelie nodded and took the woman by the arm. She

motioned to a teakettle on the sideboard and gestured at the policeman with her head. He stared at her in surprise for a moment, then turned and collected a tea tray. He followed the ladies out of the room with one last dark look at John.

Amelie's impressions on the situation would have to wait; in the meantime, John entered the office adjacent the reception area and took stock.

It was a bloodbath. A few years back, John had overseen a grisly crime scene involving gangs competing over the same territory on the docks. That was the last time he'd witnessed a crime so brutal in its execution.

"Someone brained him, all right," one of the officers in the room told John.

"Did they leave a weapon?"

He shook his head.

"Has someone sent for the coroner?"

"Yes, guv."

"Where is your captain?"

He gestured with his chin. "Down at the docks. A warehouse is on fire."

John frowned. If this murder was connected to Katherine's case, the jurisdiction would likely land on his desk anyway. "I'll command the scene here. I do not want anything touched—you, out!" He twitched his thumb at a constable who, although green about the gills, was creeping behind the desk for a better view. "Sergeant, clear the room. Please question people in these adjoining offices. We'll need witness statements."

"Guv." The man nodded and shooed everyone from the room. He passed Michael and Nathan, who were on their way in.

The two detectives paused at the threshold and stared. Michael shook his head and asked John, "Who is he?"

"A witness to Katherine Duvall's death, twenty years ago."

"Tidy coincidence," Nathan said.

"His father owned the ferry. And after the incident, the family came into an extraordinary amount of money, which they used to build the business. Two decades later, Baker, your wife and her cousin visit this man with questions about the death. He is flustered, clearly prevaricates, and now twenty-four hours later, he lies bludgeoned to death."

"Last night as we were dropping off to sleep, Amelie mentioned questioning a witness with Charlotte." He shook his head. "We'd been worried about Sophia's fever, I didn't even remember until now."

"Is she still in reception with the crying woman?"

Michael nodded. "Has she seen this?" He frowned at the gory scene.

"No, but I daresay she'd handle it with more fortitude than some officers I've trained."

Nathan scratched the back of his neck. "Do you want my wife down here to photograph it?"

"We'll contact the regular, first. If he is unavailable, you'll fetch her and the equipment?"

Nathan nodded. "She'll jump at the chance. Told me last week that her usual sittings are becoming tedious."

John almost smiled. If his father could have heard the conversation, he'd suffer an apoplectic fit. The Notorious Branch of the Hampton family, although no longer consumed with gambling and scandalous escapades, was still pointing off in its own direction. The thought led him back around to Charlotte, and his heart thrummed with increased concern.

He had to find her. There was nothing he could do now about her situation with the hospital, though, and he suspected it was only a matter of time before they'd learn that the fire at the docks had started at the Fairmont Riverboat warehouse. He had a feeling it would be hours before he could go looking for her.

There were several long impressions in blood along the floor, as though something had been dipped in ink and left a stamp. Perhaps a stick? A club? The pattern repeated in an arc next to a heavy boot print near the body.

Frowning, he thought of something Amelie had told him on the carriage ride to the crime scene. "Don't let anyone but the coroner in," he told Michael and Nathan. He retraced his steps to the reception area where Amelie sat with the stunned Miss Streatfield, who had stopped sobbing but dripped a steady stream of tears. He couldn't blame her. The scene was ghastly.

"A word?" he said quietly to Amelie, who left Miss Streatfield to the constable, who had clearly learned he would earn better results with a softer approach.

"What is it?" Amelie whispered.

"You said Fairmont mentioned slipping on a cane in the aftermath of Katherine's accident. When they'd pulled her back onto the boat."

She nodded. "It seemed like an odd detail, but with everyone gathered around, screaming, dropping their drinks and food, it's possible someone might have dropped a walking stick."

"Were they on the main deck?"

She nodded again. "I don't know, but I believe so. That's where he and his father helped the two men get Kat out of the water."

"Did he say anything else about the cane? Perhaps who might have picked it up?"

She shook her head. "Could have belonged to anyone, especially someone dressed up for a special occasion. I imagine

I'd carry my best walking stick if I were the dapper sort." She shrugged. "I suppose you'll want my notes from yesterday's interview with Fairmont?"

"Please."

"Rather a good thing I take initiative, wouldn't you say?" She grimaced. "Unless we led a murderer to his door. Either way, helps to be thorough."

John glanced at her. "Did you tell him you were a deputy? An official of any kind?"

"Of course not. But if it meant encouraging him to talk, I would have." She returned to Miss Streatfield, who was holding out her empty teacup to the constable.

The coroner arrived, and John pointed him down the corridor. He stepped outside to the increased gathering of onlookers and policemen, noticing for the first time the smoke billowing in the distance. Paramount in his thoughts was the recurring question: Where on earth was Charlotte?

CHAPTER 26

Charlotte had decided that after turning in her resignation letter and leaving the hospital she would go to Sally at the *Gazette*. Sally would provide the right amount of sympathy, enough that Charlotte would feel heard. Sally wasn't in, so she and Dirk took a cab to a café for an indulgent treat of meringues and hot tea. Charlotte sat by the window where she could watch passersby and wonder how long she should wallow in her sad thoughts. She would need to meet with John to speak with him about the current state of her career, and now that she felt a little less tired and teary, she was more than ready to see him.

She knew John would be angry on her behalf, and she didn't want to have to defend her decision to resign rather than fight. The hospital simply couldn't afford to function without the money, and that was more important than her new career. She would work something out.

Overall, she was angry. Angry at the injustice of the system, angry at individuals who could control a person's future on a whim, angry that her mother wasn't alive to lend a listening ear. She wanted to put together a plan, a list of steps she could take to pull everything back under her own control.

Shortly before noon, she and Dirk stepped outside the café

into a light drizzle. Dirk popped open an umbrella, scanning the street. He frowned.

"What is it?" she asked.

He took her elbow and began walking down the row of shops. "We'll catch that omnibus up ahead. This traffic is keeping it slow."

She caught her reflection in storefront windows as they walked, and only after they'd gone a fair distance did she realize a man was following them. Light complexion, brown hair, nearly six feet tall.

She stumbled as they walked, and Dirk held her up. "Keep going, and do not turn around. I take it you have seen him before?"

"Yes." She swallowed, forcing away her memories of having been attacked in an alleyway. It was different this time; Dirk was with her. "How would you handle this if you were alone?"

"Plant my fist in his face and drag him to the nearest police station."

"Would it help if I run ahead? I can catch the bus, and—"

He shook his head, quickening their pace. "If we separate, he'll go after you, not me."

"While he's doing that, you can—"

The streets were busy, and amidst the traffic, which was growing heavier by the minute, she heard people calling out and pointing.

When she looked behind her, she saw not only the same man, who blended into the crowd between them, but smoke rising in the distance. Something at the docks was on fire. Frowning, she turned around as Dirk urged her on, trying to find an open path despite the increasing traffic of pedestrians and vehicles alike.

"Almost there," Dirk said, as a loud *pop* filled the air. He grunted and stumbled, dropping to one knee.

Charlotte stared at him, first in confusion and then in horror as she spied red spreading against his light-colored waistcoat. She cried out and struggled to right him, throwing her arms under his, attempting to help him stand. Looking over Dirk's shoulder, Charlotte saw their pursuer pocket something and begin elbowing his way through the crowd toward them.

It wasn't much work for him, as by now people had screamed and scattered, which only spooked the horses in the street and added to the melee.

"Go!" Dirk yelled as he braced himself against her, trying to stand. He gained his feet and shoved her toward the omnibus. "I'll stop him. Go find John!"

"Dirk!" she cried out. "We must get you to the hospital!" She reached for his side where the blood continued to spread.

He shoved her hard and spun around to step in front of the man who was gaining steadily on them.

She reluctantly turned and ran toward the bus. She looked back to see their attacker hitting Dirk in the ribs. The big Scot hit the man hard in the jaw, and Charlotte thought the stranger might go down, but another punch to Dirk's midsection dropped him to one knee.

He is going to die, and it is my fault. Everything is my fault!

She told herself to stop the useless litany running through her brain. She fought the urge to run back to help Dirk and instead picked up her pace, closing in on the bus. She grabbed the railing along the back stairs and swung up onto the bottom step. The driver shouted for her to pay the fare, and she nodded, even as she climbed up a step. If she could just get to John, he would send the cavalry, and she could examine Dirk's injuries. Delaney was the closest hospital—as long as she kept Stanley's hands out of the wound, Dirk would have a chance.

She heard footsteps running behind them, and to her frustration, the omnibus slowed in traffic. Shouts rang in the air, mingling with the clop of horses' hooves and creaking wagon wheels. Over her shoulder, she spied her follower closing the distance and was relieved when the omnibus began moving again.

She didn't want to climb to the top of the vehicle—it was the purview of men, mostly because it was cumbersome to climb up and down in women's clothing—but she reassessed her decision when her follower lunged for the railing and pulled himself up behind her.

"Leave me alone!" Charlotte scrambled up two steps but stopped short when the man stepped on her skirt. His impassive expression was somehow more worrisome than a leer. He climbed the steps between them but kept a hand on her dress, preventing her from climbing to the top.

"Why are you doing this?" she asked him through clenched teeth, tugging at her skirt. Four gentlemen seated atop the conveyance turned their attention to her in confusion.

"Thought you understood your instructions the last time we met. You and your people have been putting your noses where they don't belong."

Her heart pounded. "What is that supposed to mean?" Surely he wouldn't accost her further in full view of the busy city street.

"It's a message, Dr. Duvall."

"From whom?"

"My employer."

She tried to tug her skirt free, but he remained firm. "Who is your employer? Blast it all, stop speaking in riddles!"

"Is anything amiss?" One of the gentlemen moved to the end of the bench.

The American pulled her attention back to him with a tight

grip on her arm. "Should've returned to New York when you had the chance." He moved so quickly that she didn't see it coming. He grabbed her shoulders and turned, lifting her and hurling her down the back of the vehicle. She hit the ground on her shoulder, her skirt caught in the bottom steps. The omnibus dragged her several feet before the other passengers screamed at the driver to rein in the horse.

Charlotte's shoulder burned with stabbing pain, and her vision blurred as her attacker leapt from his perch on the stairs to the street, and, despite several shouts and pointing fingers, disappeared into the crowd. One man scrambled down from the top of the vehicle and gave chase, while two others quickly followed to free Charlotte's dress from the wheel.

"Are you well, miss?"

"Where d'ya live?"

"She needs a hospital!"

Voices came at her from all sides as she tried to stand, leaning heavily on a gentleman who braced under her arm. Another man placed an arm under her injured shoulder, and she cried out in agony. She knew without looking that it had popped out of its socket and would have to be shoved back into place. She'd helped perform the procedure on a boy who had fallen out of a tree in Pennsylvania.

"Come, love," a woman said, "let's get you a cab." She stepped aside and looked down the street. At the insistent yelling coming from those stopped in traffic, she hollered back, "Get us a cab, then!"

"My friend," Charlotte told the woman. "My friend was shot!" She pointed to the crowd gathered in the middle of the street where she'd seen Dirk fall.

The yelling continued as Charlotte's vision dimmed against the blinding pain.

"Here, love," the woman said and motioned to the gentleman holding her uninjured arm. They walked her back to a cab already occupied by a woman holding a small child.

The passenger moved aside to make room for Charlotte. As she climbed inside, she gasped, "Please, please get my friend!"

Her helper shouted out to others in the crowd, and she dimly registered the driver protesting that he wasn't an ambulance as an unconscious Dirk was lifted up into the small cab.

"Take them to Delaney, straightaway," the woman told the driver. "Unless you want him dying in yer cab." The woman clasped Charlotte's hand. "It's just around the corner, love, and they'll help. Good people there—took my Tommy last week with a broken arm."

Charlotte squeezed the woman's hand, tears falling freely. "Thank you," she managed, and the driver clicked at the horse, maneuvering to the side before taking a street off to the right.

She knelt on the floor between the seats and shoved against Dirk's weight with her good shoulder to take stock of his wound. Her head buzzed, and she was nauseated with the pain of her dislocated shoulder.

The woman handed Charlotte a scarf, which she shoved against Dirk's side. He groaned softly, and she nearly cried with relief that he was still alive.

"Almost there," she told him.

The cab came to a stop, and Charlotte fumbled with her reticule, which dangled awkwardly from her wrist. She managed a coin for the driver and shoved three into the other passenger's hand before calling out to a hospital orderly standing at Delaney's receiving door. She recognized the young man, and when he saw her face, his eyes opened wide.

"Dr. Duvall!" He yelled for help, and two other orderlies maneuvered Dirk from the cab, got him to a stretcher, and carried him inside.

"He needs Dr. Corbin," she told the young man, clutching his arm. She bit her lip hard as her shoulder was jostled. "Or Mr. Leatham. Do you understand me? If Mr. Stanley goes anywhere near him, come and find me. Will you do that?"

He nodded and swallowed, running to catch up with the stretcher as they carried Dirk down the hall.

Charlotte's energy was spent, and she leaned against the receiving room wall. Her clothing was filthy, her hair disheveled, and she feared she was developing a limp from having been dragged along the road.

A nurse caught sight of her, and her jaw dropped. "Dr. Duvall?"

"Hello, Sister Thelma," Charlotte mumbled. She tried to smile, but it quickly turned into a grimace. Pain and terror battled within her, and she felt like laughing and crying at the same time. She didn't think their attacker would return, but she didn't know. Everyone in his path was in danger.

"Come, Doctor. Exam room one," the nurse called out. "Dr. Stevenson?"

"Dr. Stevenson," Charlotte murmured. "Good. I like him."

Sister Thelma nodded and guided Charlotte into the room and onto the examining table, taking stock of Charlotte's injuries. She tried to remove the coat, but at Charlotte's gasp, left it in place. Instead, she retrieved a basin and cloth and began cleaning the smudges on Charlotte's face and hand. The scrapes stung, and when Sister Thelma touched the cloth to a spot above Charlotte's eyebrow, she pulled back.

She managed a smile for the nurse and said, "Apologies."

Sister Thelma chuckled. She was a practical girl in her early twenties, and Charlotte had gotten on well with her. "It looks rather awful," she said. "The doctor will say, of course, but I do not believe it will require stitching."

The door burst open, and Matron Halcomb rushed in, her face a mask of shock. "Charlotte!"

She was followed by Dr. Stevenson. The middle-aged doctor had been among those who had first wondered about Charlotte's abilities, but he had come to respect her as a colleague. "What has happened?" His face was grim as he took in her appearance.

"My shoulder," she said, tilting her head to the left. "I was thrown from an omnibus."

"You were . . . *thrown*?" Matron Halcomb took the basin and cloth from Sister Theresa and continued the cleaning herself.

"It's become dislocated. You'll have to set it," Charlotte gritted through her teeth to Dr. Stevenson.

He reached inside her jacket and gently probed the area. Charlotte braced herself for the coming pain. She was turning to ask Sister Theresa for something to bite on when Dr. Stevenson took her shoulder between his hands and wrenched it hard back into place.

Charlotte's scream dissolved into a coughing fit of sobs, and she cried until her vision went dark for lack of breath. Matron Halcomb held Charlotte's face in her hands, her eyes filled with worry, and Charlotte dimly registered Dr. Stevenson instructing Sister Theresa to fetch him a glass of water.

He gently put the glass into Charlotte's right hand and patted her knee as she gulped in a huge breath of air. She rested her forehead on the matron's shoulder.

"Apologies, doctor," she whispered between sobs. "I thought to be brave." She lifted her head, tears still streaming against all self-recrimination she could muster.

"Sip the water," he instructed her, wiping his hands on a cloth and giving her a small smile. "Surely you must have suspected that was coming."

Charlotte sipped the water, coughed, and then drank again. She gasped out a sigh and glared at her former colleague. "I did not suspect it, thank you, sir."

He chuckled quietly and examined both the cut above her eye and her scraped hands. When the matron pulled aside Charlotte's skirt to reveal her leg, he prodded gently at a darkening bruise on the outside of her knee.

"You should stay off this leg for a time," he said. "Ice will help. As for your shoulder, we'll place it in a splint you'll wear for a week."

He paused, frowning, and then as a precaution she'd have taken herself, he listened to her heart and lungs through his stethoscope. He nodded to himself, and then folded his arms, leaning back against the counter. "You seem to be attacked on a regular basis. Who threw you from a moving omnibus?"

Charlotte blew a quiet breath between pursed lips and tried to gather her thoughts. "I was being followed by someone I don't know." She described the man and added, "I do believe I know at whose behest he acted, though."

The matron withdrew pins from Charlotte's hair and deftly braided it into an orderly plait.

She thought of Dirk and felt sick again. "My friend, my shadow here these last weeks—he was shot and is being taken to the surgical theatre." She clasped the matron's hand. "Please do not let Stanley operate or administer anesthesia. I can do it myself if there's nobody else available."

The matron nodded grimly. "I'll get Dr. Corbin."

"We should call the Met," Dr. Stevenson said.

"As it happens, I was on my way there when I was attacked. When I leave, I'll go there and give them a report." She sniffed and winced as she reached for a handkerchief with her aching left arm.

Matron Halcomb handed her one and then studied her face. "Do you give your word you will report it?"

Charlotte nodded. "Immediately."

"Do you require official signatures?" Dr. Stevenson asked.

"If I need them, I'll return."

They studied her for another moment, and Dr. Stevenson said, "Sister Theresa, give us a moment, please."

The nurse left, and Charlotte tensed. She'd hoped to avoid speaking with any of her colleagues regarding her resignation.

"Perhaps you'll consider returning as a physician," Dr. Stevenson said. "Your departure was rather abrupt, and you offered no explanations to any of us."

The matron watched her quietly. A flicker of something crossed her face—hurt? Disappointment?

Charlotte nodded. "I . . . I am . . ." She cleared her throat. "There are stipulations tied to the future success of the hospital that require my, erm, absence."

They both frowned, and Dr. Stevenson said, "What the devil does that mean?"

Matron Halcomb's eyes widened. "You—" Her mouth dropped open, and she shut it again. "Charlotte Duvall, are you suggesting the funding—"

Charlotte held up her hand. "I plan to seek avenues of redress, but not until the fundraising gala is over and the budget for the coming year is in place."

Dr. Stevenson shook his head. "What sort of enemies do you have, Doctor?"

"Wealthy ones," she muttered and sniffed again, trying to laugh.

"This isn't right," the matron said. Her face was red and angry.

"Give me some time," Charlotte said. "It was a temporary solution, and I'm hoping to broker a more amiable, permanent one. Please do not speak of it to anyone else. Not yet."

Dr. Stevenson nodded reluctantly. "Return straightaway if you experience further injury or pain. Send for me if you cannot come here yourself."

She nodded. "Thank you, Doctor."

He patted her hand and offered a partial smile. He pointed to her shoulder. "Apologies about that bit of trickery."

"I do not think you're sincere in the least," Charlotte grumbled.

"Of course, I am. I'll check in on Mr. Dirk." He winked at her and left the room.

Matron Halcomb sighed, but rather than defend herself again, Charlotte gingerly stretched her leg to the floor. The matron eased her down, and to Charlotte's relief, she was able to stand and walk, although the knee bothered her when she put her full weight on it.

"Where are you going now?" the matron asked.

"Upstairs, to be sure Dirk is well. Then I have someone to see at the Yard."

Chapter 27

It was nearly dark by the time John was able to return to the Yard. He was exhausted and worried about Charlotte. He hadn't heard anything from her all day, and he'd even had Michael telegraph Sally's *Gazette* to see if she'd stopped in. He told himself he was behaving like an old grandmother. Charlotte was probably at home. She would either visit him soon or send word that she'd sacrificed herself to the Worthingstones. He'd only learned of her resignation that morning, but it felt like days.

He climbed the steps as the day shift was changing over to night, listening with only half an ear to the conversations flowing around him.

"Sir?" The sergeant at the main desk caught his attention. He stepped to John's side and said in an undertone, "There's a woman waiting to see you. She's been in some trouble, but rather than report it to anyone, she wanted to wait for you. I told her I didn't know if you'd even be back today, but—"

"Thank you, sergeant, I'll handle it." He nearly ran to his office.

Charlotte was seated in a chair by Amelie's vacant desk, and she looked as though she'd been involved in a brawl.

"Charlotte?" he whispered, his heart in his throat. "What on *earth* . . ."

She stood when she saw him but slipped as if her knee had

given out. She didn't fall but shoved herself upright by pressing her hand against the desk. Her left arm was in a sling, and she bore a deep gash above her eyebrow. Further scrapes alongside her jaw and neck became visible as he drew closer. Her hair was in a loose braid that hung over her shoulder and whisps framed her face.

"John," she said, lifting her chin, "I have an official report to file."

"Again?" His heart thudded. "Where is Dirk?"

"He was shot." Her smile was wobbly. "But he's recovering, now. I made sure he had a good surgeon."

His relief at the news was short-lived as the sight of her hurt again nearly dropped him to his knees. "Did you see the assailant?" He put his arm carefully under her right one and ushered her into his office. He pulled out a chair for her.

She sank into it with a muted grunt and a wince. He called out to the night desk sergeant to bring a tea tray and then closed the door, moving his chair close to hers. He took her right hand in both of his and repeated, "What happened? Exactly."

"Dirk was shot, but he is recovering at Delaney." She swallowed, and her voice trembled. "I was afraid he was dead. I didn't know how I was going to tell you." She took a breath. "A nurse, Maggie Petersen, is sitting with him. She promised me she'll be his protector through the night."

She sighed and looked at him, and her chin trembled. She was pale, causing the scrapes and bruises to show in starker relief. She began explaining what he'd already guessed, that the machinations of the Worthingstones forced her resignation, and then ended with the cab ride that had brought her to his office.

He shook his head. "They will pay for this." He had not thought any anger would have topped what he'd already felt that morning.

"We do not know if the man who attacked me was working for the Worthingstones."

A knock on the door interrupted them, and John retrieved the tea tray from the sergeant. He poured her a cup and added a splash of milk with two sugars. She smiled at him, but it was a shadow of her usual spark. Her eyes were glassy, and she occasionally squinted at the light. He turned down the sconce, fretting about another head wound mere weeks after she had healed from the first one.

He rubbed his eyes. "I cannot believe he threw you from a moving omnibus." He put his hands on his hips and looked at her arm in the sling. "At least it's not the right side again."

"Small favors." She took a sip of her tea and closed her eyes.

"I do not know who it would be, if not the Worthingstones," he said.

"They have already exacted their revenge," she said. "I resigned from Delaney. They knew it was a feat for me to have secured employment in Town, and she made certain it was finished."

The corner of her mouth was raw and scraped, and she touched her tongue to it with a wince. He took her teacup when she finished, feeling completely useless and unable to comfort her without causing additional pain.

She frowned at him, then, and looked at him carefully. "Where have you been? You're looking rather rumpled too."

He didn't want to tell her, but he knew she'd hear it eventually. Probably from one of her cousins as Eva had eventually been brought in to photograph the murder scene before the coroner took the body away. "Mr. Fairmont was bludgeoned to death in his office."

Her mouth slackened, and her eyes opened wide. "That poor

man!" She shook her head. "What did we do? What if we led the killer right to his door?"

"It might have no connection to you," he ventured.

"Of course it does," she scoffed and put her hand to her eyes. "This just gets progressively worse."

"Miss Streatfield confirmed that her employer kept good amounts of cash in the office."

"Was it taken?"

He sighed. "No, it wasn't."

"Robbery, not the cause." She paused. "If the American followed us yesterday, his 'employer' would wonder what Fairmont told us. Perhaps he questioned Fairmont and then silenced him permanently."

John nodded.

"I might assume that if I stop speaking about my mother, cease any questions about that night, that this harassment will end. No new evidence has come to light that would warrant keeping the case open." She sighed. "It is finished."

John shook his head. "It is only beginning. The Fairmont murder will tie to Katherine's death. If they thought to keep it buried, they've gone about it the wrong way."

She nodded and swallowed. She rested her right arm against his desk and put her fingers under her chin, facing away from him and clearly trying to avoid looking at him.

He let the silence sit until a tear rolled down her cheek, breaking his heart. He pulled his chair closer. "Charlotte," he murmured, placing his hand on her knee and hoping belatedly it was the uninjured one. "My love, look at me."

He hoped the term of endearment would pull her attention away from the nothing she was staring at, and he was correct. She looked at him with big eyes, her tears continuing to fall.

"I have cried multiple times now in your presence, and I have cried today in the presence of total strangers and a former esteemed colleague." She shook her head and wiped her eyes. "This is not me, John. This is not my life. As difficult as things were in school, I did not fall apart and become this puddly mess."

"You came home to the death of your father, you learned that your mother's death was not a simple accident, you looked at autopsy photos of your late mother, and today you were thrown from a moving vehicle and dragged along the street. Then, a doctor who was a colleague as of yesterday, caused you an intense amount of physical pain." He paused. "To his credit, he had no choice in the matter. But you take my meaning. I do not know anyone who wouldn't have shed a tear or two given such circumstances."

She didn't nod or smile or react in any way.

"You are strong."

A muscle worked in her jaw, and she winced. "I thought I was."

He suspected that was the root of her distress. He took her face carefully in his hands. "I love you. You are among the most headstrong, stubborn, hardworking, fearless, fascinating, and intelligent people I have ever met in my life. Everything that has occurred since your return home has only reinforced my opinion of you." He brushed his thumb carefully across her cheek. "And I've learned a few additional things about you that I find most intriguing."

She rolled her eyes, and he dropped his hands as she retrieved a handkerchief from her sleeve. "Additional things," she mocked quietly. "Things such as 'cries at the drop of a hat.'"

"Additional things such as 'responds ardently to a kiss in the dark.' And 'drives John to distraction with a single glance.'"

She smiled, probably in spite of herself, and shook her head at him. "Incorrigible."

"Absolutely."

"I love you too," she whispered. "So very much."

His heart pounded. *Finally.* "I'm relieved to hear it. I'll not propose yet as it would probably send you running for the hills."

She chuckled and then put a hand to the cut near her mouth. "Perhaps I will do the proposing. I am a Woman of Independent Means." She winced. "Or rather, I was."

"We'll find another position for you, if not reinstatement at Delaney." He shook his head. "This will not stand."

"I've a plan. Something I've been mulling over since this morning. I'll share details when they're more solidified in my head." She sighed. "I am tired."

"I am not surprised. Come, let's go home. I plan to tell Sally tomorrow that I'll be a Hampton House resident until you propose to me and we move out together."

She opened her mouth and he quickly said, "No rush. I'm a patient man."

"Mrs. Burnette will be scandalized anew. The gentlemen's rooms are on the *second* floor, you know."

"A little scandal is good for the most hardened among us." He wondered if he kept up a steady stream of words they might both relax. "Hampton House has a soft spot in my heart. Do you remember the night we met? Sammy was missing, and we searched the house top to bottom."

"Quite the memory you have, Director." She took his arm, and he walked with her slowly out the door and into the great room.

"Never forget a detail," he said, relieved to hear humor returning to her tone. He hoped she would maintain it, because his had all but fled. He'd managed to bank his anger, but a day of reckoning was on the horizon. Heaven help the Friends when he was finished.

CHAPTER 28

Charlotte, despite being as exhausted as she was, did not immediately fall asleep. Her thoughts turned continually to her mother.

She eventually rose and turned up the lamps, making her way down to the pantry and clumsily climbing the stepladder to retrieve her mother's diary and letters. She returned to her room, sat on her bed, and reviewed everything again. She read each letter, some twice, but since she did not know the men well, she was hard-pressed to put a name to the ones he'd written as a young man.

She read Katherine's journal, touching her finger to the places where she'd written about her love for her new daughter, about the hopes she had for her. She had written about her love for David's sons, which rekindled Charlotte's anger at Thomas. There were postcards from Sally, who had begun her adventuring by the time Charlotte was born; Katherine had been so proud of her baby sister.

Charlotte looked again at the letters, willing them to give up the man's identity. James Carter had told John that Katherine's soft spot had been reserved for Finebough, but Charlotte wasn't certain Carter's judgment was sound. He had propositioned Mrs. Winston, after all, which spoke to his recklessness or stupidity.

He had been, however, the only person who spoke kindly of her mother that night at the Winston supper. Phillipa Carter, also, seemed kindly.

She turned again to her mother's journal entry about the planned trip to Town in celebration of the Carters' engagement. Katherine had made a list of items to pack, down to the stockings and jewelry she planned to wear. Charlotte could almost see the ensemble, and it made her smile, though it was bittersweet.

She mixed a headache powder packet in a glass of water and drank it, hoping to dull the pain without needing to take laudanum. It was as she settled into sleep that an idea formed, and she decided that if it was a sound one, she'd remember it in the morning.

When morning dawned, she realized the idea had merit. She struggled into a dressing gown and padded next door to John's room. She heard him moving around, so didn't feel too bad about interrupting his routine.

He opened the door at her knock and looked mildly panicked. "What is it?"

"Nothing, silly. I have an idea, and I wonder if it's feasible."

He eyed her with some suspicion as he fumbled with his cravat. She was of no use with one arm in a sling, but she hated watching him struggle. "Do you always have this much trouble getting dressed for the day?"

"Until recently, I had Mason, who is worth his weight in gold."

"Perhaps we can offer him a room on the gentlemen's floor."

He eyed her flatly. "What is your idea that may or may not have feasibility?"

"I propose a party that pays tribute to a bygone age."

"Ancient Egypt?" He muttered a curse and untied the cravat, stalking back through his quarters and into the dressing room.

Charlotte followed and sat on the tufted bench at the foot of his bed. "Not Ancient Egypt."

He reappeared, still looking flummoxed and disheveled. He was without jacket and waistcoat, his cuff links still lay on the vanity, and his cravat was draped around his shoulders, untied and forlorn. "If not Ancient Egypt, then what?"

She wrinkled her brow, belatedly realizing it was still sore. "The only bygone era that comes to your mind is Ancient Egypt?"

He closed his eyes and leaned against the doorframe. "Charlotte—"

She took pity on him. "I should like to host a party dedicated to the 1860s."

He looked at her blankly. "That was only twenty years ago."

"Exactly."

Charlotte's relief was immense when she approached Dirk in one of Delaney's recovery wards to see that he was awake and alert. His mouth tipped in a half smile as she sat at the edge of his bed, John standing close.

"You look like I feel," he told Charlotte.

"Quite the pair, aren't we?" She grasped his hand and gave a little squeeze. "I am so glad you are well."

"This is nothing."

"Thank you."

He nodded. "Of course. I'm sorry I wasn't able to stop him from hurting you."

She smiled. "You slowed him down." She glanced at the notes

over his headboard. "You've been free of fever since the surgery? That's good news. We may skirt infection."

"I'm ready to leave."

John chuckled. "Another couple days, perhaps." He sobered. "I'd like to assign a constable to keep an eye on things here, although I'm sure you don't find it necessary."

"You'd be correct."

"Indulge me."

"Will you convalesce at Hampton House?" Charlotte asked. "That way we can all keep an eye on each other."

"I would like to see the job finished," Dirk said.

John nodded. "I was hoping you'd say that. I could still use your insight."

By the time they left, Charlotte had elicited a promise from Dirk that he would drink his tea and not complain about the limited menu offered at the hospital.

"I've made an appointment with the sisters Van Horne," Charlotte told John as they exited the hospital. "Eva will join me, along with Constable Gundersen, who has been part of her security team."

"I'd be happier if you just stayed at home," he muttered.

"The meeting is part of a plan to bring this mess to a close. Trust me."

"I trust *you* implicitly."

"When I am finished, I'll go straight home. I promised to teach one of the constables how to play pinochle."

He sighed as he helped her into the carriage. He gave the driver the Van Hornes' address, though he needn't have bothered—the whole Town knew where the sisters lived. He sat next to Charlotte and took her hand, threading their fingers together.

There was still unfinished business between them. They had

flirted around the topic of marriage, and she thought she knew what he wanted, but tossing that conversation into the mix was too much to work through, so she set it aside. She wouldn't have the luxury of sorting it until her mother's death had been brought fully into the light. Only then could she entertain the ideas stewing about her own life, her career, and her relationships.

She rested her head against John's shoulder. Was it enough to just exist as they were? To remain in this place where they weren't forced to admit defeat, where neither of them were compelled to sacrifice dreams or familial obligations? As much as Charlotte hated not having a plan to follow, she wished they could freeze the moment. Live in a place outside time or space.

The carriage rocked to a stop at one of London's most unique residences. Charlotte opened her eyes and saw Eva standing on the wide porch with Constable Gundersen. Her cousin waved.

She stretched up for a goodbye kiss, and John obliged, but seemed reluctant.

"Please, *please* be vigilant."

"I'll meet you at home shortly." She liked the way the phrase sounded. "We are one step closer to finishing this thing."

"Give my best to the sisters Van Horne." He walked her to the porch and reluctantly left her with Eva and the constable.

Eva smiled broadly at Charlotte. "This will be wonderfully fun." She knocked on the door, the sound echoing loudly along the porch.

The door opened to a very nattily dressed young butler. "Yes?"

"Good day," Eva said. "Are the Misses Van Horne in residence? We've made arrangements to meet with them."

"May I ask who is calling and the purpose of your visit?"

"We are two of the Notorious Hamptons and have a proposition for them." Eva smiled.

The butler paused, then opened the door wider. "Please wait here in the foyer. I'll ask if they will see you."

Charlotte was making use of a cane a visitor had long ago left in the foyer at Hampton House. Using it made for awkward maneuvering, but it was better than falling over when her knee twisted just the right way. Now, she leaned on it and looked at their surroundings. The foyer held a large sarcophagus that brought to mind vivid memories.

"This is where it all began," Eva murmured. "My first crime scene photos."

Charlotte chuckled. "The first time we met Nathan, and Amelie became Michael's unofficial scribe."

The butler reappeared, and they followed him into the Van Horne sisters' palatial drawing room, which was identical in décor to Shepheard's Hotel in Cairo. Charlotte inwardly laughed, thinking John might get his Ancient Egypt wish after all.

Margaret and Ethel Van Horne were seated near the hearth, which was guarded on either side by huge palms and statues of Anubis.

"Ladies!" Margaret said and pointed to two empty chairs. "Ooh, and a gentleman! It is always an honor to host a Notorious Hampton. Two at once is a boon!"

Constable Gundersen, clearly visiting the home—and the sisters—for the first time, took up his post near the hearth and examined the room with wide eyes.

Ethel smiled and said, "Too true!" But her smile faded as she looked at Charlotte. She gestured around her face in reference to Charlotte's fresh bumps and bruises and said, "Oh, my dear girl, I do hope that happened in Pamplona."

"Ma'am?"

Margaret nodded sagely. "Oh, yes. You had very much that look about you the year we ran with the bulls, Ethel."

Eva nodded and tried to match their sincerity. "I have heard tales," she said. "Regrettably, neither of us have had the pleasure of such an adventure."

"Ah, well." Ethel waved her hand in dismissal. "There will always be another opportunity."

"To what do we owe the pleasure of your visit?" Margaret smiled at the cousins as Ethel directed the handsome young butler to bring tea.

"We have a proposition," Charlotte began, "but please do not feel obliged if it does not meet with your schedule or inclination."

She gestured to Eva, the polished spokeswoman, to continue. Eva looked briefly startled but gamely picked up the baton. "Our proposal requires a bit of background," she began. She took the sisters back to Katherine's death, which they remembered, up to the present day, including Charlotte's current state of cuts and bruises. Her recitation took nearly twenty full minutes, and the elderly women's attention remained rapt.

"Our aim," Charlotte said, "is to draw out the perpetrators. It is only supposition, but it is my opinion from observing the Friends at the Winston supper that at least one of them may become rattled enough by such memories to crack, if you will. We're also aware that this may take some time to arrange and will be of assistance in any way you require."

Ethel rubbed her hands together and Margaret chortled. "Absolutely, we will host. What do you have in mind?"

CHAPTER 29

Nearly a month had passed since the warehouse fire and Mr. Fairmont's murder. In that time, John had worked tirelessly to hunt down every lead, and his efforts had yielded some results. Witness testimony of a man fleeing the scene—a man who matched Charlotte's description of her attacker—had led him to a tavern, which turned up a tip from a newsman on Fleet Street, which directed him to a nondescript building with decent housing.

John stationed detectives at the location, and the American, who gave his name as "Mr. Brown," was finally spotted returning home one evening. He was arrested for the assault and attempted murder of Charlotte Duvall and Mr. Dirk. In addition to Charlotte's testimony, several omnibus eyewitnesses to the assault also identified the man.

Yet the man refused to give up the name of his employer. He wouldn't admit to killing Mr. Fairmont, although an incriminating boot print matched a pair found in his flat, complete with spots of blood on the sole. Short of having the man beaten, a tried-and-true method but one that sometimes caused a case to fall apart at trial, John wasn't sure they'd have enough for a conviction. When Mr. Brown hired a very good solicitor, John could only assume the "employer" had secured the pairing.

One morning, Michael arrived with the surprising news that the solicitor indicated his client may be willing to negotiate. Also surprising, but perhaps not, was the news that arrived that evening: Mr. Brown had been killed in his cell, with no known culprit. Disgruntled guards? Fellow inmates? Nobody seemed to know, and John fumed, knowing money had crossed the right hands.

The solicitor, oddly enough, immediately took an extended leave to the Continent.

Now the night of Charlotte's Bygone Era party had arrived, and John stood before the mirror in his Hampton House dressing room, successfully tying his cravat with a sense of pride but chafing at the fact that his key witness had been killed in his jail cell.

The doorbell sounded downstairs, and he heard muted voices, footsteps on the stairs, and then a knock at his door. He opened it to see Mrs. Burnette, looking slightly perturbed. "A letter for you, Director."

"Thank you, good lady."

"You and Miss Duvall are going out this evening?"

"We are."

"Is she ready to go?"

He smiled. "I wouldn't know. I do not enter her bedchamber for any reason. I wait for her to knock at my door and then retreat a safe distance after I open it."

He thought he might have detected the hint of a smile, but the woman hid it well with a sniff as she turned away. "I do hope you'll take every precaution. Danger follows the Hampton girls when the Metropolitan Police invade."

"Thank you, Mrs. Burnette." He looked at the letter and his heart skipped a beat at the return address. He opened it and read the words, written in a firm hand, by Sergeant Dane, formerly of

Thames Division and the officer who took the incident report for Katherine's death. After the accident, Dane had moved to France to be married and had stayed there with his wife's family. He'd been extraordinarily hard to track down, a fact that may have kept him safe from Charlotte's enemies.

Sergeant Dane's letter was cordial and professional. It stated that he did indeed remember the night in question, the circumstances, and the testimony of the witnesses he had personally questioned. One of those had been the younger Mr. Fairmont, who was understandably shaken. The reason Dane recalled the testimony in particular was because it had brought several questions to mind. Fairmont told Dane that after Mrs. Duvall had gone into the water, he'd heard arguing, screaming, and chaos.

Several people had run up the stairs to the deck, and he'd followed. A couple were pointing overboard at a body in the water, and Fairmont was nearly trampled in the ruckus. It was during the melee that he'd slipped and fallen on a gentleman's cane, which was rolling on the deck. When he put his hand down to stand up, he pushed against it and came away with blood on his fingers. It was then he noted a small puddle of it in the middle of the deck.

He was nearly stepped on, then, and when he stood, someone had picked up the cane and disappeared with it. He did not see who dropped it or who picked it up.

John sat down in the common area, unable to believe what he was reading. Blood in the middle of the deck meant that Katherine hadn't hit her head on the railing or on her way into the water. And blood on the head of a cane matched what Dr. Neville had noted in his autopsy records.

"Blunt impact, cracked skull," John murmured to himself,

remembering their conversation at the morgue. "A deep, circular wound."

Dane also expressed surprise that the young man's witness statement had gone missing from the file. He closed his letter by saying he was willing to testify to the contents of the lost report at a future date, if the need arose.

John held the paper in his hand, feeling that it might as well have been gold. It was invaluable, and while Fairmont was no longer alive to testify—indeed, he had likely been murdered because of what he knew—the investigation suddenly had new life.

Charlotte's door opened, and John's breath caught in his throat. She'd followed the notes in her mother's journal exactly in preparation for the soiree at the Van Horne mansion, and while the dress was two decades out of style, it looked brand-new. Instead of a streamlined skirt with noticeable bustle at the small of the back, the skirt was wide, as were the sleeves with dropped shoulder seams. Jewels sparkled at Charlotte's wrists, throat, and ears, and her glorious auburn hair was elegantly done by Sarah, parted down the middle and secured at the back of her head as opposed to the curls piled high on her crown as she usually wore. The maid hovered anxiously behind Charlotte, apparently awaiting approval.

"Stunning," he breathed, and both Charlotte and Sarah smiled.

"Excellent," Charlotte said and patted Sarah's hand. "Thank you, as always, dear."

As Sarah left, Charlotte made her way to John, who still sat bemused in the common area. "We do plan to be fashionably late, of course, but you look unsettled. Are you ready to go?"

"Sit down."

She did but frowned. She took the letter he handed to her

and read it, eyes widening. She put her fingertips to her lips. "John!"

He nodded. "I have an idea, but we'll need to drop it carefully tonight into conversation. We must keep Sergeant Dane's name out of it."

She nodded. "Absolutely." She grimaced. "Poor Fairmont."

"Proves what we suspected. Someone paid his father large sums of money to keep his son from repeating his testimony."

John thought about Fairmont and Dane as he and Charlotte rode in his carriage to the Van Horne residence. A mostly healed Dirk had already left for the party with an additional contingent of seven constables dressed in undercover clothing twenty years out of date.

Charlotte fidgeted in the seat next to him, and he reached for her hand.

"Are you all right?" Her wounds had healed, but he knew she still occasionally felt a twinge of pain.

She shook her head. "What if some of the Friends do not attend? This will be for naught."

"Can you imagine anyone who is *anyone* in London not attending a Van Horne event?"

"No, but perhaps we've been too obvious. A party celebrating the 1860s? It feels rather transparent."

"Perhaps, but the invitation came from the Van Hornes and said nothing about you or your mother or any Hampton at all. There is no direct tie between you and the Van Hornes other than you move in the same circles and attend the same events. I daresay even our esteemed Friends often covet invitations they do not receive. They can besmirch your name all they like, but 'Hampton' is old, much older than some of theirs. Your family will receive invitations no matter how 'notorious.'" He smiled and kissed the back of her hand.

She huffed impatiently and turned her face away.

"What is it?"

She turned back to him and studied his face for a moment. "I've been quite healed for at least two weeks, and you still act as though I am made of glass."

"I—" He paused, unsure of how best to respond. "Charlotte, you were very wounded. Everything hurt, no matter which direction you moved—I saw it every day."

"Have you seen such pain lately?"

"Sometimes, when you descend stairs."

She rolled her eyes. "My knee hurts now and again."

"You've brought a cane." He pointed to the walking stick at her side.

"As a prop! John, have you forgotten what we're doing?"

"No, Charlotte, I have not, and the thought of you in the same room with any of those vipers makes me want to spit venom of my own."

"An apropos analogy." She shook her head. "What I am saying is I am no longer in pain, and you do not need to treat me as though I am."

He studied her carefully. "Very well, what would you like?"

"This, foolish man." She put her hands on the back of his neck and pulled his face closer, pressing her lips to his and stealing his breath away.

She pulled back and looked at him. "I like that. Call me brazen, if you must, but I am who I am—"

He silenced her with his lips, kissing her fully, deciding he ought to accommodate her wishes. He'd not kissed her thoroughly in more than a month, and perhaps he had been waiting for her signal that she was no longer hurting.

"I would never call you 'brazen,'" he said, smiling against her lips, "unless you wish it."

The carriage came to a stop, halting any further conversation and additional quips. He was disappointed; he would like to know what she might have said. As it was, she kissed him again, firmly, and touched her forehead to his. "On with the show," she whispered. "Isn't that the phrase?"

He paused. "I believe it's said if something goes horribly wrong, first."

She frowned. "Let us assume that the 'horribly wrong' has already happened."

He nodded. "Let us step into the ancient past," he said, gesturing to the door. "Lead the way, my lady."

They stepped from the carriage and approached the house, which was glowing with lights from within and glittering with guests visible in the windows and in the front garden. John tried to shake the nerves that settled in hard and fast when he looked at the crowd and considered all the things that could go wrong in the space of a few hours.

He put his hand on Charlotte's back, noting that the gown was a bit loose because in the month since she'd ordered it, she had not been well. She *had* been hurt, and badly, and although she had picked up work as a personal physician to some private clients, her heart was still back at the hospital.

If nothing else, he hoped tonight would shake something loose. It was time to move forward.

CHAPTER 30

Charlotte roamed the perimeter of the Van Horne drawing room several times, first with Amelie and then with Eva at her side. Michael and Nathan were on opposite sides of the room, and John maintained a close proximity to Charlotte despite her assurance that she'd be fine in a house where the crush of guests threatened to blow out the exterior walls. She spied Dirk and a few constables she recognized mingling among the guests and tried to still an onslaught of nerves.

"How many people were on the original guest list?" Eva asked as they made another circuit.

"I thought fifty, but this appears triple that amount." Charlotte frowned. If she couldn't get close to the Friends, how would she read their reactions to her appearance? She had worked hard to resemble her mother down to the last glittering jewel. She'd followed the list, commissioned a seamstress, and hunted down old images of just the right hairstyle.

"When the activities begin," Eva said, "the crowds will spread more evenly into different rooms. Are we still planning to use the ballroom for best effect?"

Charlotte nodded, feeling her stomach tighten. "Have you seen them? Are they here?"

Eva nodded. "The Paddletons and Carters are near the foyer.

I've not seen the Fineboughs, but I think I saw the Worthingstones in the sitting room on the other side of the foyer."

Charlotte blew out a quiet breath, trying to steady her nerves. She spied John across the room and caught his eye. He winked at her and then continued his perusal of the guests around her.

This will work . . . This will work . . .

She clutched the brass head of her cane. It was in the shape of a duck, which was ridiculous, but probably not so far removed from the instrument that had wounded her mother so gravely. The thought made her feel queasy, and her hand grew damp in her glove.

"Ugh," she muttered and flexed her fingers, tucking the cane temporarily under her arm.

"Attention, esteemed guests!" Margaret Van Horne stood up high on something Charlotte couldn't see, and its invisibility added to the older woman's sense of wonder. She felt a swell of gratitude for the sisters, regardless of the party's outcome.

"Welcome to 1869! The theme we've designed for this event took much planning and preparation, and we hope very much it has been a challenge for you! It is not often we reach back into the wardrobe only to find that what we need, we've already donated."

The guests chuckled and murmured their agreement.

"We will award prizes throughout the evening for the best representation of two decades past, and we take this responsibility very seriously. We've also resurrected our famed Treasure Hunt to entertain and delight—" At this, the crowd applauded and laughed. "—and each room contains objects that can be identified by a riddle written here." Margaret reached down and grasped a bundle of papers from Ethel, holding them high. "Mark each one as complete and return to this room for a delightful prize."

"They are truly accommodating," Charlotte whispered to Eva. "This must be the most absurd Bygone Era gathering to date."

Eva grinned. "I enjoyed going through my mother's old dresses. She keeps everything in a cedar closet. If you're *our* age, this is delightful." As the crowd began to move and disperse, she whispered, "Now is our chance—upstairs, quickly!"

Charlotte followed Eva out of the drawing room through the doors leading to the servants' staircase. They quickly climbed up to the first story, entered through the back hallway, and followed the corridor to the ballroom, which was empty. The lights were turned down just enough to remove any harsh glare.

"I'll be in the corridor," Eva said. "And here are your Treasure Hunt paper and pencil. You just wander and scribble things, and the rest of us will herd the crowd." She took Charlotte's shoulders and looked into her eyes. "You look so lovely." Her eyes misted. "This will work, dearest." She clasped Charlotte in a quick embrace and then left the room through one of the two entrances out to the corridor.

Now that Charlotte was alone, the ballroom felt cavernous, and she felt very small. She clutched the cane in one hand and her paper and pencil in the other and wrapped her arms around herself.

The ballroom's high ceiling reached the home's upper story. A staircase led from where Charlotte stood to the second floor where it connected with a small Juliet balcony and glass door. She wandered to the huge windows on the wall and looked out over the back gardens. The gazebo was forlorn in its dying foliage, and frost covered the ground.

She tried the handle to the door leading to the outside balcony, and it opened without a sound, allowing the cold air to steal in from outside. A staircase led down to the lawn in a sweeping curve, and Charlotte imagined she would like to attend an event here during the summer.

Voices sounded in the corridor, and she quickly closed the door. She made a show of writing something on her paper as she looked at the walls, noting the light stream of guests who entered, laughing and talking to one another.

More people came and went until finally James and Phillipa Carter entered the room. Steeling herself, Charlotte approached them with a bright smile. "Well, hello, Mr. and Mrs. Carter. I did not see you here earlier."

Phillipa's lips parted in shock, and even Mr. Carter paused mid-step.

"By my *word*, Miss Duvall," Mr. Carter finally said, an astonished smile breaking across his face. "You so resemble your mother!"

Charlotte smiled and patted her dress, moving the cane from where she'd tucked it under her arm. "Imagine my surprise when I found my mother's favorite dressmaker! She knew exactly what to do when I described what I imagined my mother wearing. I hoped to feel a little closer to her by wearing it."

Phillipa's eyes were riveted to Charlotte's cane, and then her gaze shot to her face. Mr. Carter did not seem fazed by it, other than to say, "Are you walking with an impairment, Miss Duvall?"

"Oh, yes. I was in an accident some weeks ago, and my knee occasionally gives me trouble."

He nodded. "I hope you recover quickly. Now, then, about these riddles . . ." He wandered to the center of the room, looking at the painted murals on the walls.

Phillipa moved closer to Charlotte tentatively, and then, looking over her shoulder, put her hand on Charlotte's arm. "My dear, you must . . ." She frowned, looking pained. "You must take care. You don't know what kind of—"

She broke off as other voices sounded at the door, but she remained in front of Charlotte, effectively blocking her view. "You mustn't be here, dressed like this, with these people."

"Mrs. Carter, I absolutely must. If you bore my mother any affection, please do not hinder me."

Her eyes widened. "It is *because* I bore your mother affection that I hinder you. If I could, I would whisk you away in an instant."

"Carter," a voice sounded, and Charlotte saw Mr. Worthingstone approach the center of the ballroom. "Don't know why we let ourselves get dragged out to these things."

"Mrs. Carter," Charlotte whispered, "why did you react to my cane?"

She shook her head. "I can explain, but not now. Perhaps another time. Later."

"Phillipa?" A feminine voice sounded behind Mrs. Carter, and she turned slightly as Mrs. Paddleton approached.

"Oh, hello, Winifred," Phillipa said shakily.

"Have you solved any of the—" Winifred Paddleton stopped cold when she saw Charlotte. Her face blanched of all color, and she stumbled back.

Phillipa Carter grabbed the other woman's arm and supported her weight as Charlotte heard the main doors quietly click shut.

She moved out from behind the two women to see the rest of the couples in the room. They'd only just entered, and some looked back at the doors in confusion. Amelie stood guard at the Juliet balcony door, keeping it open a crack, and the ballroom's other set of double doors showed a sliver of light from the corridor.

Charlotte stood near the center of the room, allowing each of the guests to have a clear view of her, knowing she looked like her mother in the hours before her death.

"Hello," she said, and her voice echoed to the ceiling and back.

If only she hadn't been nervous, if only the moment hadn't been fraught with meaning, she might have laughed at the expressions pointed at her. They ranged from shock to panic, and on some, anger.

"What is the meaning of this, Miss Duvall?" Anastacia Worthingstone hissed. Little wonder that she would be the first to find her voice. Of all the Friends, she was the most headstrong.

The four Jameses approached Charlotte slowly, as if pulled in by threads.

"Astounding," Mr. Worthingstone said. "Miss Duvall, are you aware—"

"Of course, she is aware," Mrs. Worthingstone snapped. "She has done this very deliberately!"

"I'm sure I do not know what you mean," Charlotte said to the woman. "I was invited to a themed party, and so I dressed accordingly."

"You . . . you saw no picture of your mother?" Mrs. Finebough now approached, the color high in her cheeks and her eyes like chips of obsidian in the low light.

"Of course I saw no picture of my mother," Charlotte said evenly. "At least, not like this. I did see a picture of her on the autopsy table, however, with a wound in the back of her head that was made with something that probably looked like this." She held up the cane, and Mrs. Finebough froze.

"You all seem to recognize the cane," Charlotte continued. "Oh, not this one, certainly, but I am assuming one very much like it."

She looked around at the people who were slowly forming a lopsided circle around her. "The point on this cane isn't nearly sharp enough. I imagine the original must have been another kind of bird, or a shape with a much tighter point."

Winifred Paddleton sucked in a breath and stared wide-eyed at the others. "You—"

"Not a word out of you," Mrs. Worthingstone snarled.

"Anastacia, I think it is time for us to leave," her husband said. "Enough of this charade." His gaze lingered on Charlotte as though he still couldn't believe his eyes.

"You loved my mother?" Charlotte asked him. "The consensus seems to be that your love for her exceeded her love for you, even as you all grew into adulthood."

He swallowed visibly. "She loved me, as well."

"James!" his wife hissed. "We are leaving."

"The doors are guarded," Charlotte said. "None of us are leaving this room until I have the truth." Her voice was strong, and she was glad, because her knees shook. "My mother received two letters just before her death, both referring to an event on a ferry meant to celebrate an engagement."

Phillipa cleared her throat and made her way closer to Charlotte. "That is true," she said.

"Phillipa," Gwendolyn Finebough growled. "Not another—"

"I've had enough of you!" Phillipa cried, her voice ringing high. It was clearly an unprecedented outburst from the woman because it startled everyone into frozen silence. "You will no longer do this thing!"

"What thing?" Charlotte asked quietly. "What is she holding over your head?"

"My son," Phillipa said, her voice breaking. "I saw something that night, and she has threatened me into silence ever since. First with James's life, and then with our son. Soon, I suspect she will threaten my grandson."

"Phillipa?" James Carter stared at his wife. "What is this?"

"Oh, James. You have never known anything."

"Did you see blood in the middle of the deck that night, Mrs. Carter?" Charlotte asked. "Someone did, and he gave testimony to that fact. Now he's dead, so I suggest we air all that we know right now in this room."

Mr. Finebough shifted his feet, and Charlotte looked at him. When he glanced away to his wife, some of the pieces fell into place for Charlotte.

"She was in love with you, Mr. Finebough," she said in wonder. "You were the 'James.' The one she called James, not Jim or Jamie." She shook her head. "Right there all along, and I didn't see it."

"I loved your mother to distraction," Mr. Finebough said. "But we could never marry. Her dowry wasn't enough, and my parents didn't want ties to the least hint of scandal."

"Shut your mouth, James," his wife snapped.

He looked at her in disgust, and Charlotte guessed he was another man who usually remained in the shadows.

Mrs. Finebough stared at him in open-mouthed shock. "After all I have done for you!"

"You have done nothing for me, Gwendolyn, but bring grief and destruction on everyone."

"You sniveling coward!" Mrs. Worthingstone moved closer to Gwendolyn and stared daggers at her sister's husband. "You would have ruined everything we worked for!"

"*You* worked for?" Charlotte asked. "Husbands in positions of power, I presume? That was your pinnacle?"

Both women turned to Charlotte as one, and the hatred was palpable.

Phillipa Carter edged closer to Charlotte. "I did see blood on the deck that night," she said. "And it dripped from the cane belonging to Finebough. Only he wasn't the one holding it."

Mr. Finebough ran a hand along the back of his neck with a quiet sigh. Amazingly, Charlotte thought, it sounded like relief. "I asked Kat to meet me on the deck once the party was underway and the drinks had started flowing. I only wanted a moment alone with her, but she met me there to tell me goodbye. She said she wouldn't attend functions anymore where I was present, that it wasn't fair to her husband. She asked me to refrain from any further contact, told me that in another life, things might have been different."

Charlotte felt a lump form in her throat.

Mrs. Finebough moved forward, mouth open as if to speak, but Mr. Carter spoke first. "I want to hear this." He crossed to stand next to the two women who were so full of ire.

Finebough looked at Charlotte. "I argued with her, begged her, but she was resolute. Your mother was a woman of integrity. She did not play your father false, not with me." The sorrow etched on his face was deep. "It is because of me she is dead. Gwendolyn noted my absence and came up on deck to find me. When she saw Katherine with me, she stormed over, but Kat moved away. She said she was leaving, but she only made it as far as the middle of the deck when Gwen grabbed my cane and hit her in the back of the head."

His voice broke, and he swayed on his feet. "Katherine fell, and from the severity of the wound, I felt sure she must be dead." He rubbed a hand over his eyes as if to dispel the memory. "I panicked. I picked her up and shoved her over the railing at the back of the boat. Just as I turned back around, Phillipa came up the stairs."

Phillipa Carter had tears streaming down her face, and she pressed her hand over her mouth.

"Soon after, Anastacia arrived. Phillipa left, but of course, she had seen too much, even if she didn't hear the confession that Gwendolyn spilled to Anastacia. I knew the two of them would orchestrate everything that followed. Anastacia started screaming, and then it began."

Silence fell hard in the room, and Charlotte saw the door crack open. John made eye contact with her, but neither of them moved. The situation felt volatile, brittle, like everything would crumble if she moved.

"What happened to you?" Charlotte asked Phillipa, whose tears continued in stream down her face. She put her arm around the woman, understanding finally why Phillipa had tried to encourage her to leave.

"They threatened me." She glanced at the two women her husband stood guard over. "Soon after we were married, they had my husband's assistant—his young nephew—killed to show they could get to James any time if they wanted to."

Mr. Carter stared. "That was a robbery at my office!"

Phillipa shook her head with a sob. "And once we had our son, they knew my compliance was assured. I would never breathe a word of what I saw that night. Within two years, both of their husbands were elected to Parliament."

"She is delusional," Anastacia said, drawing herself up and smoothing her dress.

"We have another witness who will testify to Mr. Fairmont's original police testimony," Charlotte said. "Phillipa isn't the only one who realized my mother's death wasn't an accident."

"Who?" Mrs. Finebough demanded.

"Why do you ask," Charlotte said, her shock wearing off and anger settling in its place. "So you can have him murdered also?" She glanced at James Finebough. "Unless you orchestrated Fairmont's death."

He shook his head and looked at the two women. "No. No, I did not."

"He's lying," Anastacia whispered as Gwendolyn Finebough began backing away from the others.

John opened the main door to the corridor, and Michael and Nathan entered from the other direction.

Gwendolyn broke away and ran for the balcony door that led outside, and Charlotte cursed herself for not locking it.

The woman tore open the glass door and dashed out into the cold. Charlotte, fueled by fury, chased after her, ignoring the chorus of shouts behind her. Gwendolyn was at the bottom of the stairs and running across the garden by the time Charlotte had made it halfway down the stairs.

Then she slipped.

With effort, she pulled herself up using the icy wrought-iron railing. She kept running, following the woman who disappeared around the back of the gazebo. Charlotte tore after her, only to be caught in her stomach by a tree branch clutched in Gwendolyn's fingers. Her breath left in an agonized wheeze, and she pulled at Gwendolyn's hair as she doubled over.

Charlotte barely recognized the litany of words the woman hurled at her as she struggled and struck out at Charlotte again and again. In her mind's eye, she saw her mother as she turned her back on the man she'd loved in order to honor the one she married. She saw an angry, vengeful, jealous wife strike out in fury, and it suddenly matched Charlotte's own rage.

She tightened her fingers around the cane she still clutched, then swung upward, catching Gwendolyn on the chin and knocking her to the ground. Charlotte screamed at the woman, feeling all the painful years without her mother as she lifted the cane high.

Arms wrapped around her from behind and hauled her back as she brought the cane down, narrowly missing Gwendolyn's head. Charlotte sobbed, robbed of coherent thought and so filled with sorrow and rage that she could hardly breathe.

"I have you," John whispered in her ear. His arms were secure, his face against hers, and he shielded her from gusts of wind that blew through the garden. "Shh, darling. It's over." Nathan Winston and Michael Baker were close on his heels to handle Gwendolyn, whose angry sobs filled the air.

John held her close until Charlotte's breathing had evened out. Then he walked her back into the house where the ballroom was a swarm of activity involving constables, the detectives who had hidden among the guests, and the Misses Van Horne who had watched the entire melee from the ballroom doors. John said something to Michael that Charlotte didn't hear, and then he guided her from the ballroom and down the corridor to a library that was warm with a fire and the soft glow of lights.

She sank down onto a sofa, and he followed, pulling her up against his side. She rested her head on his neck, and he brushed her hair and tears away with his thumb. She did not know how she would ever stop crying, for everything. For her mother, for her father who had spent so many sad years locked away in his own grief, and for herself. She tightened her fingers in John's waistcoat until they ached.

She eventually quieted, more because she was spent of energy than resolve.

"There," he whispered, "it's all right. It will all be right."

"She's not coming back," Charlotte whispered, her voice breaking. "I found the answers, and she's still gone."

"I know, darling. I would fix it if I could. I wish I could. But you made it right. She is still gone, but you put the questions to rest, and you found justice for her. They will be tried, each of them, for their part in the crime."

Her breathing eventually slowed, as did the tears. "I've cried in front of you again," she muttered.

His chest rumbled with a quiet laugh, and he produced a clean square of pressed fabric from his pocket without her having to ask.

She mumbled her thanks. "I suppose I need to start filling my hope chest with embroidered handkerchiefs. I'm depleting your supply." She sat back and looked at him, the fabric pressed to her nose.

He smiled and tucked a curl behind her ear. The entire side of her face was damp with tears that had matted her hair to her skin. "I'll have Mason get more."

"Thank you," she said, finally wiping away the rest of her tears and holding the handkerchief loosely in her lap. "You solved my mother's case. I shall be certain to give your superiors a good report." She smiled, trying to be light, but her effort was weak.

"You're welcome," he whispered. He paused. "I love you."

She nodded. "Will you marry me?"

He raised one brow and was silent for so long she felt insulted.

"Well?"

He nodded slowly. "Are you certain you're not under severe emotional duress? Perhaps we should wait for clearer thinking before asking questions of that sort."

"John Ellis, if tonight has taught me nothing else, it is that love is not guaranteed, that one doesn't always love someone who will return it, and that with one blow, a life can end. I do not want to have regrets, and right now, this very minute, I want to know you are mine and I am yours." Tears gathered again, just when she thought she'd never manage another. "I want to be your wife and live with you and share—"

He kissed her, holding her face in his hands and relishing the moment. "Yes, Charlotte, I will marry you." He smiled and placed a kiss on her forehead.

"I did not envision having to talk you into it," she groused quietly.

He laughed. "I asked you first, if you'll remember."

"You said you wouldn't ask me 'yet.'"

"Semantics." He paused. "What of your career?"

She smiled. "I'm thinking I'd like to start a clinic for women and children like the one in New York. I've already mentioned it to the Van Horne sisters, and they are set to help me gather a cadre of potential donors. It's where my heart is, and with female benefactors and staff, we can structure the bylaws as we see fit."

He smiled. "I'm so glad."

"John Ellis, are *you* crying?"

"Do not be ridiculous." He kissed her soundly, and she suspected he was trying to distract her. "Are you ready to go tell our friends the good news?"

She sighed, still sniffling and feeling as though her head was stuffed with cotton. "Yes. However, I must confess that I have wanted to get you alone in a library again ever since the Fulbrights' party."

"Oh, darling. I'll not tell you how many hours I've wished

for the same thing. That was when I realized I wanted you for my personal physician."

She laughed, grateful she still could. She stood and tugged his hand, and they walked slowly to the door.

"Do you want to speak to anyone else?" he asked.

"You mean the Friends?"

He nodded.

"I would like to hug Phillipa Carter. I would like to visit with her again soon."

"Many burdens were lifted tonight, I believe."

"Yes." She nodded and managed a smile. "Thank you, Director Ellis, for lifting mine."

CHAPTER 31

Charlotte stood in the lovely, blooming garden at Hampton House and turned her face to the sun. The weather had cooperated beautifully, and as her family and friends gathered to celebrate her wedding after the ceremony at the church, it was picture-perfect.

Eva had just finished photographing the wedding party, the guests, the unruly children, and a grumpy Mrs. Burnette who had fought tooth and nail against having her picture taken but, in the end, posed nicely.

John scooped up Eva's toddler, Henry, into the air and placed him on his shoulders. In the months during their engagement, John and Charlotte had spent countless hours with the cousins and their children. Director Ellis had transformed from someone fairly uncomfortable with children to one of their favorites.

Sophia, Amelie's four-year-old girl, tore past Charlotte with a spoon full of cake icing in pursuit of fourteen-year-old Sammy, who tried to hide behind Eva's camera. John intercepted the shrieking child and scooped her into his other arm, then hauled the wriggling little girl over to Michael, who took her with a stern look that soon gave way to smiles as she offered him the icing.

John deposited little Henry on Nathan's shoulders and then looked over the garden until his eyes met Charlotte's. They warmed, and she decided she would never tire of that moment when, after searching a room, he found her. Crossing the yard, he reached out and took her hands.

"Are you ready to leave? We must be at the docks in two hours, and we still need to change clothes."

Charlotte laughed. "Now that we're married, you can change your clothes in my bedchamber and Mrs. Burnette will have nothing to say about it."

He laughed. "She will still have something to say about it, make no mistake."

John had moved out of Hampton House after the Van Hornes' Bygone Era celebration, and the months until the wedding had felt long. The only bright spot was the pace of his work that kept time moving forward.

Charlotte worked with the Van Horne sisters, Mrs. Winston, Phillipa Carter, and even Winifred Paddleton to build a solid board of benefactors for her vision of a women's clinic. Redesigning and restructuring an old building in the East End provided the perfect home for the new clinic, and the Van Horne Center for Women and Children was nearly ready for opening.

Anastacia Worthingstone's fall from grace had been dramatic. Her hiring of a criminal in England with an American relative—Mr. Brown—came to light, along with her directives for Mr. Brown to harass, assault, and if necessary, dispense with Charlotte. A new investigation into David Duvall's death had opened. Mrs. Worthingstone and Mrs. Finebough had been among his final visitors just before his death, and John suspected they'd had a hand in hastening his end. Charlotte hoped they could reach the truth without an exhumation, but also hoped that, if necessary, her brothers would agree to it.

The Fineboughs awaited sentencing after a lengthy trial, and

Charlotte was glad she would be out of the country when it happened. It was a chapter she wanted to close. The silver lining to the entire dark cloud was that Charlotte's fractured relationships with her brothers were beginning to be repaired.

Dirk had attended the wedding ceremony but was on his way to the Continent to meet with a potential client. He'd given them wedding gifts before the ceremony, and Charlotte had been delighted to see a new rugby ball among them.

John and Charlotte made their way across the garden, and Charlotte stopped by Eva and Amelie, who both smiled and pulled her close. The three of them stood together in the warm sun—brown hair, black hair, and red hair—gleaming. Charlotte kissed them both and promised to send postcards, and then she found Sally, who clasped her tightly.

"I am so proud of all you've done, sweet girl," Sally told her as she ran her hand over Charlotte's hair. "And your mother—she smiles on you each day."

"Thank you, Sally. For everything. For giving me a family." She kissed her cheek and said goodbye, joining John on the stairs into the house.

They waved to friends, family, and loved ones, and finally broke away, entering the house and climbing the stairs together. John paused every few steps to kiss his bride, and she finally laughed and smacked him away.

In the seating area that anchored the bedrooms, dappled sunlight played on the carpet through the wide windows that overlooked the front square. Charlotte tipped her head back and threw her arms wide, finally feeling peace.

John grasped her around her waist with a laugh, and she wrapped her arms tightly around his neck as he spun her in a circle. It was her turn to laugh when he spun them into her bedroom and kicked the door closed with his foot.

"Mrs. Burnette won't check on us for at least thirty minutes," he said, kissing her soundly. "By then, we'll be on our way, and she'll be none the wiser."

Charlotte laughed again, and in the back of her mind, she had to admit Amelie had been right all along: True love was worth every effort.

Acknowledgments

I've had so much fun spending time with the Hampton cousins and am continually humbled and gratified at the positive reader response. The Victorian era is endlessly fascinating, and especially toward the end, saw so many changes. I will never tire of doing the research, although I admittedly get details wrong on occasion.

My thanks, as always, to Jennifer Moore (The Blue Orchid Society series), Josi S. Kilpack (Mayfield Family series), and Rebecca Anderson, (*The Art of Love and Lies*). The moral support, not to mention the brainstorming video calls, have kept me sane. I love you each dearly.

Special gratitude to Lisa Mangum and Heidi Gordon, for continual cheerleading even while finding plot holes and spots for improvement. You are so good at author hand-holding, and I am grateful. The whole Shadow Mountain team—Chris Schoebinger, Heather Ward, and Rachael Ward—you are wonderful and so much appreciated.

To my family, who go without my time and attention during deadline sprints and conferences, your love and support sustain me. I am so lucky, and I realize it every day. My life is rich and full because of you—Mark, Nina, Anna, and Gunder. To Nichole and Bruin, you are such bright spots, and I am so lucky to have you in my life! To my siblings, my adorable nieces and nephews, and my sweet dad and step-mom, I love you more than words can express. We are close, and it is such a gift.

Last, but not least, to my readers who show up at signings, post beautiful things online, and message me with kind thoughts and questions, my heart is overflowing with gratitude and love. I could not do what I do without you, and to be able to share my daydreams with all of you is as wonderful as I ever imagined it would be. Maybe there will come a day when I can write as quickly as you all read, but I doubt it. In the meantime, thank you for patiently waiting! I will keep imagining stories as long as I live, and it is my fond hope that they will always find a home with you.

Discussion Questions

1. Charlotte goes to medical school at a time when few women did. How have societal conventions changed for women? What kind of changes do you hope to see in the future?
2. Life these days moves at a much different pace than it did in the Victorian era. Do you feel the changes are positive? Negative?
3. Part of the beauty of Charlotte, Eva, and Amelie's relationship is their closeness; they are cousins but also a kind of "found family." What relationships in your life take on these elements?
4. In what ways are the relationship challenges John and Charlotte face similar to those we handle today as couples or families?
5. In fiction, we often see a rosy view of historical settings. Even knowing it wasn't always picture-perfect, would you like to live in an era different from ours?
6. It has been said that if a society wishes to strengthen itself, its women must be educated. What is the significance of this idea, and why?
7. Romances almost always have a happy ending. Do you find value in this? Do you agree or disagree with the idea that it is often unrealistic?
8. What is the value of consuming fiction? What argument would you make to someone who feels fiction is a waste of time?

About the Author

NANCY CAMPBELL ALLEN is the award-winning author of twenty published novels and several novellas, which encompass a variety of genres, ranging from contemporary romantic suspense to historical fiction. Her most recent books, which include Regency, Victorian, and steampunk romance, are published under Shadow Mountain's Proper Romance brand, and the What Happens in Venice novella series is part of the Timeless Romance Anthology collection published by Mirror Press. She has presented at numerous conferences and events since her initial publication in 1999.

Her agent is Pamela Pho of Steven Literary Agency.

Nancy loves to read, write, travel, and research, and enjoys spending time with family and friends. She nurtures a current obsession for true crime podcasts and is a news junkie. She and her husband have three children, and she lives in Ogden, Utah, with her family and an obnoxious but endearing Yorkie-poo named Freya.